FOUR CORNERS

FOUR CORNERS

WALLY RUDOLPH

SOFT SKULL

BERKELEY

Library of Congress Cataloging-in-Publication Data

Rudolph, Wally.
Four corners : a novel / Wally Rudolph.
pages cm
1. Addicts—Fiction. 2. Repentance—Fiction. 3. Life change events—Fiction.
4. Violence—Fiction. 5. New Mexico—Fiction. 6. Southwestern States—
Fiction. I. Title.
PS3618.U83F68 2014
813'.6—dc23
2013047513

ISBN: 978-1-61902-297-3

Cover Design by Jason Snyder
Interior Design by Domini Dragoone

Soft Skull Press
An Imprint of Counterpoint Press
1919 Fifth Street
Berkeley, CA 94710
www.softskull.com

Printed in the United States of America
Distributed by Publishers Group West

10 9 8 7 6 5 4 3 2 1

FOR ILENE

COLORADO

I *want to surprise you. You're young and deserve more.*

I was cold and drunk. Maddie lay next to me asleep, the brown drapes above our bed covered her face. It was just the start of morning, and in the wink of that late December daylight, all I could see was Maddie's black-blue hair on the uncovered pillow. I got up still speedy and right and pulled my army duffel out of the closet. I packed it tight with sweaters and jeans and a jacket for the both of us. I smoked in the kitchen listening to Ben breathing heavy on the couch. He sounded awake by how loud he was, but when I checked him, his eyes were closed. It was just the noise of air scraping down his throat.

I finished three sips of bourbon from the night before. I poured one more to make sure I was awake and another to steady my hands. I went back into the bedroom and did a study on my sleeping girl. Maddie was four months into her twentieth birthday. Her head barely came up to my chest. Her pale skin glowed in that dawn, and her black-purple eye shadow was smeared over the freckles on her cheek. I put my lips on her sharp chin and pushed the drapes away from her face. I picked up her little sleeping body and carried her out to my truck.

We left driving out of Santa Fe on all the big new roads and then caught Highway 285 and started our way north. I swore at myself and didn't stop until I lost the drought-cursed town in the rearview mirror. Just as New Mexico's all God-painted sunsets can hum you a lullaby every night, the town takes to drunk spectres when it wants you to leave. The hum turns to a clipping static, and the sunsets say nothing but *freebase, freebase, freebase.* I was hearing sirens from all across the city. They were the sounds that woke me up. Their howl was reason enough to go scarce in my book. Real or not.

When Maddie woke up, we had just passed Pueblo, Colorado—forty miles from her folks' place in Cañon City. She wiped the sleep from her blue eyes not even surprised we were on the highway and rolled her hand over mine on the steering wheel. The diamond on her ring looked huge and fake on that clear winter day.

'I took the liberty,' I said. 'I figure we should break the news proper to your family.'

'My mother's not going to believe her little girl is engaged.'

Maddie said her family's home was an heirloom of Cañon City. The rot-shingled, two-story yellow house was a gift from an old mayor to her grandfather, the town's only optometrist, in the fifties. She said her grandfather gave sight back to the mayor's wife, a woman who was born blind by all accounts. Maddie's grandfather taught the woman eye exercises, told her to stare into the corners of all the lacquered wood rooms for hours on end. In a year's time, the woman recognized blurry shapes, and by the end of her life, she could tell her grandkids apart nearly perfect. That's all she ever wanted, the mayor said at his wife's funeral. He left his home to Maddie's family when he died five years later. When they moved in, Maddie ran her tongue on every grainy wall and bumpy bannister in the entire home. She told her father that the whole house was painted in sand and dirt. Her father took her small hand, walked her around the house. He ran her fingertips on the walls, the brass door handles, the flaking window frames, and wooden-carved angel at the top of the stairs.

'This is the constancy of Christ,' he said. 'Long prayers to Saint Lucia, the Bible in braille.'

They never touched a thing. Maddie said she used to walk the entire home eyes closed, blindfolded, in the dark. I didn't believe her until I was standing in their sitting room, cinnamon roasted apples cooking inside my nose. I ran my hand up and down the wooden mantel and felt psalms biting back between the plastic Christmas holly that hadn't been taken down. While Maddie spooned instant coffee into four boiling mugs in the kitchen, her folks stared at me in silence. Her father was one of them tall balding numbers—older than his wife with big hands and uncomfortable with his own size. His eyes were kind, then scared, then angry. He whispered into his little wife's ear instead of speaking to me straight, and when she opened up her arms to embrace me, this substantial man shot me a look of womanly envy and hate. I stared back with my worn-out red eyes, and Maddie's mother smiled and smiled till she took all of me in. She hounded me around their sitting room—tapping at her perm, watching my pockets, straightening her jeans. I didn't let down. I groped every single one of their decorations down to an ancient portrait of Father Christmas, his tiny glasses barely curbing his bloated greedy nose.

They asked me how we met, and why I loved their daughter. Why me, Francis Bruce, a declining ox with a rough cough and scarred hide? A thirty-five-year-old land surveyor who made no airs, predictions, or promises for Maddie's future. I sipped my cooling coffee and didn't tell them the truth. I was thirty-seven, and Maddie had worked up the bit about the land surveyor. I told them Maddie clippered my early gray hair short at a cheap haircut spot in a strip mall, and I fell in love. I didn't say when she was drunk or high their little daughter seemed lost but turned hungry for sex. I didn't say we met two years prior in a dirty hippie den outside Española—how we drank vodka and sucked on tangerines, and how we held our breath till the liquor and drugs betrayed us, flushing our faces red then pink—I didn't say any of it. And her mother thought the haircut yarn was straight till her husband whispered into her ear something wise.

Her face went white, and she took Maddie upstairs by the arm. I stood alone in the kitchen with her old man. He looked at the ground, and I don't know if he thought I was laughing—because I was coughing. But he looked up at me, pulled his thin red lips back, and told me to get the fuck out of his house. I didn't fight and walked out making sure not to touch a thing. I waited in the truck for Maddie to come storming out, crying all over her face. She was huffing and puffing and then three steps from the car door, she bent over and got sick all over the sidewalk. She didn't stop though. She just finished up, spit, and slammed the truck door hard. Her father stood at the window shaking his head back and forth. He turned his head to the side and said something over his shoulder. I lifted my hand to him, but he didn't move. I understand. He was no coward. I would've just sipped my coffee the same and closed the drapes slow like he did, not wanting to be the first one to turn away.

'You okay?' I asked Maddie.

'Do you want to know the truth?'

'Never.'

'Then I'm a fucking wreck.'

The plan had been to spend New Year's with her parents celebrating our new family, but now we were driving in light snow on Highway 25 to Maddie's best friend's home in Denver. My cell phone vibrated in my pocket. It had been ringing off and on since we crossed the Colorado border. I pulled it out and threw it on top of the dash.

'Who is that?' Maddie asked.

'Ben. He's been calling all morning.'

'Aren't you going to answer it?'

'No, I don't want to hear it. Don't want to hear any of it, that's why we left.'

Everyone needed to dry out. Maddie and Ben knew it, but I wouldn't tell a soul I was trying to go straight. I had quit the speed— all of it—going on two weeks and was nursing myself with half-bottles of aspirin crushed in my drinks. More and more often, I'd been closing my eyes with every breath and had to lie down when I was in the middle of nothing because my lungs fell short while I braved the spins. My hope was I could get clean enough to start over again for myself, for Maddie. Brand-new houses were going up near the highway on the south side of Santa Fe. We could throw out everything we owned, buy leather and cans of clean white paint.

Ben had been on a bender, hitting anything that would keep him up. The week before, his father, Marcus, had served him papers, trying to take his son away once and for all. I didn't think much of it— it wasn't the first time. But then, it all came together when Ben nearly took off two of his left fingers with a band saw in the garage. He said he was daydreaming about the ancient Olympics, racing to cut off his father's head, and when he came to, the saw was well into his left palm. The skin flapped back, revealing muscle and white bone. I held him on the floor of the garage, rocked my old friend like a child while he cried and bled. When he could speak, I stapled up his hand, wrapped it in the legal papers, and cinched the mess together with a spider strap from my truck. I held his face in my drunk hands and promised him we'd never lose his son.

We left him alone passed out on the couch, high enough on painkillers and smoke that he'd be downright scared when he woke up and found Maddie and me gone. *He'll numb out again,* I thought. *He always does.*

We knocked on Noni's door in the early afternoon, and when she opened it, I saw why she and Maddie were so close. They dressed just alike. Noni was a twenty-two-year-old single mother. Her dyed red hair was short to her shoulders, and when she and Maddie were standing together, you'd think they were in some sort of club. They both wore heavy black makeup on their eyes, dirty torn-up jeans, and a rainbow of plastic bracelets on their wrists. Noni went to all sorts of trouble for us because she hadn't seen Maddie in so long. The two of them grew up together in Cañon City, but after Noni had her baby, Margaret, a year out of high school, they barely spoke. The baby's father was a bum from their hometown—an ex–grade school teacher who trolled the H-E-B parking lot for older teens who liked beer but didn't know about rough sex.

Noni cooked all of Maddie's favorites—macaroni and cheese from the box, a canned sweet ham, and a big plastic bowl of mashed potatoes. She even bought me a bottle of Irish whiskey and set it at the end of the table next to a handle of store-brand peppermint schnapps. We ate, and we drank. The girls talked in voices that only made the two of them laugh. I stared at the sleeping baby, drunk and happy my Maddie had forgotten about the sore morning with her folks. The night slipped away into smiles and beeping shit rock, and then Maddie came to me in Noni's old prom dress. Lace and green velvet cradled her breasts before it fell into a sparkling liquor-stained pool at her feet. She told me it was ten minutes before the year 2000, and she wanted us to be holding each other because the world might end. Noni woke up Margaret and carried her out to the backyard. We all watched fireworks from Mile High Stadium across the city. Right there was a beautiful young girl and barely a man kissing each other on an overcast night. Silver-purple rockets painting the black sky.

The shame is, Ben drove through the night. His hand wasn't healed. He'd been taking blood thinners and a crapshoot from the medicine cabinet back home. I call that God's work. It'll never heal. His legal paper cast was soaked black. Blood collected on Noni's kitchen table. His eyes were swollen shut, and his face had been insulted by a heel. Ben's head was thrown back in a dead man's pose. His long, dirty hair matted to his cheeks while his clotted breath barely kept him alive in this New Year.

The shame is, Ben forgot we spoke. He said he heard my voice calling to him from a private parlour in downtown Santa Fe. The type where once a year, cash is paid to a quiet house manager who keeps your liquor stocked and a silver cigar box filled with up-and-comers and proven champs. I did call him to wish him a Happy New Year. I heard music and women laughing—tough timbres of sex and booze poured through Noni's kitchen phone. Ben didn't remember hiding in the bathroom talking for an hour on the depth of highway cement and the best disappearing act we'd ever seen. We spoke on all of it. I told him about Colorado and Maddie's parents, how we ended up at Noni's. I said I was tired outside of Denver.

The sight of Ben put Maddie in a hiss. She took Ben at face value. All she saw was a strung-out deadbeat father. She stood behind him still in her dress from the past night. She propped his head up on her sequined chest and wiped his face with a wet kitchen rag. He kept on trying to babble through. He was at the parlour. We spoke while he was at the parlour. He drove out to his old house. He wanted to make things right.

'I had to make things right,' he mumbled.

It was thievin' talk. The whole speech stank of it. Maddie wanted him to repeat what he said, but I wanted to hear the truth.

'Why'd you go out there, Ben? *Why would you go out there?*' I pushed.

Ben grabbed the rag from Maddie's hand and held it over his right eye. He rolled his head around and opened his other eye as wide as he could.

'Look at me, Frank. Things have changed. I won't let him take my son.'

Maddie took his arm and helped him to the couch. He stumbled forward, his feet falling like he was wading on sticks. He kept saying, 'Thank you. Thank you for everything, Maddie.' I picked up his car keys from the table and went out the front door.

Ben Shenk was born Polish, but his Daddy bought some Pueblo blood into the family soul. The Shenks made their family fortune from partial ownership in the Native casinos peppered throughout the Southwest. His father, Marcus, had only one son, was white, and claimed his Pueblo blood through a five-year magic spell called 'The Admission Thread.' Back when the casinos were just breaking ground, Marcus paid in fifty thousand cash and signed over a 27 percent stake in all of the Shenks' assets worth over five thousand dollars to the Pueblo nation. For that, a tribal elder 'sewed' the Shenks' white blood into the tribe. Ben told me he was just a kid, but he remembered when the man-witch came to his house wearing a one-piece work suit cut off at the knees. He said the medicine man milled dirt in their backyard till dead Pueblo told him when the Shenks arrived in the States. He burned driftwood and ate carrizo until he was sure Warren Shenk, Ben's great-great-grand-father, never spilled any Pueblo blood in The Great Revolt, swindled land deals, or raped their squaws under winter moons. When the check cleared, the medicine man ran a stone knife across little Ben's chest and collected his six-year-old blood. He mixed it with a vulture's egg, desert rock fungus, and trickled drops into all the New Mexican rivers surrounding Pueblo land. The Shenks were now tax-exempt tribe, able to claim federal money and profit share in one of the richest Native gambling empires in the nation.

When Ben got out of university, Marcus set him up with a mansion in a gated community outside of Santa Fe. He hired Ben on to look after all the family interests in the local casinos—Camel Rock, Big Rock, Sandia. Over the years, Marcus had started think-ing less and less of his tribal business partners. The old man smelled numbers cooking and peace-piped accounting. He bought estates all across Arizona and New Mexico to keep an eye on all the Shenk money. That was Ben's job for a long time before we met. He was put together, mean, and greedy. He said his father always told him to say,

'Take it easy, Chief. I'm just looking out for all of us in the tribe.'

Everything was breaking the Shenks' way until Ben met the

blonde Miss New Mexico 1987, Ali Sharpe. Nothing but a steady, calculated whore with a numbed-out cunt for hours and hours of ragged-out sex. Five months after they met, they were married. Four months after the wedding, their son, Sean, was born, and when Ben looked on his baby for the first time, he saw a grand wager for himself—the chance to change his selfish route and forget the Shenk virtues of jealousy, envy, and unhinged greed. Ben enrolled Sean in a private bohemian school. Taught his son to read, himself. Took him into the canyons and showed him the shallow rivers in drought. Gave him a mutt and a bicycle and turned him loose. Marcus fumed, and Ali got her angle. She opened a separate bank account and started shaving off the monthly stipends from the family trust. One by one, she changed the locks around the house and sent pictures to Marcus of his grandson—sole heir to the family gold—shirtless in a Pueblo headdress learning a rain dance at The Private Academy of Youth Education and Holistic Wellness.

The old man flew to Santa Fe that night, punched Ben in the face, and put a .25 pistol in Sean's hand.

'Don't let your father ruin you, Sean! Define yourself!' is what Marcus screamed.

But Sean couldn't do it. He ran into the empty dark desert outside the mansion's gates and did his small rain dance around a pile rotted-out chamisa. Ben said Sean's dance saved his life. A neighbor driving home called the police when he saw the six-year-old half-naked with dirt and tears on his face, and when the cops took Sean home, they came on Marcus and Ben and a hunting rifle.

I was all Ben had. He came to me and fell apart, telling me how Ali stole custody of Sean, how she had turned him on to Los Alamos cocaine. He said Marcus had moved into the mansion, hired his big Jew accountant to tutor and bodyguard Sean, and was now fucking Ali day after day. Marcus told Ben, his own son—to his face—that he couldn't help himself. Ali's pussy made him feel close to God.

It was just past seven in the morning, and Ben's Saab was crusted with frost. Sean was asleep in the backseat, his head resting on Ben's welding bag. His face and body were barely covered by an old peacoat. When I first met him, he was a two-year-old shooting across the polished cement of the mansion. He must have been eleven by now. I knocked on the window, but the kid didn't move. I was worried he'd frozen to death, so I unlocked the door and shook his legs. He screamed and threw the peacoat off his head.

'Hey, it's all right. You're gonna freeze up,' I said.

Sean sat up and looked out the window, not recognizing one thing around him. The angles on his cheeks were from his mother, but he had Ben's round eyes and the start of the pointed Shenk nose. He pushed his fine brown hair from his face and stared at me, trying to blink off his sleep.

'Where's my dad?' his voice scratched out.

'Inside.'

He followed me into the house holding the jacket tight against his chest. He was smart to be scared. I wasn't going to ask him what happened just yet. I'd wait till he met Maddie and Noni, let them care for him a while, get the color back in his face. Maddie was in the kitchen washing dishes. She had changed and was back in her jeans and a white T-shirt with all sorts of paint stains. Her blue hair was tied back from her face, and with all her faded makeup, she looked old and famous.

Ben was still passed out on the couch taking short sharp breaths in his sleep. The sight made Sean stop. His eyes watered up. His father looked beaten-up and dead. This poor boy never asked for any of this. He still believed in the word of his father, despite Ben's swollen jaw and near-collapsed throat. Maddie turned off the sink and took Sean by the hand. She sat him down at the kitchen table and then went through the cupboards and made him a plastic bowl of Cheerios. She put the cereal in front of him with a crusted honey bear and a soup spoon too big for his mouth.

My jaw started to shake, and my hands went cold. I was already getting restless for booze. Maddie motioned for me to follow her into an empty bedroom that stank like must and wet carpet. A comforter and a pillow were balled up on the ground. Maddie closed the door, threw her arms around me, and kissed me on the neck.

'Do we have to take Sean back home?' she asked.

All I wanted was distance right then—a cheap bus ticket, a ferry ride to the Midwest. Anywhere. I'd take framing houses in Minneapolis or stumbling through Chi waiting for those cold beaches to open up. Marcus Shenk was already hunting by now. He'd beat Ali, and then find a lackey to come after Ben and Sean. I kissed Maddie on the cheek.

'We'll wait till Ben is up. I want to hear him tell the story straight.'

Then I planned to slap him and make him tell it again.

It was quite an affair. Marcus had a bunch of local Mexicans dressed in cheap tuxedos working a two-story bonfire. Big fucking teepee burning outside Taos marking the spot for his new casino. The whole fire department was there, nervous as all hell 'cause there ain't a drop of water on that land. The poor sons of bitches—you could see the sweat and grease coming off their faces like they were staring at the end. All the investors and Canyon Road gallery hogs were lined up at the buffet line. Money just dripping out of them. I licked the fucking pistol, that's how hungry I was. Should've turned the cock on them. Bastards. And Ali—she looked like a fucking painting. Satin white gown. Fur around her neck. Those big fake tits Marcus bought her. I have to catch my breath . . .'

Ben turned around and made sure Sean was still asleep on the ground in front of the TV.

'I got worked, damnit. I just wanted to see Sean. Talk to Ali for a minute. I know what I look like. I can still taste the speed in my mouth. I was starving. I just wanted to ask Ali if we could work things out, and then my old man comes out, waves that big fucking Jew away. He puts his hands on me and starts whispering all this sick shit about Ali. Spitting in my ear. The thing is—'

Ben got red in the face, started to choke up. He swallowed down hard and pushed out the words.

'I dream of killing that fuck every day. Taking a jigsaw to his fat face. He's behind all of this. He already fired me. Now, he wants to cut me out, steal my son—I chop him in the goddamn throat. And nobody's hearing shit yet. They don't want to lose their place in the fucking buffet line. He falls down, hacking on himself, trying to wail. His Jew comes and lays me out—stomping on my fucking stomach, working my face. I can't see. I can't hear. I was blessed right then, because I found my gun and stopped the whole goddamn celebration. I got Sean, though. I don't remember driving here.'

Ben went to Sean and lay next to him on the floor. He took his wallet from his back pocket and set his keys on top. My ears stung from his story. I wanted to leave him right there, holding his sleeping son in a stranger's house. I'd take Maddie and keep driving my little pickup north. We'd stop at every rest stop, take pictures with our tongues hanging out. We'd drive until we hit a border—any border. I'd try foreign food, drink water that didn't run clear. Maddie would take a job on some beach. They'd give her a bullhorn, and she'd warn people to stay away from the shallows. She'd come home satisfied, and I would love her too because I'd have a loose throat, dry hands, and when I breathed, my chest would fill to my chin and empty free of fiend and past.

But it wasn't deserved. No one looks like me anymore. My mother and father died a long time ago. Both cooked in Texas, knives hanging from their bodies like penny keychains at a dollar store. Next to Maddie, Ben was all I had. We mixed blood a long time ago, watched sunrises gripping the other's hand. I had no children but knew they are true love. The truth is if Sean was mine, I feared I would have done all the same things.

'We'll have to leave soon,' I said. 'You know that, right?'

Ben looked up from the ground and caught himself before he started in again with all the nonsense.

'After Maddie says her goodbyes, we're gone. Your daddy is gonna want Sean back—even more than Ali.'

'Ha. Ali doesn't want him back,' said Ben.

Ben put his arm around Sean and pulled him close. His heart was broken, and he knew he had just stirred up a mess.

'Wake us up when it's time to leave,' he said, closing his eyes.

I went to the front porch with cigarettes. These times, more than ever, I wished more of myself. More smarts. Some kind of wisdom. I felt confused and not much else. Just sifting all the ideas was a task. Marcus Shenk would have reported Sean kidnapped by now—that I knew. As each hour passed, he would call in one favor after another because his money afforded him that. Not a bit of mercy in that old man. If Maddie and I were picked up even close to Sean or Ben, the bastard would send us all up.

Right then, Maddie and Noni pulled up in Noni's little Toyota. They both got out, and Noni went to the back and unfastened Margaret from the child seat. The baby was bundled up in a tiny purple winter coat and matching hat.

'We went shopping for Margaret,' said Maddie, walking up the driveway.

Margaret was awake, pawing on Noni's face. Her fat cheeks bounced up to her popping blue eyes. The little girl was nobody's business. Since she woke up that morning, she hadn't stopped smiling. Noni stopped and turned her towards me.

'Who's that, Margaret? Who is it? Is that Frank?'

Margaret reached out slow, then pulled her arm back and turned away.

'I should get her inside. It's getting cold,' said Noni.

Maddie sat down next to me. She took one of the Parliaments from my pack and lit up.

'Did you get high with Ben?' she asked.

'I had a hankering, but thought better of it,' I said.

'Where are they?'

'Inside—asleep.'

'You know, you can get high if you want to. I can drive.'

'Don't say that. I ain't getting high.'

'Sorry, I just thought it might be easier. You could wait—'

'I'm not waiting to kick. I had plans for us, Maddie. A ceremony—some sort of day.'

Maddie scratched at the back of her leg, not wanting to ask a question she already knew the answer to.

'Does that mean we're done with them?'

'I don't know . . . Ben's father is gonna stick on this.'

I shook my head, angry with myself. Even to me, my words rang bull. I wanted Maddie to believe me, to know that I meant to give her a life. Maddie grabbed my hand.

'Frank—Sean is important to you, huh?'

'Ben's been a good friend to me for a long time. He's seen me through. Saved me more than once. I owe him as much. I mean, if there was a way—'

'Shh. It's all right. I get it. He's your Noni.'

'Yeah. Yeah, he's my Noni.'

She kissed my hand and set it back down.

'Wherever we go, we need to get you some gloves,' she said. 'Don't worry, we've seen worse.'

Maddie stood up but started to stumble back as soon as she got to her feet. I grabbed the back of her leg and held tight.

'Whoa, you all right?' I asked.

She bent over and held on to her stomach, taking deep breaths.

'I've been feeling like shit all day. I think I drank too much of that cough syrup last night,' she said, smiling. 'Probably just need some water.'

When we went back inside, Sean was awake. He sat in front of the television, staring at me as I walked through the front door. He looked better, not so scared like before. He was warm and had decided he was safe for the time being. Maddie got a glass of water from the kitchen sink and sat at the table with Margaret in her high chair. The baby held on to Maddie's fingers and moved them up and down. Her smile got bigger and bigger until she just gave up and started laughing.

'Wake up your dad, Sean. We have to leave soon,' I said.

Sean looked at me to see if I was serious and then started shaking Ben.

'Wake up, Dad . . . Wake up.'

'What about dinner?' Noni asked from her bedroom. 'It's almost ready.'

'Dad, wake up. We're on TV.'

The woman on the news was already laying into Ben. I didn't want to look. I fixed my eyes on Margaret's dancing smile. The way her cheeks flushed every time she laughed. A New Year's Day kidnapping is what the TV was saying. A desperate father stealing his son. Series of bizarre events. Erratic behavior coupled with methamphetamines. Bounty on the child's head. The lady said Ben attempted murder. He kidnapped Sean for fix money. When I heard Ali crying, I turned to the screen. She was standing next to Marcus Shenk in a white fur jacket that fell to her feet. Her blonde hair was pulled away from her face, and her right eye was swollen shut. Her lips were pink, cracked, and beat-up. Marcus put his arm around her shoulder and stepped to the bouquet of news station microphones. He took off his glasses and tried to cry, wiping at tears that weren't there. His fat cheeks looked red on the TV, tiny veins stretched purple across his pig nose.

'I wish I could say I was surprised,' he said. 'I wish I could say I was shocked. But for myself and for Ali, this kidnapping is just the latest tragedy in my son's destructive fight with addiction. For the first time, I've lost hope.'

Noni crouched behind Sean and tapped him on the shoulder.

'Why don't you come help me make dinner?'

Sean turned to Ben, not sure what to do.

'It's all right, Sean. Go ahead,' said Ben, his eyes not moving from Ali's busted face.

He waited till Sean was in the kitchen before he turned to Maddie and me.

'I didn't do that to Ali,' he whispered. 'It happened just like I told you. I wouldn't have hurt her.'

'Would you even know if you had, Ben?' asked Maddie, shaking her head.

On the TV, Marcus broke down. He closed his eyes, squeezed Ali close, and looked to the sky. His giant assistant, the Jew Goldstein, handed him a white handkerchief, and Marcus wiped at his face again before he looked directly into the camera and spoke.

'Benjamin, if you're listening, I want you to know I still love you, but, son, I can't let this go on. You're sick, Ben. You need help. Please know I will not rest until Sean is out of harm's way. I will do everything in my power—*use all my resources*—to get my grandson back.'

Marcus kissed Ali on the cheek, pet at her blonde hair, but before he could leave, a reporter shot out a question.

'Mr. Shenk, will this affect the groundbreaking of the new casino?'

For a second, Marcus dropped his crocodile tears and smiled, unable to resist the scent of money and business.

'No, of course not, all my investors and the entire Pueblo Nation should have confidence that the casino's construction will continue as planned despite my family's duress. I will not have a worthless drug addict derail my business. You hear that, Ben? You worthless piece of—'

Ben switched the channel to a Mexican game show with a tall woman in heavy makeup and stripper heels. He turned the volume down before he cocked his head back and winked at me with his one good eye.

'He's full of shit. He probably paid that reporter to ask that question. The Pueblo are getting nervous. That casino's not getting built. Land's too dry.'

'Ben, you're a fucking idiot,' said Maddie. 'Did you hear a word your father said?'

Maddie picked Margaret up from her high chair and went to the kitchen. She stood next to Noni as she finished up dinner. Sean sat alone at the table, staring blank at a pile of silverware and dishes. Ben sat up from the ground and moved close.

'Frank, I need a favor,' he asked.

'Isn't that what I'm doing right now?'

'I'm serious.'

Ben checked again to see if Sean was listening before he leaned in and whispered in my ear.

'I need you to call Santer. We're going to Mexico.'

'What the fuck's that got to do with Santer?' I asked.

'He can get us across, can't he?'

'Us? I ain't going to fucking Mexico. *Maddie ain't going to fucking Mexico, Ben.*'

'Can you call him?'

I leaned back. If he weren't already hurting, I would've thrown him through the window to get him thinking straight.

'You know I can't do that,' I said. 'Even if I wanted to, I wouldn't know where to find him.'

'I know where he's at. I got a number.'

Ben sat back and rubbed his hands on Noni's stained carpet, excited to let his mouth run loose.

'I figure we've got all that money in the garage back home. We call Santer, blow through Santa Fe like a breeze, pick up the cash, and in two days, we're on a beach in San Marcos.'

'Ben, I'm not taking Maddie to Mexico,' I said. 'That ain't in the cards.'

Ben pulled his hair back from his reddening face. His eyes welled up, and his hands shook in his lap.

'I'm scared, Frank, and I'm sitting here just trying to keep it together for Sean. I don't see a way out of this is what I'm saying. You know Marcus.'

I checked over my shoulder at Sean. He was staring at Ben, lips trembling, ready to run over and fall apart. The words came out of my mouth before I could think.

'Look, I got money. Don't worry about that,' I said. 'We'll get you to Phoenix. After that—'

'We're gonna need more. We need everything, Frank.'

'I got plenty, Ben. I've been putting away for me and Maddie. I wasn't planning on coming back.'

I'd never said it out loud before, but as soon as I said it, I knew it was true. So did Ben. Until that moment, he took for granted we were going to be a family forever, married in spilled blood and speed. He dropped back to the ground and turned up the volume on the TV. The Mexican game show exploded into the living room. Horns and carousel drums filled the room. The woman in high heels kissed at the camera. Her tongue darted out of her wet red lips, nearly touching her nose.

'Ben, we're gonna get you to Phoenix,' I said. 'My money is yours. You got my word.'

'Yeah, and we all know what that's worth.'

He said it loud so everyone could hear.

We waited till Sean was asleep. After dinner, Ben picked him up from the couch and set him in the backseat of the Saab. Noni had filled two paper grocery bags with ziplocked leftovers. She carried them out to my truck, holding Margaret in her other arm.

'I'm not the best cook,' she said. 'But I know you two like my mac 'n' cheese.'

Noni looked over at the Saab. Ben was high-revving the engine, trying to warm it up.

'Where are you guys going to take Sean?' asked Noni.

'They have to get rid of their car,' I said. 'State police will be looking for it. After that, Phoenix.'

Maddie stared at me, confused. I hadn't told her the plan.

'What's in Phoenix?'

'Don't worry,' I said. 'That's as far as we go.'

'Promise me you'll take care of Maddie, Frank. She's my other baby,' said Noni, tears filling her eyes.

'I will. I promise.'

Noni smiled and blotted her tears with the bottom of her scarf. Maddie hugged her, took her by the shoulders.

'Don't worry. We'll see each other soon,' said Maddie.

'What? Like another five years from now?'

'*Noo*—I'm gonna need a maid of honor.'

'More like a maid,' said Noni. 'Honor left with respect a long time ago.'

'Thank you for everything, Noni,' I said, kissing her on the cheek. 'We'll call you when we stop.'

Noni took one of baby Margaret's mittened hands and waved at us.

'Say goodbye to Aunt Maddie and Uncle Frank, Margaret. *Can you say, bye?*'

I got in the truck while Maddie held and kissed Margaret one last time.

'Watch out, she's a natural, Frank,' said Noni, winking at me.

I started up the truck, rolled down the window, and waved Ben up next to me.

'We'll trade your car in and get you a new one in Alamosa,' I said. 'Maybe stay the night—then head south on the 285. Sound good?' I asked.

'I still don't see why we can't leave the car in Santa Fe and take off from there. We can get everything from the house. We need money, Frank—'

'Goddamnit, Ben!'

Maddie leaned over my lap, making sure to look Ben in the eye.

'You still don't get it, do you? You fucked up! The whole of New Mexico is looking for Sean, thanks to your dad.'

'Fuck him,' said Ben.

'Just follow me to Alamosa,' I said.

'I know how to get there.'

Ben turned on his lights and pulled away. I jammed the pickup into first and turned the defrost on high. Noni watched from under a street lamp in front of her house. I glanced in the rearview one last time before we turned and caught her kissing Margaret on the cheek and dancing up her driveway, trying to make her baby laugh. Her shadow cast long off her body—moving back and forth, getting short and long—then, like any other animal, it was gone.

If the weather held, Alamosa was only four hours away. We would drive the interstate as long as we could and then cross onto local roads, zigzagging west and south till we made it to Arizona. Ben was playing stupid. If anything, he just didn't want to believe he had endangered his son. In his eyes, Sean was better off with him. Maddie twisted back and forth on the torn-up seat, taking off her jacket in the tiny cab.

'Do you care if I sleep?' she asked.

'Go at it.'

Maddie moved the radio dial back and forth, looking for a station.

'Can you tell me now?' she asked.

'What's that?'

'Why we're going to Phoenix.'

She found a Spanish station and turned the volume down low.

'Ben's taking Sean to Mexico.'

'What?'

She sat up straight and leaned forward, trying to look me in the eye.

'He's Sean's father, Maddie. I can't stop him,' I said.

'So you're just gonna help him? He's a fucking degenerate, Frank.'

'We're taking them as far as Phoenix—that's it. Then we're done.'

Maddie balled up her jacket and put it against the window.

'He's lucky he has you,' she said. 'Does he realize that?'

'And I'm lucky I got you.'

The taillights of Ben's Saab were a quarter mile ahead as we got on the highway. He wasn't speeding—a good sign. As I caught up behind him, I gave him my brights. The snow was coming down light and wet as we passed through downtown Denver. The lights from all the business buildings hit the snow, and at once, my whole life was thick and fat. I cracked the window and stuck two fingers out. I tasted the warp and the anatomy and the fog. I needed my luck. We all needed some luck. Ben's fortune was falling fast. I turned the defrost down to low and left the window cracked, letting the cold air fill me up. My friend was born into this fuckery. I was due a fair shake.

Ben bought the Saab in cash a few months after I met him. It was the summer of 1986, and at the time, his father was sending his big Jew accountant, Goldstein, out to New Mexico with leather duffels of cash every three months. Marcus made his man red-eye the trip straight through from Rapid City, South Dakota—no stops. I remember sitting in the dirt in front of Ben's just-finished mansion drinking wormwood vodka. Goldstein pulls up in a big two-door Benz, road rot all over it. He gets out in a rumpled suit, his usually trimmed beard looking all bearcat and wily. He walks over to a hallucinating Ben, drops the gym bag onto the ground, and gets right back in the car and leaves. Not a word. Not even a piss. I don't even think he was high on anything unless you count his obsession with the Shenks' accounting and cycles of Russian juice—none of that horse racing bullshit, either. Ben said he took the heavy sauce every six weeks. A doctor-managed program with a silver gear setup he kept on his body at all times. Goldstein mainlined the shit into both arms, both legs, and Ben said he caught him once with a tube letting some black blood from his shrinking dick. Ben tried to make a joke about it—tell him he knew an easier way to get off—and that just made Goldstein bananas. He put Ben's head into some bathroom tile, ripped his pants off, and threatened to fuck him with his rotten snail cock. If anything, I admired the Jew's dedication—the steroids, the fourteen-hour money drops..Goldstein worked any scheme in front of him right to death.

As soon as we could see straight, Ben and I walked the gym bag into the only Saab dealership in Santa Fe. We drove away an hour later in the floor model, a light tan turbo convertible. We drove up the ski basin, watched the sunset, and smoked crack until our lungs hurt. I dropped the pipe and burned a hole in the Saab's new carpet, but Ben didn't say a word. He waited another hour till we were well past his house and Tesuque. He said he found something with me and not just another kindred knob.

'Together, we're worth something,' he said. 'Alone, we're a disgrace.'

We had been driving for two hours. The snow was still light and didn't seem to be getting any worse. We were behind Ben in the right lane. Four semis with pictures of McDonald's breakfast food passed us. The trucks put eddies in the falling snow. The salt and slush kicked up from their back tires and left wide tracks in the left lane. As we got into Colorado Springs, Ben exited to a Chevron station. Sean was awake and in the front seat now. He stared at me blankly as we pulled in. He was wearing Ben's peacoat again and had that same scared look on his face as when I woke him up. Ben pulled up to a pump and motioned for me to come over. When I opened the door, Maddie's eyes opened.

'Where are we?' she asked.

'Not far. Colorado Springs. Ben needs some gas. You want anything?'

'No, I'm fine.'

I closed the door and walked over to Ben. He was clapping his hands together, shifting from foot to foot. His forehead was shiny with sweat.

'It's really coming down out there,' he said. 'I can barely see. Ain't no snow in Old Mexico, Frank. Isn't that a song?'

Ben pulled the pump from its holster and unscrewed the gas cap. I walked around to Sean's side, opened the door, and crouched down next to the Saab.

'Hey, you doing all right?' I asked.

Sean looked around the driver's seat to see if Ben was listening.

'It's really cold. He won't turn on the heater.'

'You want to ride with us?' I asked. 'There's not much room, but it's warm.'

Sean nodded his head.

'All right. I'll go talk to your dad.'

I went back around and took a hard look at Ben. He'd tied

back his hair with a rubber band, and even with his black eye and scraped-up cheeks, I could see his skin was pale and pasty. He'd been dipping into some crank.

'Ben, Maddie wants Sean to ride with us. She's getting bored with me already,' I said.

'Want me to spank her for you?'

Ben smiled, waited for me to laugh. I ducked my head down and checked on Sean. He was sitting with his back to us, dangling his legs out the door.

'Sean, who do you wanna ride with?' Ben shouted. 'Your dad or Frank in that piece of shit?'

I heard the passenger door of my truck slam behind me. When I turned, Maddie was walking over.

'Hey, Sean,' she called out. 'Let's go get some snacks.'

Sean ran to her outstretched hand, and they weaved their way through the other cars into the gas station. I walked up close to Ben—close enough so he'd listen.

'Sean was in the car.'

'What are you talking about?'

'I'm talking about trying to get you two safe, and you're doing bumps with the kid in the fucking car.'

'I didn't give Sean any—'

'Can you just take it easy till we get to Alamosa?'

'You jealous, straightedge? I bet you're just starving for a taste.'

From his front pocket, Ben pulled a baggie choked tight with meth. I turned around and started back to my truck. Ben laughed at my back.

'How's your cock feel now, big man? *Important?* Frank's in charge, everyone! Frank the man!'

Maddie watched everything through the gas station's dirty windows. She was leaned forward under a lotto sign, eyes wide, both hands on the glass like she was going to bust through and tear Ben apart. I climbed into the truck, turned the key, and switched the radio to an oldies station. Maddie walked Sean back and opened the door. He looked at me before he got in. His whole face trembled, trying not to cry.

'Thanks,' he said.

The air was dry after Pueblo. As we drove, the clouds cleared out of the night sky, leaving only the white moon freezing the top of the snow. I could see the land again—Colorado forgiving itself this far south. The mountains and trees slowly moved aside for flat ground and the penance of the desert. We had stopped only one other time. Maddie forced me to. Sean was cramped up trying to sleep in the cab, and Maddie made me pull over so she could fashion a bed for him. She pulled two dead car batteries from the truck bed, stuck them between the tiny seats, and covered them with her jacket. They were both back asleep before we hit the juncture with Highway 160 and started heading west to Alamosa.

Ben knew we were safe, driving local road now. He slowed to fifty, pulled the latches on the ragtop, and shoved it back with a free hand. He let me pull in close to see the scarf muzzled on his face, then he gave me the finger and let the Swedish turbo whistle him away. By a seven count, he was a dash and a glow and gone. A smile pasted onto my face watching him tear away. I pushed the pickup to a hundred without even noticing. I'd be lying if I didn't say I wanted a fix right then. Ben was too much. Maddie was too much. Sean was too much. I wanted to be the lesser man in the gas station bathroom fumbling with a pile of meth on the lid of a toilet, blasting it up my nose, trying to forget about kidnapping and winter.

In 1983, I was twenty-years-old and doing face time for a shut-in hippie farmer named Aspen. His farm sat on a chunk of rolling land outside of Española, New Mexico. For years before he came out to the high desert, Aspen was an old-school computer programmer in Texas. He said he had too much money and time on his hands in Dallas, so on a whim, he bought a side of a hill—sight unseen—and proceeded to slowly load the property with two double-wide trailers, a solar power setup, water pumps, and a roughly used but working C-class backhoe. He let everything sit for five years and used the time to order boxes of high-grade plant seeds over BBS boards on the computer. He had everything shipped to the empty land in Española and let it sit there for another two years before he threw up his arms one day at work, grew a beard, sold his Porsche, and retreated like me and so many others to the cool barrens of the Southwest.

He took the nicer of the two double-wides and made a home for himself and paid a well digger to drive down from Abiquiu. The man hit paydirt after an hour. The whole property sat on enough water for the state. After the first snow, Aspen sparked up the backhoe and demolished the hill at the back of his property. He said it took him two months just to level it off, but the work was proving something to him every day. The hours in the freezing wind, the diesel soot blowing into his face—it was all feeding a very quiet and, up to then, ignored part of his body. He was down to sleeping only one or two hours a night. Just after midnight, he woke up, rubbed his torso with dirt, and then worked himself into an exhausted mess with toe touches and arm hangs off the rotted lip of his trailer. He sat naked at his tiny trailer table eating dried fruit rolled in instant coffee, then slathered his body in Vaseline—face and all—and slipped into his flannel-lined coveralls for the day's work. The routine made his chest swell and withered the puny part of his soul every day.

He towed that second trailer into the flattened hill and covered it with the same dirt and finished rebuilding his heap before the thaw. By the time spring rolled around, the red dirt hill looked untouched save for the jimmy-rigged steel door he had salvaged from a train depot in town. In the sun, the hill was the same hill, and you would never know he worked a blister. Aspen had never grown a flower or bean in his life, but by the time I met him, he was letting his marijuana rot in garbage bags next to his compost pit. He didn't give a damn about it, he said. It was too strong for him. I told him he was lucky he was never caught, being well into felony territory and all. He looked at me with a pair of homemade brass knuckles on his fist and said,

'Them in them helicopters? Is that what you're speaking of?'

I nodded my head.

'Shit, I barely can speak English as it is anymore. I've dined on raw four-inch steaks. I've eaten rotten catfish. In both cases, I should've known better. Look at this watch.'

He pulled up the sleeve of his dirty coveralls and showed me his oyster-faced Rolex.

'I'm trying to grow something out here, Frank, and it ain't weed.'

He helped me load the fresher plants into my car, gave me a brand-new pistol, and told me to bring back a case of Fiddle Faddle from the Walmart in Albuquerque. By the books and by the end of six months, we were well into tens of thousands. I had never seen cash you couldn't spend until then. I had messed around with hand-fuls of pansy deals before. Boxes of Valium, tupperwares of cocaine—one-night drug runs that left me with a month-, two-month-long stack of cash. When I met Ben in '86, I was already well into my 'treasure mountain' investment scheme. I couldn't deposit the cash into the bank without being arrested, so I took some lined steel bar-rels, filled them with money, and buried them on Aspen's land with the backhoe. Aspen didn't care. He was burning all the fives and tens with books of matches from local restaurants. He took the time to record the dates and weather for each of his cash bonfires, writ-ing down the temperature of the fire, color of the flame, and ori-gin restaurant of each match—Baja Tacos, Bobcat Bite, Horseman's Haven. Aspen believed the blue tips burned faster than the reds, and the reds burned faster than the whites.

I was burying my eighth trash can and Aspen was beginning to track fine-dining establishments when Ben shut the whole madness down. Up until then, Ben's and my friendship consisted of chance silent drug sessions. We'd run into each other on the street or stalk the other to a restaurant and lie. One of us would be holding, the other would be hurting, and two days later, we'd be at each other's necks threatening Babylon and Gomorrah if the other didn't bow out their stash. No last names, no 'brothers,' 'partners,' or 'dicks'—that was all we had. When Ben finally saw how I made my living and, more impor-tantly, what I did with my earnings, he spoke straight with me and gave me better ideas for the cash. We could wash it through his father's casinos, put it in a bank proper, and let the Shenks' accountant, Gold-stein, make the investments. Ben offered the same deal to Aspen, but the hippie laughed in his face and told us we'd be better off in South America where the cocaine was wet and the majority of the country still drank black rum and prayed to stone calendars.

'The American economic model is based on bloodlust and nudist colonies. Look at this watch.'

He showed his Rolex again and said he hoped we found what we were looking for in coke and speed, because he was sending a message into space and his first communicado involved dynamiting his underground growing operation. In one night, he sent it all up, left me the deed to the land, and disappeared. Ben yelled, but I didn't blink. From the beginning, I thought I had more or less stumbled onto Aspen. So when he pushed on, I figured he must have stumbled onto something with his cash bonfires. Aspen was only looking for God like the rest of us.

After Aspen left, I took to the pistols and beatings. I was twenty-four, and Ben still hadn't met Ali, so I grabbed him, and we started running quantities of speed for white trash outfits between Arizona, Colorado, and Utah. We shaved what we could on every trip, and when asked about coming in short on weight, my answer usually began with a piecemeal of cash but quickly fell to Aspen's homemade gauntlets, his parting gift. All I ever had to say back then was: this fucking sex, this fucking money, this fucking murder.

Police lights broke into the night in front of us. By the highway signs, we were ten miles from Alamosa, and Ben's Saab was skidded out on the shoulder with its nose in a farming fence. A police cruiser had the whole scene lit up with his flood lamp and flares. I let off the gas and tried to see if I could catch Ben doing a sobriety test or lying dead on the pavement, but all I caught was the pig's dead stare scoping to see who the fuck I was. As I sped back up, an ambulance clipped by with its sirens going. The wail echoed inside the tin interior of the pickup. Maddie's eyes opened, and she straightened herself up in the seat.

'What was that?'

'Looks like Ben wrecked a few miles back,' I said.

Maddie turned and looked through the back window.

'You're kidding—why didn't you stop?'

'We can't,' I said, motioning to Sean sleeping in the backseat.

We drove the last fifteen minutes to Alamosa in silence. Maddie leaned her head against the window and stared up at the electrical wires the whole way into town. There were no cars on the street, barely any street lamps. I stopped at a Days Inn before the main drag and got us a room at the back of the motel. Maddie woke Sean up and walked him half-asleep into the room. I popped the hood of the truck and checked the oil. I didn't want to go inside and have to look at Maddie and Sean and still not have any answers.

'I know you don't want to talk about it—'

I looked under the open hood. Maddie was standing just outside the motel room, smoking a cigarette.

'But can you tell me what we're going to do?' she said. 'So I can at least start coming up with a believable lie for Sean?'

'You should go inside. You're gonna catch a cold.'

I closed the hood and went to the passenger side, looking for something to wipe my hands.

'Frank, will you just talk to me?'

'We're going to Arizona.'

Maddie followed me to the driver's door. She was getting mad but trying not to yell.

'Fuck Arizona. What if Ben is fucking dead or if he's in jail right now?'

'We'll go to Arizona and get everything straightened out.'

I closed the truck door and stood in front of her, not knowing where to go.

'How? How, Frank?'

'Maddie, if you ain't realized it yet, we're in. We were in as soon as Ben walked through the door. If Marcus or any of the cops he's bought off find us with Sean, we're fucked. He'll have us locked up so fast, ain't nobody will find us. Not Noni. Not your parents. He can make us disappear.'

Her eyes darted left and right as I spoke. She was taking it all in, getting scared. I was trying to level with her, but I'd just made it worse. I tried to think of something to calm her down, but she stared right through me, knowing I had nothing.

'I want to go back to Santa Fe,' she said.

'We can't do that.'

'*Yes, we can.* We'll take Sean back and just give him back to Ben's father.'

I didn't want to hear it. I slapped her across the face. Her head snapped to the side and stayed there like I'd thrown a crick.

'I'm gonna help Sean,' I said, quietly. 'I'm gonna do right by Ben.'

It was bright and dark—the way it can be in parking lots at night—but I could still see Maddie's freckles drowning in a swelling red and tears flooding her cheeks. She turned, went back inside the motel room, and locked the door. The tips of my ears numbed out in the cold. I couldn't go inside. I couldn't watch her cry and hate myself. I wanted to feel right. I wanted to feel like I was doing something right. But all my gut had for me was fear and shame, those rotten fucking truths.

The smell woke me up. I'd fallen asleep in the truck eating the cold leftovers Noni had packed for us. The open container of macaroni and cheese sat on the passenger seat next to me. I opened my eyes and didn't move. An older Mexican woman, already in her brown housekeeping skirt, got dropped off for work. She kissed her husband on the cheek and waddled across the empty parking lot to an unmarked door three down from our motel room. She went inside and, after a few minutes, propped the door open with a glass ashtray and rolled her cleaning cart around the corner of the building. She sang a song I couldn't hear. From inside the cab, it was just a sketch of melody.

My cell phone buzzed in my pocket. The screen lit up with 'Unknown ID.'

'Hello?'

There were a few loud clicks on the other end, then a woman's automated voice came on the line.

'Hello. You are receiving a collect phone call from the Alamosa County Corrections Center. Will you accept the call from—'

The woman's voice stopped, and Ben came through loud and clear.

'602-264-1341. Call Santer, Frank.'

He was talking low, breathing heavy right into the receiver.

'I'll get there.'

The automated voice asked me to clearly say yes if I wanted to take the call, but Ben was already gone. He only called to send me away. I wrote the number down on one of the napkins Noni packed with the food and got out of the truck. I went to the door of the motel room and started tapping away until Maddie let me in.

Sean was still asleep in the bed. His eyes were squinted down tight, and his mouth was barely open. Maddie didn't say a word. She took my hand and led me into the bathroom. She dropped her pants with one hand and rubbed herself until she was wet. She stroked me until I was hard and wanting her. We fucked over the toilet seat until she came quietly, and then she sat down and sucked me off into her mouth. She spit it out in the sink and went back to sleep in the bed with Sean. I didn't try to stop her. We didn't even kiss. I pulled my pants up and washed my face with the motel bar soap. I snuck back into the room and lay on the floor at the foot of the bed. I held my eyes closed, trying to go back to sleep, but ended up just staring at the ceiling.

Ben was still flying on that crystal. It wouldn't have let off an inch.

As much as I hated to admit it, he did think a whole lot clearer on the mess than sober. The usual amount of bullshit that flew out of his mouth was significantly less, and when he lied, at least you could see the guilt pass over his face immediately. He disliked himself when he was straight, but high—there were moments between all his big-timer talk that he couldn't downright stand his own existence. A horrible lot for anyone, but when old-man Marcus took Sean away, Ben was no longer able to follow all his righteous principles. He wasn't capable of it. His father burned him for greed and spite, and the grind of the drugs ate any good that was left.

I hoped Sean would sleep till noon, but after twenty minutes, he got up and went to the bathroom. He pissed, flushed the toilet, and then came out and sat Indian-style next to my head.

'Frank, are you awake?' he whispered.

'Yeah,' I said, opening my eyes.

'Where's my dad?'

I wanted to lie to put him at ease, but I knew he was wise on most of it.

'Your dad—Ben's in jail, Sean.'

He took the news in slow, not surprised.

'Are you scared for him, Frank?' he asked.

'Honestly? . . . No, Sean. I'm not scared. He's gonna be fine . . . He loves you a lot, you know?'

'I know.'

'I don't want to lie to you, though. Your grandfather and mother are here. They're looking for you.'

'That means we're gonna have to get going, huh?'

'It's up to you, Sean. Do you want me to take you back?'

He stared into the hands in his lap and shook his head no.

'Then it's settled. So to answer your question, yeah, we're gonna have to get going.'

He stood up and crawled back onto the bed with Maddie.

'Can I turn on the TV?'

'Sure. Just keep it down for Maddie.'

I wasn't going to be able to rest. I went to the bathroom and started up the shower. For a few minutes, I bathed in the hot steam, rubbing my shoulders and stretching my neck and back. My body was starting to cramp up from being in the car for so long. The bathroom door opened.

'Sean?' I said.

'No, it's me.'

I turned off the water, and Maddie handed me a towel from around the curtain. When I got out, she was tying her hair back and undressing, getting ready to wash. In the mirror, I could see her cheek wasn't red anymore. She wouldn't look me in the eye.

'Sean's going to need to bathe,' she said.

I grabbed her by the hand, but she pulled away and stepped into the tub.

'I'm sorry, Maddie . . . about last night by the car—'

'I don't want to talk about it. I feel like shit.'

She closed the curtain and hummed the same bag of melodies that only made sense to her in the mornings. I dried off, pulled my jeans back on, and went back out to the bedroom. Sean was on the bed wrapped up in the polyester blanket with the TV down low.

'You need to jump in the shower and wash up once Maddie's out,' I said.

'Okay, I will.'

He turned up the volume on the remote control.

'Your phone was buzzing the whole time.'

I picked up my cell phone from the dresser next to the television. There were five phone calls and three voicemails from a 505 area code—New Mexico. I started to call the voicemail when the line beeped with the same number.

'Hello?'

'Frank? Frank, it's Marcus—Marcus Shenk. I'm here with Ben. Quite a pickle he got himself into. He's lucky he's not dead. The car is useless, though. How's Sean?'

'He's fine. We're just getting up.'

'Good. Good. Still heading to California? Don't worry, Ben told me everything.'

'No, we haven't decided. We're just getting going, like I said.'

'If you'd like, I could send my assistant over to help. He could take Sean off your hands, then you and Maggie could be on your way in that little pickup of yours.'

The old fucker was flexing on me already.

'I think you'll have to get fucked on that one, Marcus.'

'Me? Son, you're in the thick of it. Look, I understand, you're only doing what you think is right for Ben . . . As a friend, of course. It's quite admirable on your part. Quite irresponsible on Ben's—putting you and Sean and that girl at risk and all. I've got authorities looking all over for you. Kidnapping across state lines—these are felonies, Frank. But you know that, given your past—all that business in Nogales and such. I'm more than willing to let it go, if you'd just return my grandson to me.'

'Be happy to, Marcus. Can you just tell me one thing—what do you call it when a man is screwing his own son's wife?'

'Excuse me?'

'I've been sitting here thinking, and I think you're a right real *motherfucker*. I mean, I've met some *fuckers* in my time. And hell, I've got my share of *asshole* running through me. But you may be the only true *motherfucker* I've met in my entire life. That should be the name of your new casino. Can't you see it, Marcus?' *True Motherfucker* in gold.

The phone went quiet. Marcus cleared his throat and drank something down like he was swallowing glue.

'Frank, are you listening?' he asked.

His voice was quieter now, hollow.

'I'm going to string him up, Frank. I'm going to string Ben up and beat him until you return Sean—'

I hung up the phone, took the battery out, and tossed it in the garbage. My chest and hands shook with anger as I finished dressing. Marcus Shenk was spitting plenty venom and meant every word of it. He didn't stutter, grab for air. He was seeing the whole future with all its color and blood.

'Was that my granddad?' asked Sean, eyes still fixed on the TV.

'Yeah, it was, Sean.'

'I don't want to go, Frank.'

'Then we need to leave.'

Maddie came out of the bathroom drying her hair with a towel.

'I'm starving. Can we get something to eat?' she asked.

'Get Sean cleaned up. I gotta get us another car. You two, don't go outside.'

I grabbed my jacket and pulled the blinds to the side, looking for Goldstein in that Mercedes tank. I cracked open the door and peered down the wall of motel doors. The housekeeping woman was just getting to this side of the building. Marcus knew we were in the pickup. Alamosa is a small town, and he'd have Goldstein and the local police combing the streets for us. In the parking lot, there were eight cars pulled up in front of motel rooms. A couple came out as I was standing there and started loading their Toyota up with bags. I walked around the back of the building to the motel's office. The balding death's-door night manager had been replaced with a bright-eyed brunette. She was typing steadily into the computer in front of her. When I opened the door, her head shot up with a crooked-tooth smile.

'Good morning,' she announced. 'Just so you know, we have complimentary coffee and donuts in the lobby.'

She pointed to a folding table against the wall. A steaming plastic urn sat next to a silver tray of yellow donuts and brown fruit.

'I'm gonna need to check out,' I said.

'That's not a problem. What room are you in?'

'I'm in 178. I've got cash.'

She drummed into the computer, bringing the bill up on the screen. I reached over and stopped her creamy little hands.

'Can I ask a huge favor?' I said.

'Of course, sir. What can I help you with?'

Her voice pitched like a Texas debutante through a cloud of cheap vanilla perfume.

'I think my battery died overnight, and I need a jump.'

She turned and grabbed my bill from a printer behind her. Her face screwed up like I'd asked her for a lung.

'I kinda can't leave the desk. I'm the only one here.'

She slid the bill across the counter and offered her crooked teeth again, trying to make it better.

'Your total for the night is $86.95,' she said.

I pulled out a hundred from my pocket and dropped it onto her keyboard.

'The thing is, we really need to get going. I guess I'll have to knock on some doors.'

She handed me back the change and looked me up and down. I tried to sparkle my eyes at her, but more than anything, I was glad I took the shower.

'Tell you what—How about I give you my keys and you go start your car and bring them back? I've got cables in the trunk. Funny thing: my dad put some in there on Christmas. Can you believe it?'

'Would you really do that? That would help us out so much. I'm Frank, by the way.'

I held out my hand. She smiled and shook it.

'I'm Bethany.'

'Thank you, Bethany. You're really helping me out. There's just not that many people to ask this early in the morning, and not everyone's a Christian before their coffee, know what I mean?'

She laughed as she went into her purse for the keys.

'Oh God, do I. You know we get this weather out here, and I swear, it just freezes people's souls. I go to Faith and Rally Presbyterian, and Pastor always says, 'The Lord's light can melt the coldest and hardest of hearts.' And I believe him. You have to these days.'

'Bethany, you're preaching to the choir. I'm from Texas, and I tell you what, you guys got it easy down here. Sometimes I think the whole state was born into hell.'

'What part of Texas? I've got family down there.'

She handed the keys over, dying to hear my answer.

'Stockton,' I said. 'Be right back. God is truly great.'

'It's the red Cavalier with the crucifix around the rearview mirror.'

'Of course.'

I gave her a big smile and backed out of the office. I felt guilty for grifting her, but I wasn't interested in the Jew mincing my face in front of Maddie and Sean. I pulled the Cavalier to the back of the motel and parked it next to my truck. I grabbed our bag, the tire iron from the pickup, and threw it all into the backseat of Bethany's car. When I went back into the motel room, Maddie and Sean were sitting on the edge of the bed, fresh-faced and worried.

'Let's go.'

'I'm hungry,' said Sean.

They threw on their jackets, and Maddie grabbed her purse.

'I hear they got good food in Utah.'

We took the side streets as long as we could. It was barely two days into the New Year, and Alamosa was already back to work. As we drove past the small houses, cars and trucks sat running, warming up before their commutes to Pueblo or the tiny local airport. One man salted his driveway while his neighbor started up a wood splitter in his front yard. They stared at us. The man with the splitter sipped from a steaming mug of coffee while his machine kicked fist-sized clouds of black into the gray morning. He looked pissed, but then as we drove by, he smiled and waved. Sean waved back through the back window. His fingers hit against the glass and left clear dripping spots where there'd been fog.

'Don't we have to get back on the highway?' asked Maddie.

'We gotta get out of town first.'

We stopped at the intersection of Main Street and Denver Avenue. In two miles, the main drag would turn back into Highway 160—one left and then it was a clear shot west, west, west.

'Well, I need to stop at a drugstore soon,' said Maddie. 'I need to get some Advil and some girly things, and Sean needs underwear.'

Sean blushed in the backseat.

'I don't need underwear.'

I eyed a sheriff's cruiser pulling behind us in the rearview.

'We all need underwear,' I said.

'I'm fine with mine,' said Sean.

The cruiser flashed his brights and laid on the horn.

'Frank, it's green.'

'Damnit . . .'

We took a left into the right lane and headed down Main Street into traffic. The cruiser stayed behind us for two more blocks before it turned off to another residential street.

'I'll find somewhere to stop on the way,' I said. 'Maddie can get her girly things, and Sean and I can get underwear.'

'That's disgusting,' said Sean.

'You know what's more disgusting, Sean? Walking around like a poor man with dirty underwear. You don't want that, do you?'

We pulled up to the intersection at the center of town. Three college kids walked in front of the car with backpacks over their winter parkas. Two of them had scarves wrapped around their faces. The third wore a full ski mask and danced in front of the other two as they walked.

'Sean, look at this crazy guy up here in the road,' I said.

Sean unlatched his seatbelt and pushed himself forward between the front seats.

'Why does he have that mask on?'

'Maybe he's a criminal—'

Across the intersection, a black Mercedes pulled to a stop heading towards the motel. It was a newer model, but I'd be damned if a local was driving a front-tinted, snowshoed Benz this early in the morning.

'Sean, I need you to sit back and put your seatbelt back on,' I said.

'Can I get a mask like that when we stop?'

'Now, Sean!'

I shoved him back with my right hand and hit the gas.

The Mercedes turned into us from the left lane, trying to cut us off. I cut the wheel to the right, barely missing its front end and sending our rear end all over the road. Maddie slammed into the passenger door, and Sean flew around in the backseat.

'Get him into the belt!' I yelled.

I floored the gas. In the rearview, the Mercedes jumped onto the curb, making the U-turn.

'Frank, slow down!'

'Marcus's man is behind us.'

She turned, checking the back window. The Mercedes was coming on us fast. There wasn't a chance in hell we could outrun him. Bethany's Cavalier could barely stay on the road.

'Sean, are you all right?' I asked.

He held his head and cried out in a long high whine.

'Maddie, is he bleeding?'

'Sean, baby, look at me. Put your hands down,' said Maddie, leaning into the backseat.

The right side of his face was red and swelling up like Maddie's the night before.

'He hit it pretty hard, Frank.'

I looked into the rearview trying to catch Sean's eyes.

'Sean, look at me. It's going to be okay—Maddie, give me that tire iron—It's going to be okay, Sean.'

We were almost out of town, the Benz was right on us. Ahead, the road opened up to another lane as it turned into the highway. I slowed down and took the last right onto a gravel farming road.

'What are you doing?!' Maddie screamed.

'Give me that iron! Sean? Sean, listen to me. *I need you to lie down across the seat, okay?*'

Sean wiped his eyes and lay across the backseat, holding his head. I shoved the tire iron up the sleeve of my jacket and slowed the car to a stop. Maddie looked at me wide-eyed like I'd lost my mind.

'It's going to be okay,' I said.

'Don't go out there, Frank.'

In my side mirror, a fatter but still-huge Goldstein got out of the Benz with his pistol in hand. He wore a brown leather bomber jacket and tight black gloves that made his hands look like a pair of giant spiders. His sunglasses were way too small for his bearded head. They balanced on the tip of his nose, threatening to fall off. When I opened my door, he already had his gun leveled on my heart.

'Don't move unless you want to die out here,' he said.

I held my arms up and stepped out of the car.

'I'm not doing anything. Listen now, Sean's hurt. He needs help.'

I walked towards him, my arms still raised.

'Stop. Stand at the back of the car, Frank.'

I listened, stayed at the trunk. Goldstein walked slowly to the driver's door and checked on Sean in the backseat, then he puffed up, stared Maddie down.

'Try anything, you little bitch, and I'll shoot you right in front of the kid.'

'I don't care!' she said. 'He's hurt. He needs to get to a hospital.'

Maddie was holding her hands up, looking scared. When Goldstein bent over to pull the front seat forward, I was to him in two steps. I landed the iron on his back three times in that morning daylight. The fuck took all three and dropped the pistol to catch himself on the ground. He was barely broke. I swung into his knee with all I had. He grabbed at his leg, screaming.

'I'm going to fucking kill you!' he yelled.

He was red-faced and bloodshot already. I grabbed his good leg and dragged him behind the car. I crossed his face with the iron, breaking his nose. His hands filled with blood, and his screams turned to hissing groans.

'Maddie, where's his gun?' I called out.

'In here on the floor!'

I leaned into the car and picked up the pistol from the floorboard. Maddie grabbed my hand.

'What are you doing, Frank?'

'Make sure Sean doesn't get up from the seat.'

I went back to my crying man, yanked up his fat head, and laid the pistol on his cheek.

'This ain't no fun, Israel. You tell Marcus to keep coming as long as he wants. Sean ain't coming back. Ya'll don't know a damn about me.'

I snapped his head back as hard as I could. He bucked, trying to grab my hand and pull it down. But it was all nothing. I held the pistol to the side of his face and pulled the trigger. After the explosion, his bloody ear fell into a puddle of black road rot on the ground. I dropped him crying and wailing onto the Colorado dirt. Blood spilled from between his fingers like how it's supposed to, like every time I'd done it before.

I dug his keys from his jacket pocket and walked back to the car. I picked up Sean, covered his face, and carried him to the Benz. I didn't want him to see a person he knew bleeding, eyes rolled back, screaming for God. A mile away in town, sirens started up. Maddie and I climbed in the front. Bethany would get her car back in the end, I thought.

We turned back onto the 160, and I laid into the gas. We passed the last of the farm roads and a lone ranch house before Alamosa and its two sheriff cars were gone. Sean, his face swollen, stared out the tinted window in the backseat. I wanted to tell him everything was fine, remind him of the ski mask he wanted, but he was wise, like I said. He saw Goldstein squeal and kick and cry. He saw my face go blank and hungry when I swung the tire iron with everything on the man's back. Sean couldn't sift the ground I stood on, but right then, I'd say he recognized that what separated me from any of the other violence he had known was small and slight.

I hope I was more than a brute to the both of them. But damn it all if I didn't feel a pressure lifted when I took off the Jew's ear. As if my heart doubled in size, I felt everything in the world—even the overcast sky.

Marcus's boy had just about every option on the Mercedes, and that included a fuzzbuster that smelled the highway patrol more than a mile away. For the first hour after Alamosa, I resolved myself to being caught. I figured Marcus would buy a helicopter and run us down on the highway. He'd shoot us up with his golden nickel cannon and send us into a snowdrift, dead before we hit the wet. But as we cleared Durango, I realized he wasn't coming—not for now. I slowed down, and my nerves went back to craving a grand fix, thick like sugar. My palms sweat. My chest shook, and I chewed on my cheek, fighting it with all I had.

Sean and Maddie were stretched out on the backseat. Sean lay on top of Maddie, and she held him tight with her small arms. My gut was always to write Maddie off because she was barely twenty. She listened to shit music and still binged on ecstasy and pot. But in truth, her mind and body weren't rotted like mine. She spoke clear to herself and didn't fiend like me. She was grown up, had her own stories. I feared she would come around and see me standing with the remains of my life around me. I told myself if I loved her enough, she would never be able to throw me away.

The 160 ducked down into Arizona at the Colorado border. This is the four corners of the Southwest, where Colorado, Utah, Arizona, and New Mexico meet respectively and alone in the United States.

The Navajo still run the place, and as midday hit, the few wagons and RVs that had been with us since the end of Colorado exited off for the tourist trap on the side of the highway. A large new Airstream honked at us as it pulled off. The young couple inside smiled at us, thinking we were something we weren't.

It wasn't safe to head straight to Phoenix. Marcus would wait. He had Ben and his broken man with him now, and if it was just a hateful game before, the work on Goldstein made it dark and personal for Marcus and his bottomless bank. At the time, I had thought the hurt I put on his man would scare him away. But now—with me and my sore fists—I realized I had just made all the outcomes worse. No, we'd follow the 160 till I found a highway breaking back north, and then Utah and rest.

Maddie climbed into the front seat and kissed me on the cheek. She pressed buttons randomly on the center console. Lights and fans turned on and off.

'How do you turn on the radio?' she asked.

'I don't know. I tried to figure it out and gave up.'

She reached over and rubbed my hands on the steering wheel.

'Are you all right?' she asked.

'I'm fine. Why?'

'I mean your hands. Do they hurt? You're shaking.'

'No . . . Yes, a little bit.'

She reached behind my seat and got her handbag from the floor.

'Will this help?'

In her open palm was a small plastic baggie of meth.

'Where did you get that?'

'Noni had a bunch on New Year's, but we didn't do any. I kept some.'

'Put it away. I told you already—Christ, I have to drive.'

I watched as she folded it and put it in her change purse.

'Well, it's here if you need it.'

Maddie found the right button for the radio and clicked it on. Tinny pop music blared before she found the volume control and turned it back down. Sean woke up in the backseat, startled by the noise. As soon as his eyes opened, fear broke over his face.

'What happened?' he asked.

'Sorry, it was my fault. I was trying to put on some music,' said Maddie.

I felt his eyes on me in the rearview mirror. When I glanced up, he looked away.

'Sean, you should start thinking about what kind of jacket you want,' I said. 'You're gonna need some warmer clothes where we're going.'

His eyes stayed out the window.

'Like that ski mask that guy had, remember?' I said. 'You still want one of those?'

'I don't want a mask.'

'I just thought you liked them—'

'Where are we going?' he asked.

He met my eyes, demanding an answer.

'Utah. We're going to Utah. I know a place up there that's really—'

'When am I going to see my dad?'

He was terrified. He had slept and rest, and now was realizing he was in another car with another man given to violence and a girl he barely knew. Maddie turned around and held out her hand.

'Sean, give me your hand,' she said.

He reached out, voice shaking.

'I'm scared. I miss my dad.'

'I know, baby. I'm scared too,' said Maddie. 'Frank and I are going to get you back to your dad as soon as we can. But right now, it's not safe. Your granddad sent that man back there to get you. He was going to hurt you. We can't take you back till we know that everything is going to be safe—for all of us, okay?'

Sean wiped the few tears from his face and gave Maddie half a smile.

'Okay.'

When Maddie turned back around, I saw she was crying too. She swiped at her tears with the cuff of her jacket, and what was left of her eye shadow streaked purple across her pale cheek. She ejected the CD from the radio and threw it at her feet. She turned the volume back up and rolled through the stations till she found some oldies with plenty of static. I wanted to pull over, take them both in my arms and tell them no matter what, I would keep them safe. I would tell them I had a big good heart. I would tell them I was going to save Ben from that pig, Marcus. But I didn't know if I could. I could tear and rip and claw, but I knew better than anyone that didn't mean jack. It only gave one guarantee: more running and more blood.

The Supremes came on quiet on the radio when we passed through Kayenta, Arizona. Highway 98 North was thirty more miles away.

'Sean,' I said, 'I don't know how, but I promise everything is going to work out all right. It always does.'

He didn't say anything and lay back down on the backseat.

'I mean it. I'm going to get you back to your dad, and I'm going to take care of your granddad for you. I'm not going to let either of them be mean to you no more. I promise with everything I've got.'

To this day, I hope he heard me.

UTAH

'The drought air and red dirt make the crystal mean,' Santer used to say. He was a crank cook with all his fingers, and when I met him in Santa Fe, all he asked for was ten thousand dollars to buy a broken-down trailer to start up his new kitchen. Santer was a white man on the back end of his fifties with a giant *MT* branded on his back below his neck. From a distance, the letters looked like two hand-sized black tumors. You could always see them because he kept his hair short and only wore torn-up wifebeaters to show off his tattoo of a burning Jim Beam bottle on one arm, and on the other some old, forever-healing tracks. It was five years ago—the spring of 1995— and Ben was well on his way down. Ali was swinging murder and driving up to Los Alamos on the weekends to fuck some local dealer for Ziplocs of uncut coke. She was filling Ben's desk drawer with blow and telling him that it turned her on when he drank Everclear straight. Ben would fuck her until she cried and then lock himself away, blasting at the coke for days. Always, he'd show up at my door with a greasy bag of gas station burritos and the handle of Everclear. Once, I tried to hide in the bathroom, hoping he'd give up and go away, but that just sent him into a fit. He screamed 'fuck all' in my front yard and took a gardening shovel to the kitchen window. This was all fine by Ali. She knew after three hours of work on the blow, Ben would sign any check for any amount as long as she let him spit on her asshole and then take her—a more-than-fair trade.

Always, three days later, Ben would come-to on a bed in my garage—nose dried with blood, hungry. He'd do his business over the phone, checking the numbers on the casinos, and then break into a rage saying somebody was on the take. He never said a word about Ali's angling until he put the cheat together himself. By then, Sean was calling Marcus 'Pappy' and Ali was having at the desk drawer all by herself.

The sad thing is, when he told me, I didn't believe him.

While Ben was raging in the garage, Santer was cooking in the middle of Santa Fe. If nothing else, the old man was resourceful. He was from Montana but had to leave because he killed his only family in a kitchen fire. He didn't suffer a scratch, but he watched a fireball burn his fourteen-year-old son alive, turning the boy into scorched driftwood. He rode a piece-of-shit Harley and said that every morning after the accident, all he smelled over the whole of Montana was Jon Jr.'s burning chestnut hair. He loved the boy more than anything. For years, he'd been putting away for a vocational school in Spokane. They had planned to open up a motorcycle shop together, father and son. He said, on the day, the fire burned in a rainbow, and Jon Jr.'s screams were the color of flame.

No more than five months later, Santer was set up off Cerrillos Road cooking the same shit that toasted his son. By the end of the summer, he had paid me back double what I loaned him and offered me another stack to make trunk runs of his 'Burning J' meth to trash all over the four corners. He vacuum-sealed the kilos in red bags and handwrote 'In Memoriam, Jr.' on each of them. I reminded him, if anything ever happened, he had ratted on himself with the fucking inscriptions. That made him smile, then cry, and say,

'It would be a fucking honor. This is all that's left of Jon J. If anybody changed it, I'd gut 'em from teeth to toe.'

Ben thought we could make more money skimming from the memorials. I never saw it. I just knew the first time I touched Santer's Burning J, I saw God inside a fat pregnant white girl. She asked me if my cock got harder on crank. I told her I never noticed. She bent over and put a line on her lower back. I snorted it—sweat and all—and fucked her for another day. I wanted it every day like that, and it didn't take much to get me to thieve from Santer and his dead son.

I emptied the last four thousand dollars out of my bank account in Page, Arizona. I still had another three thousand on me, but for now, I wanted Marcus to think I was desperate, closing out all my accounts. The teller at the Wells Fargo called her manager over, and he squared me up and down for half an hour, trying to figure what I needed with such a grip. I told them Sean was dying, and in a last-ditch effort, we were heading to Mexico to get frozen deep-sea water pumped through his veins. Both the teller and manager cried while they counted out the money in wrapped stacks of fifties as I had asked.

This whole area was foreign to me. I had made runs for Santer around these parts and still never learned all the south Utah back roads.

All the drops I'd done were on the side of the highway in burned-out refrigerators or abandoned cars. One time, I stayed at a drop a couple miles back, binoculars in hand. I watched a long-haired kid—couldn't tell if it was a boy or girl—pick up three keys of Burning J on a dirt bike. He or she didn't give a damn and sat right there in a ditch with their bike still running. They snorted key bumps until they were shaking, then stuffed the whole package under their jacket and lit off straight towards the mountains. The little Honda spat dust to the sky, and for a moment, you couldn't figure if it was rising or falling.

We stopped at a Walmart just inside Utah. Sean still wasn't talking, and I hoped taking him around some toys would loosen him up. He had slept on and off in the backseat for the past eight hours. The last thing I had heard him say was, 'I need to go to the bathroom.' If he were ten years older, I would have cuffed him to the doors by now. He was clear—I scared him. He didn't trust me no matter how many times Maddie squeezed his leg or made him smile. He needed something familiar. I feared he would up and run on me or scream out, bite my arm, and tell the world I kidnapped him. None of us could afford the beatings and the jail personally served by Marcus Shenk. I aimed to buy Sean's trust back as much as I could.

The Walmart parking lot was still packed at this hour of night. Rows of ragged-out trucks and economy-sized hatchbacks were packed tight in every direction. People walked past us, coming in and out as we parked. It was probably the only useful store in fifty miles, very much by its own design. And while some returned the wrong-sized particleboard shelving, others came out with New Year's deals on televisions and computers. They all stared at us and the dirty

Mercedes. We looked like zombies with Maddie and her red lipstick, piercings up and down her ear. Sean was still wearing Ben's peacoat to his knees, and my face was in a steady scowl because every time I moved, my entire left side shot out with busting pain from throwing the tire iron to the sky. When we walked into the store, the noise of clamor and borderline human grief woke me up. The three of us stood just inside the entrance, lost and useless inside the zoo.

'Sean, you can pick out whatever you want,' I said. 'Just make sure to get a jacket and a hat.'

Maddie looked at me and mouthed out, *Go with him.*

'You know what? I could use a jacket too. You mind if I come?' I asked.

Sean stared at a family leaving the store. There were two boys about his age, and a husband and wife. The family was poor and didn't look much better than us, but they were happy. The worn-out father pushed the cart and yelled at the boys, who were close if not already in a fight. The kids were wired up from the liters of Mountain Dew in their hands. Their mother was a hard thirty carrying another baby at her waist. While all I saw was a beat couple capable of only passed-out sex after their ninth flip-shift at work, Sean looked at the whole thing and wanted to run up, hold the woman's legs, and cry into her chest.

'Sean . . .'

He turned and looked at me, still dazed.

'Does that sound good?' I asked again. 'You wanna go pick out that jacket?'

I stood up straight and held my face up so he could see me

smile. I tried to forget about my wretching back and the cold pistol cramped under my shirt.

'Come on. It'll be fun,' I said. 'And I won't talk about the fucking ski mask. How's that?'

He smiled and took my hand.

'We can still look at them, can't we?' he asked.

'Of course we can look, but you made such a big deal about it. I thought you didn't want one anymore.'

'We just have to find the right one,' he said.

'We'll meet at the front, then?' asked Maddie.

'Maddie, come with us,' said Sean.

'Yeah, come with us.'

'I have to go the girl's section, and I need to get some medicine. I feel like I caught a cold. We'll meet up front, and don't forget to buy underwear—both of you.'

Sean and I walked into the aisles with their blue signs and yellow smiley faces pointing out the weekly daily forever deals. The whole place smelled like wet candy, and the linoleum was scuffed with dry mud and boot marks. The lights were too bright, and the chatter and the yelling from the whites and the Mexicans pinched at my ears. The noise needled into my brain. I heard Ben's voice, spitting and saying, 'If this place was aflame, we'd all be better off. What I would do for a bulldozer right now.' *Laugh. Laugh. Chuckle. Chuckle. Burn. Burn.* I didn't listen to any of it, not a word. I felt Sean's hand inside mine and, in my chest, the worry fell away. He held tighter, but not out of fear or fright. I want to say he felt safe right then between all the racks and shelves. We could have been anywhere, and he didn't care.

Sean and Maddie were asleep when we pulled into Big Water, Utah. I had wanted to find a remote horse ranch off the highway. During the day, Sean would ride an old mare in his new blue Walmart parka while Maddie and I ate steaks and had sex till I was healed. But when we pulled into the parking lot of the Cowboy Inn, I saw no stables or restaurant. Across the road, a drive-through liquor shack flashed a fluorescent '24-Hour Cheap Drunk' in its window. My eyes burned. We'd been driving all day. My back and side were cramped-up from sitting, and my right leg was numb from holding down the gas pedal. The cruise control in the Benz was either broken or I just didn't know how to set it. I parked the car in front of the motel office and squeezed softly on Maddie's thigh. When her eyes opened, I took out some cash and set it on her lap.

'I need you to get us a room.'

'Where are we?' she asked.

She sat up and looked out the tinted windows.

'Utah, a few hours in,' I said. 'I can't drive anymore today.'

'Is it safe?'

'I haven't seen anybody on the road for the past couple of hours.'

'I think we should keep going.'

'To where?'

'I don't know—Salt Lake. Somewhere with more people.'

'We ain't going to Salt Lake. I need rest. I don't feel right.'

'What about Marcus and the police?'

My palms started to sweat, and my mouth went dry. The car felt like it was still moving. The back of my head pounded away. My bet was any minute my jaw would start shaking and then the rest of the tremors.

'Go get us a room, all right? I'm going across the street for some aspirin and something to drink.'

Maddie took the cash from her lap and stuck it in the pocket of her jeans.

'What about Sean?' she asked.

'Take him with you. I'll be right back.'

The cold air felt good on my face. My legs were shaky, and all the aches on my side slapped with pain. My fiend had been rolling through me all day. One moment, I felt fine—happy the heat worked in Goldstein's car—then my stomach would turn. I felt exhausted, angry that I was responsible for Sean, the little shit, and my little sleeping tramp in the backseat. I needed to sit down with my nurse, take some worry off the edge.

The wind flew into my feet, hit my body, and went straight up into the sky.

I stood at the side of the two-lane highway scared to cross, as if my weight on the asphalt would trigger a speed train or stampede. I took in a full chest of cold air and blew it out quick, trying to get my wits. I focused on the front door and lights of the The Old Mine liquor store and tried my best to walk in a balanced stride across the highway.

Inside the store, there weren't any customers. The cashier sat in a fold-up chair by a space heater behind the counter. With one eye, he watched satellite on a thirteen-inch TV, and kept the other on a smaller black-and-white security monitor.

'You guys sell liquor?' I asked.

'That's what the fucking sign says,' he said, not looking up.

'I need some bourbon, some beer, aspirin.'

He muted the television, picked up an empty wine box at his feet, and stood up, holding a shotgun in his other hand.

'Whiskey's in the back. If you aim to rob me, I'll shoot you. So I'd prefer if you didn't wander around while I get the bottle.'

'I'll need two.'

'What's your poison?'

'Nothing cheap.'

He lifted the counter, walked to the back of the store, and unlocked a closet next to the last refrigerator.

'I've got Beam, EW, Crow, and a few others,' he yelled.

'Give me two bottles of the Crow.'

He put the bottles in the box, walked over, and set it next to the register.

'Fill it up with whatever else you want,' he said. 'It's on me. This is my last night.'

I got a six-pack of Olympia, chips, aspirin, Tylenol, and some chocolate bars for Sean. For a moment, the cashier eyed me down the two aisles, but then he got bored and turned the television back up. I didn't say a word of thank you to him as I left. In the reflection of the door, I saw him glance at me one last time. He pulled his lips back and sucked at his teeth, lonely and pissed.

Across the street, Maddie had moved the car in front of one of the rooms and left on a light. Just like before, I took a deep breath before I crossed the highway black. Call it what you want, but that night, I had coward's sight. I felt like garbage, a dead pile of leaves waiting to get kicked, burned, or stuck with each step. I was close to tears like I knew something was coming. By the time Sean opened the door, I was crumbling, out of breath.

'Where'd you go?' he asked.

'I've got a bad headache. I needed to get some things. Where's Maddie?'

'In the bathroom.'

'You want a chocolate bar?' I said, pulling a Nestlé Crunch from the box. 'Don't eat it all. Save some. That shit will make you sick.'

He sat on the bed while I took off my jacket and turned down the heater. The room was stuffy and cramped. All the Walmart bags were piled up at the end of the bed. The bathroom door was cracked open, and a steady blanket of steam poured out from the top. I knocked on the door.

'I'm almost done,' Maddie said from inside.

'I got you some beer.'

'What'd you get yourself?'

'The same and some more.'

'Just give me a minute.'

I took one of the glass tumblers from next to the sink and poured three fingers of bourbon. I sat on the edge of the bed gulping it down, trying to straighten out my nerves. Sean smacked on the chocolate bar while he flipped through the channels like a madman. It wasn't two minutes before I poured another tumbler and moved the only chair to the front door and cracked it open. Maddie came out wrapped in a towel.

'What are you doing?' she asked. 'It's freezing outside.'

'I want to smoke a cigarette. I didn't want to stink up the room.'

'Well, close the door. I'll catch a cold if I don't have one already. I don't care if it smells.'

'I need some air. I've got a mean headache.'

'Why are you smoking, then?' asked Sean.

'Sean, get under the covers,' said Maddie. 'Frank—'

Before she could finish, I grabbed the bottle of bourbon and walked out, trying my best not to slam the door. The window still shook. I could hear Maddie talking to Sean in a low voice. He asked what was wrong with me, and she told him to take it easy, get ready for bed. I was just tired, she said, and we all needed rest.

Across the empty parking lot, the blinds pulled back and the manager of the motel looked out of her den office. She stared at me with no shame. I mad-dogged the old broad right back, took two swigs from the bottle, and sucked on the cigarette until it was out. That made the drapes fall back, and the lights switched off over the whole building, leaving only the blue glow from the television set inside. My arms should have been shivering with cold, same with my hands. My legs were numb, and my whole upper back was a knot of cramps—that same snake swatting at my fat marbled brain. Like a stale machine, a groan leaked from my chest as I squatted down and put my back against a three-foot-tall finger-painted cutout of a whooping cowboy.

I didn't need this right now. The fight with the Jew had bellied me up. My body was jamming, demanding a big nasty fix.

For the past couple of years, these shakes had gotten worse and worse. D.T.'s, watery shits, busted vessels in my eyes—every single time, the fiending stopped me from going dry. Right then, I would have given anything to cake my nose with blow or smoke glass till my teeth sang Gospel. The only resolve I'd come to was to 'stay off the hard stuff' and try to calm my nerves with hooch or sex or sleeping pills, hot showers, hamburgers, milkshakes, lines of rocks of Ritalin, diet pills, green chile stew, unfiltered cigarettes, or plates of pancakes soaked in maple syrup and a stick of butter.

My plan to kick had been to sneak off to Jemez when time and life allowed. I'd heard of an Indian sweat lodge in the low hills that was doling out ibogaine treatments to 'lics and heads. For two days, you'd stay out there eating young cactus salads and drinking watered-down tequila before they dosed you with the ibogaine and sent you off with a teenage kid to keep watch. For three more days, you sweat it out with God, Africans, and African Gods in a PVC-pipe teepee. Story was, you would rise from the dead fifty pounds lighter but lacking any whiff of craving or fiend.

Maddie cracked open the door.

'You coming in anytime soon, or should I come out?' she asked.

'I just finished my smoke, but I can have another.'

'Let me just get my jacket. Do you want a beer?' she asked.

'Yes ma'am.'

She stepped inside and came back out wearing her jean jacket with her hair wrapped in a towel. She handed me a beer and pulled out a cigarette.

'You all right?' she asked.

'I'm just wound up from all the driving and the whole day. I'm worried about Ben, ya' know? How about you?'

'I keep feeling like I got a cold coming on,' she said. 'My stomach hurts, but then I feel okay—just need sleep, I think.'

She sat on the hood of the car, worried and not knowing what to say.

'You got Sean that chocolate bar?' she asked.

'He didn't eat all of it, did he?

'No.'

'I told him not to. Not right before he goes to bed.'

She turned around and stood in front of me, staring at the ground between us. I held up the bottle of whiskey.

'You want any of this?' I asked.

'No, I'm going to bed. You coming in?'

'In a minute.'

'Well . . . I love you.'

She dropped the smoke and let it burn on the ground. She went back inside and shut the door tight. I heard their dulled voices again through the bricks and plaster. The TV got quiet. One of the lamps switched off. I rubbed my knees. I felt my bones. I turned my collar up and fastened the top button. I drank again from the bottle and then again and again. I was cold, and now I was sorry. I sat on my ass and pulled my knees to my face. I told myself I wouldn't sleep outside again, trading my dreams with the cold. I would slip into bed and hold my Maddie close. I'll tell Sean I love him and get out of these clothes.

No, I won't sleep outside tonight. I made myself promise.

My eyes closed out of habit, but all I heard were girls singing on lust. I was drunk and sweaty on the ground of the Cowboy Inn. The carpet made me itch—all the lint and dirt. There was an awful must in the place. A vagrant's fungus from all the piss-poor travelers taking a night in Big Water, Utah. They left it for me. All those bums. Left it on the cardboard sheets and the dust-stained drapes. They shat the carpet, rubbed it in with their hobo boots.

I threw the blanket off and rolled onto my side. I tossed on the ground, trying to think better of myself, but gave up and went to the bathroom. I threw off my shirt into the empty tub. I took a washcloth and wet it with warm water. I wiped my neck, my face, my chest. I washed my hands and face with the chip of soap. *I am sick enough right now*, I thought. *My skin is pulled tight over my bones. I'm just barely getting on.* I wanted to cry or scream, but instead I locked the door and turned up the faucet.

Maddie's giant purse was on top of the toilet. The black leather was patched with punk bands and pieces of denim. I picked it up and dug until I found that New Year's stash. Sweating meth, like I said. I poured it all on top of the toilet and shaped it into a triangle with my finger.

'This is more than enough.'

I felt my lips move and was surprised when I heard my voice, deep and loud in the tiny bathroom. Like I was in a tunnel. Like

I was back in Mexico with Santer in that dry tunnel, every sound jumped back to me whistling sin, carrying death. I wet my lips and leaned over, putting my face to the crank. I snorted deep with my right nostril until the bridge of my nose burned hot. I pulled away, breathed deep, and bent over again for my left nostril. I buried my face in the pile. The pedigree was gone. I was Nero. I was Caesar. String me up. Drink your blood. There was a second before the world started tumbling, and then the rush set in. Gasoline's garnish, this stuff—the devil's dick all over my face.

When I picked up my shirt from the tub, the fluorescent above the mirror got bright and warm. My jaw grew in my face, and my heart pounded in my chest.

I snorted another chunk off the porcelain, wet my fingertips, and shoved them up my nose, cleaning out any leftovers. I ripped off a scrap of toilet paper, rolled it through my nostril, and pulled out specks of blood, hair, and crystal. I smacked on the wad like Sean had with the chocolate bar, but instead of sweet, crisped rice, it was bitter salt, bitter hair. I wiped the back of my neck again with the rag and snorted another bump. I looked on the ground for the cigarette cellophane Maddie had packed the shit in. The dirty grout breathed out to me, making the floor a mess of white squares bordered in black maggots. I gave up and pulled my smokes from my pocket and took the baggie from my own pack. I scraped the rest of the crystal in, folded the cellophane over twice, and sealed it back up with my lighter. I put it back in Maddie's change purse. She wouldn't miss a thing.

I turned off the bathroom lights and opened the door. My pupils ratcheted in my face. Squares of rainbow lights floated in the room. I stood frozen, waiting for them to fade.

'What are you doing?'

Maddie's whisper came out from the black in front of me.

'Frank, what are you doing?' she asked again.

'The fucking light blinded me is all.'

I saw her face and her eyes. She was standing in front of me. I couldn't figure out if her hair was just tied back or melting into the stinking dark behind her.

'Did you see where I put that bourbon?' I asked.

'No, I was asleep when you came in. What were you doing in the bathroom?'

'I was cold. I took a shower.'

I tried to get past her, but my foot got caught up in one of the Walmart bags, and I tripped to the floor. The corner of the TV console cut into my hip. I knew it should hurt, but all I felt was a pinch.

'Jesus! Are you okay? I'll turn on a light—'

'No. No. I'm fine. I don't want to wake Sean up. We need to get going in a few hours.'

Maddie went into the bathroom, turned on the light. She was still half-asleep. I heard the toilet seat drop and her feet shuffling as she sat down. I crawled on the ground, feeling around in the dark, and found the bourbon next to my boots. I sat back and took two hard chokers. The toilet flushed, and Maddie opened the door.

'Come lay down with me,' I said.

'Sean's sleeping.'

'He won't hear anything.'

'No, Frank.'

She tried to walk past me to get to the bed, but I grabbed her arm and pulled her down.

'Ow! What the fuck are you doing?'

I put one hand over her mouth, cupped her pussy with the other, and started grinding with my palm. She kicked at me, screamed, bit at my hand.

'Get it wet for me, Maddie,' I gnashed into her ear.

I was hard. I stuck my hand down her pants. The more she struggled, the more I wanted to fuck. I pulled out my cock, rubbed it on her stomach.

'Let me fuck you, baby.'

She reached down and took my cock. She stroked it up and down, and her body relaxed underneath me.

'That's it, Maddie. That's my girl.'

She gripped tighter and then yanked my cock straight down. A line of deafening pain blasted through my body, drowning out the crank. I pushed her off, slamming her into the bottom of the bed.

'Is that what you fucking wanted?!' she screamed in a whisper.

I folded up on the ground, both hands over my dick. She kicked at me with both her legs. Her voice cracked as she started to cry.

'You piece of shit! You do my fucking crystal and think you're going to fuck me?!'

She hammerfisted me hard on the face and then went to slap me, but I caught it.

'Stop—I'm sorry,' I said.

Her right hand flew around and slapped me on my cheek. Before I could think, I punched her in the jaw.

'You quit it, Maddie.'

She didn't wail. She just stopped, closed her eyes, and then opened them on me. Her chin dropped to her chest, and she looked up at me in the little bit of light. Any part of her that loved me ran and caucused with that pain. This is what I have to say on shame—her arm went limp in my hand, tears dropped down her face.

'Let go of me,' she said.

'You hit me, Maddie . . .'

'Let go of me.'

'Let me see your face.'

She stood up, buttoning up her jeans.

'Maddie, let me see your face. I'll get some ice.'

She crawled back into the bed. I grabbed the bottle and took another big mouthful before I lay back on the ground. The mattress shook with Maddie's sobs. I felt around for the pistol. I would have shot me in the face, if I were her. I would have stomped my face and pressed the barrel to one of my sockets. I found the gun behind my boots and slid it close to my hand.

Dawn filled the room with blue-gray light. Not enough to read by, but enough to see the stains on the ceiling and the welts on my chest. I sat up and looked at the bed. Sean was turned away, sound asleep. Maddie was on her side facing the window. Her arms wrapped around a pillow, eyes open, face wet and red, staring out a crack in the drapes. I got up and put on my jacket and boots.

'We need to get going once the sun's up.'

I went outside and watched the sky slowly warm. I held my head, trying to make sense and forget what happened at the same time. I waited till the single flood lamp in the parking lot shut off before I started to walk two miles away from the Cowboy Inn. I only thought, *heel and toe,* but my heart stomped and my chest filled with a loathing and revolt that soured my stomach. When the sun rose and I felt a bit of heat on my face in that cold air, I knew another night was gone, and I was worse off. Blood clots came from my stomach on the side of the highway. Then the red lessened to just whiskey and bile. I didn't hear any cars or see any grand sights. The clouds were uniform and steady. I wiped my mouth with my hand, turned back, and stared at the dirty snow and rutted-out road. My body burned. My face screwed up like I was born from acid and glue.

Sean was still in bed, curled up under the sheets watching television.

'Where's Maddie?' I asked.

He shrugged his shoulders without breaking his stare at the local weathergirl.

'Sean, was she here when you got up?'

'She was getting dressed.'

The TV's speaker buzzed every time the weathergirl squawked in her high little voice.

'And then she just left?' I asked.

'Yeah.'

'Did she say where she was going?'

Sean's eyes wouldn't move from the blondie. I walked over and stood in front of the screen.

'Sean, look at me. Did she say where she was going?'

'*Nooo*,' he said, rolling his eyes.

'You need to get up. We need to get moving.'

'Can I finish watching this?'

'The weather? No. You gotta wash up and get dressed.'

He ignored me and rolled his head to the side, trying to see the screen around me. I slammed my hand on the knob, turning it off.

'Come on. Move it,' I said.

He groaned, flipped the covers down, and swung his legs out to the floor. I threw one of the Walmart bags at his feet.

'Put on your new stuff. It's warmer.'

He picked up the bag and went into the bathroom. In only one night, the room already smelled like we'd been there for years. The open bottle of bourbon and half-drank beers mixed with the heat from the furnace and bankrupted any hope. I shut off the heat, cracked the door, and started looking around the room for Maddie's things but remembered all she had were the clothes on her body and that purse.

'Sean, is Maddie's bag on top of the toilet?' I asked through the door.

'No, I don't see it.'

I was still moving on the crank. My face hurt, and my stomach was rolling on me. I emptied a water bottle into my mouth and sat down on the edge of the bed. I would have left too. I wouldn't have said a thing and walked out just like she did. Sean came out of the bathroom in his new jeans and sweatshirt with the tags still on.

'I can't get the prices off,' he said, straining to reach his back.

'Come here.'

I ripped the plastic threads off his collar and back pocket.

'Get your jacket on.'

Maddie didn't have any money—not enough to get anywhere. All our cash was folded and paper clipped in my jacket pocket.

'Aren't we going to wait for Maddie?' he asked.

'She'll be here. Help me get everything into the car. Did you put all your old clothes into that bag I gave you?'

'Yep.'

'Good.'

I rinsed out a glass tumbler and drank some more water, hoping in vain to flush the meth and bourbon. I brushed my teeth, wet my face and hair, and patted dry. I kept thinking we had more bags, but when we left the room, I was carrying two and Sean had just the one. I threw the bags in the backseat of the Benz and took Sean's hand as we walked across the gravel parking lot to the motel's office. I squinted down both lengths of the interstate hoping to see Maddie hitchhiking, but the road was still quiet and the land moved up and down in this stretch. When we opened the door, the old woman I had seen at the window the night before was carrying a potted plant to the back.

'Just a second. I'll be right back,' she said over her shoulder.

I dropped the motel key on the counter and went back to the window to look for Maddie.

'There she is,' Sean said, pointing across the street.

Maddie was walking from the liquor store with a brown bag in her arms. She headed straight to the car.

'Looks like we might get a break from the snow today,' said the old woman, carrying out a small radio.

She plugged it in under the counter, picked up our room key, and hung it on a numbered rack behind her.

'You didn't mess the place up, did you?' she asked.

'We didn't make the bed,' I said.

'Where are you headed today?'

'West.'

'If you want, you can put a pin on the map. The kids like doing it.'

She pointed to the far wall where a United States map was scotch-taped to the fake wood paneling.

'There's some pins up here in this jar,' she said.

I picked it up and held it out to Sean. He fished out a yellow pushpin and walked over to the map.

'Where are we?' he asked.

'See where the gold star is?' I said. 'That's us.'

'Where are we going?'

I took his hand and moved it down to Chihuahua, Mexico.

'It's more fun if you let him do it,' said the woman behind me.

She glanced over, smiled, and then went back to wiping the leaves on her plants.

'Put it wherever you want,' I whispered.

Sean scanned the whole map before he shoved the pin into the middle of the Pacific. The old woman frowned, insulted we had ruined her game.

'We're going sailing,' I said.

When we walked out, Maddie was sitting on the rear bumper of the car. Her bottom lip was black and blue, split and scabbed with black blood. Sean ran ahead and started punching on her arm.

'We're going to the ocean! We're going to the ocean! What happened to your face?'

I walked slowly, avoiding Maddie's glare. I wasn't looking right. My face was pale. I felt my eyes bloodshot and wide. All of me was still high.

'There's a phone ringing in the car,' said Maddie.

'Where?'

'In the car—I don't know.'

As I got closer, I heard a muffled electronic dance beat.

83

'Is it yours?' I asked her.

'No. Unlock the car,' she said. 'It's fucking freezing.'

I pressed the unlock button on the key, and Maddie put the paper bag in the backseat with Sean.

'Be quiet for a second,' I said. 'I gotta find it.'

Maddie slammed the back door and got into the front.

'It's in here,' she said, opening the glove compartment and pulling out a ringing flip phone. 'It's Marcus.'

'Give it to me.'

I closed the driver's door and walked to the front of the car. The disco beat stopped, and for a moment I felt relief, as if somehow Marcus gave up looking for Sean, but after a couple of seconds, the screen lit up again, and I answered.

'Hello?'

'You still got it, I can say that much.'

'Ben?'

'What the fuck, Frank?'

He was chewing, eating. His lips clapped with spit as he spoke.

'Where the hell are you?' I asked.

'What the fuck were you thinking? *His ear?* You took off Goldstein's fucking ear?'

'He came at me.'

'Fucking right, he did,' said Ben. 'And now he's laid up in some Colorado hospital sharpening his fucking chalef carving your face into the wall.'

'Like I said, he came at me.'

Ben laughed, and I smiled. For a moment, I wasn't in Utah, and it was old times. We giggled like brothers who'd just pulled a death-trap stunt. There was no blood, no tears—if the world was falling on top of us, we didn't care because we had each other.

'Did you call Santer?' he asked.

'Where are you?'

'Did you call him, Frank?'

'Where the fuck are you, Ben?'

'I'm back in Santa Fe. Marcus had a trooper drive me back. I was fixing to ditch out at a rest stop, but then I flashed some cash, and guess who's driving me down to Phoenix?'

'The trooper?'

'My new best friend. How's Sean?'

Maddie sat in the front seat of the Benz staring past me through the dirty windshield. Her eyes blinked, and her busted lips moved as she talked to Sean bouncing around in the backseat.

'He's all right,' I said. 'He's fine, misses you.'

'Tell him we'll be together soon.'

I walked to the back of the car out of Maddie and Sean's sight and took a deep breath, talked low.

'Ben, I'm not calling Santer,' I said. 'I got money out, and I know where to find the coyotes—the good ones.'

'I knew you wouldn't call—'

'I'm telling you, we don't need him.'

'So I did.'

'Fuck you, Ben.'

'No, fuck you, Frank. This is my son. I'm not leaving this up to some goddamn Home Depot van in a back alley. You gave me your word you'd get us to Phoenix. Don't make me start counting off favors. Do I have to remind you of Nogales?'

'I don't want Maddie around Santer, and you sure as hell don't want him around Sean.'

'Then leave them at a fucking motel—done. This only works if we do it now, Frank. Marcus is driving back with Ali and the Jew right now. I gotta be gone.'

'I don't like it.'

'It ain't yours to like, Frank.'

I wanted to drop the phone, crush it under my boot, but just like before—before I could stop myself—I heard the words come out my mouth.

'All right.'

'Do you remember where he's at?'

'As long as he hasn't moved, yeah.'

'He hasn't, Frank. He's excited to see you. They both are.'

'When are you getting there?'

'Tonight,' said Ben. 'What about you? Where are you guys?'

'Pray to the sun, and you'll see me soon enough.'

I closed the phone before he could start in with another jackass demand. Ben didn't know who he was getting in bed with. He thought he would just wave some money in Jon Santer's face, and the old biker would float him and Sean into Mexico like a pair of ghosts. He didn't understand that for folks like Santer, things always go wrong. *There's no straight lines in the world*, Santer would say, and he was right. There's no more level. I took out the battery from the phone and got back into the car. I stuck it all in the glove compartment and slammed it closed. As we pulled out of the parking lot, Sean pushed himself forward between the seats.

'Where are we going?' he asked.

Maddie looked at me. She wanted to know as much as Sean. I turned back onto the highway. The engine knocked hard, still cold.

'I want to go home,' said Maddie.

'I know. We're going to Arizona, and then I'll take you home.'

'If you lie, Frank, I'll run.'

'I'm not. No more lies.'

She didn't believe me and turned back to the window. She wiped her eyes and shook her head back and forth. I couldn't tell if she was crying.

'Don't worry. We're almost done.'

ARIZONA

Maddie held a cold beer to her lips, hoping the swelling would go down. I didn't want to tell her it was too late, that you have to ice the insult while it's fresh, otherwise it's just about cold on broken skin. She didn't need to say a thing. I made her sick. She'd seen the coward inside me that pissed and shit all over itself like some sort of conviction. I couldn't look at her and say, *I'm so sick, baby. I squared you in your face. Believe it. I want your scared ass and cancer. Love me.* She stared out her window, didn't move. She wanted to be back in Denver with Noni, getting high herself, wondering how much she deserved and how much I'd just up and taken. She wanted a guitar, her father, and a gun—that's all she'd ever need. She would write songs, kiss her daddy, and shoot at the birds and drunks. She would come up with a stage name for herself, take another woman for her wife. That's how a lady would do it. Break all the shits down at once.

In front of us, the shadow of a single-prop Cessna appeared on the road. A deputized crop duster clocking speeders in northern Arizona. I swallowed hard, wet my lips, and as soon as I opened my mouth, I wished I hadn't.

'Just so you know, I'm not expecting anything from you, Maddie.'

'That's good, Frank. I'm glad I don't have your fucking expectations floating over me or what the fuck would I do? Fuck you and your sorry bullshit.'

91

She caught herself before she started yelling. She opened the beer and took one long pull.

'It ain't right what I did, Maddie. I'm sorry I hit you.'

'You're a fucking liar, and what's worse, you know it—how much longer before you just go crazy and beat me down? You think you're the first? Like I don't know you and your bullshit. I'll run. I will leave you with this shit and run.'

She dropped the empty can on the floorboard, pulled the diamond ring off her finger, and dropped it in the ashtray. It knocked dull against the plastic.

'. . . like you're somebody,' she said.

I hated myself as a child, and I hated myself as a man. I was weak as a child, and I was weak as a man. I wish I could say mine and Maddie's hearts were all wrapped up together in lust and sickness and mess—that if she left, she'd cripple herself and feared that more than anything else. When you jam up your loves, squeeze them until there's nothing left, there's little to turn it around. I had poisoned Maddie, blacked up her heart. Begging wouldn't do me any good. Same with lies. The rub was, if she ran—if Marcus got a hold of her—he'd dangle her over my head until I gave up Sean. Then, he'd chop us both up, making his eternal point: I am Marcus Shenk. Everything is mine. *Everything.*

An hour after the Utah border, the 89 South took us past Page, Arizona. We crossed the top of the Colorado River and followed it south. All the knolls and marble canyons were to the west. I never hiked, but in 1982, before all the calamity and New Mexico, I was a nineteen-year-old running from Texas, ripping through this land by myself. I was looking for all the old mining roads and their groves of young jimson plants. Always, I'd end up lost and hungry and would make my way to the highway we were on now. I would drive till I saw a car with people my own age and then tail them close, make them stop. We would exchange names, philosophies, but even back then, all I wanted was a cheap, handsome high. I followed the hippie trucks and bohemians. They all talked the same—folk music, the immaculate glow of Garcia. I'd nod my head, smile, and hope for their dirt weed and mushrooms. *Ain't that the truth? Ain't it?!*, I'd say. I wish I could see any of those strangers now. We'd share some strong black coffee, and I'd listen this time when they said,

Man, this fucking ground, these moments are sacred. That's what I sing about, brother. Heaven is here, always.

Sean woke up in the backseat and started playing with his window, sending it up and down. I was going to stop him, but the blasts of cold air were keeping me awake. I hadn't slept since Denver, and three days later, the speed was almost off and my body was starting to turn.

'Sean, cut that out,' said Maddie.

The cold had woken her up. Sean kept on clicking the button.

'You're going to break it, and then it's going to be stuck,' she said.

'I'm hungry. Can we stop?'

All we had eaten since morning was some crap food from a gas station. Fried pies for Sean, and Maddie took three bites from a dark red apple before she tossed it.

'Sean, we'll stop at the next place we see,' I said.

'I feel sick,' he said.

'It's probably just from all that soda. Lie down, and you'll feel better.'

'I need some fresh air!'

He started in with the window again. Maddie turned around and grabbed him by the leg.

'Cut the shit, Sean!'

I watched him in the rearview mirror staring Maddie down. His hand didn't move from the button.

'Don't think I won't slap you,' said Maddie.

'Come on, Sean,' I said. 'Give it a rest.'

He put his hand back in his lap. Maddie turned around and locked up her jaw. Sean stared at the back of her head with all the anger he could muster.

'We're all just hungry,' I said. 'We'll all feel better when we eat.'

'I'm not *just fucking hungry*, Frank.'

'Stop being so mean!' Sean yelled.

'Shut up, Sean!' Maddie screamed.

'You can be angry with me. Don't go and take it out on him. He didn't—'

'Fuck the both of you!'

Sean leaned forward and spat into Maddie's hair. In one motion, she unlocked her seatbelt, grabbed him, and slapped him hard twice on the face. Sean shrieked, squawking like a raw alarm.

'What the fuck are you doing, Maddie?' I yelled.

I grabbed her arm, pulling her back.

'Get your fucking hands off me!'

She slapped me on the face. Her nails cut deep into the bottom of my cheek. My skin stung hot.

'Get me out of this car! Pull the car over!'

'No, Maddie! Calm down!'

'Pull the fucking car over, Frank!'

'We're in the middle of nowhere. I'm not letting you run!'

Panic broke across Sean's face. He made fists on his cheeks, and his lips stretched to the side of his mouth. His eyes filled red with tears as he wailed louder and louder.

'Let me out of the fucking car!'

She grabbed the door, putting one hand on the handle and the other on the latch.

'Pull over!' she yelled again.

'Stop fucking around, Maddie—'

She leaned into the door, cracking it open. Cold wind roared into the car.

'You know I'll do it, Frank.'

I yanked the Benz onto the shoulder. The car filled with the sound of the tires rutting over the corrugated cement. Before we stopped, Maddie was out the car, running into the snow.

'Stay here, Sean.'

I threw the car in park and went after her. The sun bounced blinding white off the ground. My lungs filled with cold dry air down into my gut. She was already twelve yards away heading for a lone patch of bare trees when she slipped and fell. She pushed herself back up and kept running as fast as she could. She cried loud, and I could hear her breathing hard and fast.

'Maddie, please—'

She turned around, wiping the tears from her cheeks and pulling her jacket closed.

'Fuck you, Frank! I don't want to be here!'

'I don't either.'

'Take me home! I want to go back!'

'I can't—'

'Why?!'

'Marcus will send us up, Maddie. All he wants is Sean. He doesn't even care about Ben—'

'Fuck Ben! He's a piece of shit!'

'If I let you go, he'll use you to get Sean.'

She dropped to the ground crying. She sat back on her knees and sobbed into her chest. I walked up to her and crouched down.

'I'm sorry, baby. I can't.'

'Fuck you, Frank. This shit—'

I put my arms around her and held her to my chest.

'I'm sorry, Maddie. You don't gotta love me anymore. I don't want you to. I'm no better—I'm just trying to do right.'

She pushed off me and stared at the Benz. The passenger door was open, and the big single windshield wiper moved back and forth. I turned and headed back. I heard her feet shuffle then follow me, crunching on the snow. When we got to the car, I looked over the top. She stared at me with the same steady boiling rage.

'I'm sorry,' I said.

'Too much . . .'

I took another chestful of the cold air hoping it would cool the old sorrow in my chest. We both got in, and I turned to check on Sean.

'Hey,' I said.

His tears had dried out, puffed up his cheeks.

'I'm sorry I hit you, Sean,' said Maddie.

She stared out at the highway, still not ready to look at the kid.

'I shouldn't have spit on you,' he said.

'No, you shouldn't have. You can't do that. You can't do that to anyone, Sean,' she said.

I started the car back up and waited for two cars to speed by. I pulled back on the highway and turned the heater up. I heard music right then. Those rich hippies singing in my head. I begged to hear it all. What's he singing? High, drunk, coming down just like now— *Heaven is here. Heaven is here.* Forget it all.

t doesn't change no matter how many times I tell it.

In '96, the drugs took me to Phoenix. There is black space in my memory when I demand Arizona. I say everything is familiar since Maddie. The rest is spots and clips—tinfoil faggots playing broken guitars, blonde-hair clowns going down on me, bus tickets folded into valentines stuffed with ten-dollar bags of drugs. There came a time when Jon Santer outgrew the small market of Santa Fe. He had quit cooking crystal altogether except for small batches of the Burning J. After only eight months, the crystal methedrine ghost of Jon Jr. had scraped through rural Colorado and New Mexico like a giant dirty rake. Mothers were offering up their babies and pussies for just a square of the stuff. They smoked up, shot up, and snorted any table scraps from Jon's kitchen—barely a fingernail, I'm saying.

Day drunk and clipping on Rohypnol, Santer came over and told Ben and me that crank was a wash. He said he wanted a month away and, right then, set to tuning up that piece-of-shit Harley in our driveway. Two hours later, he set out for Phoenix and left me counting all the cash he didn't know what to do with. I got Ben to bring in some locals from the casino with four counting machines to help me go through it. Ben told them to pull all the two-dollar bills and set every third five-dollar bill aside for a family jackpot at the end. I broke it as even as I could, and we still were clearing a grip for the both of us and the Indians, but mainly us.

When Santer came back two weeks later, he didn't even count it all through. He was quiet for a good day, and then got chatty and offered up his shack and kitchen to Ben and me. He said his money went further in Arizona. He'd met Mexicans, he said.

'The fucking real ones too—a whole goddamn family. None of that west Texas *chingón* bullshit going between them. No offense, Frank. I mean, I talked to them through another American Mexican, but my boy barely made out a word. I don't give a shit, so I just set three thousand in front of the mother to try and expedite our goddamn dealings. Let me clarify: I have no fucking clue what these folks were into, but I'm falling in love with the daughter who's waiting at the door. So I put the stack down. Grand Madre calls over to baby boy who can't be but ten. I've been watching the little bear the whole time cause he looks like he's fixin' to pass out from humping this pack around the yard. Sure enough—Madre calls him over, unzips the boy's pack, and pulls out a brick of brown cheeva smack. Little man gives me a smile, and in any language—I don't give a fuck—I know he's thanking me for giving him a goddamn break—cute little bit of sugar that fucker was.

Right then, I punched the dumb shit in the face who was supposed to be translating because if I'd known that—that the whole family was iced enough to keep their stash so close—I'd a dosed all four of 'em, mickey'd their goddamn drinks, cut up their bellies, and ran with it. But, oh, that girl—skin looked like fresh tobacco. Mark it, I'll fuck her in the end—shit, maybe Madre too. Let me tell you,

I've got a new respect. The family was honest the whole way through. Madre's oldest son picked up the stack, counted out twelve hundred, and set it back down. They left me the brick and told me I should come visit 'em in Nogales. Now this shit . . .'

From his duffel, Santer pulled out a large Ziploc baggie filled hand-deep with cheeva and set it on the kitchen island in front of Ben and me.

'This shit ain't the future or the past, boys. This is a healthy habit and honest business. God bless my Jon Jr., but I can't take the tweakers dying on me all at once. That family showed me a sort of courage I've been seeking . . . I lost it all when I killed my son.'

Ben couldn't wait any longer. While Santer collected himself, he poured a finger-fat line of the cheeva on the counter, blasted it, stood up, and fell down.

'Do you see?' said Santer. 'That's no fucking speed, Benjamin, you fucking thief. You aren't capable of much right now besides counting the wrinkles on your dick. I feel better about it already. I'm not trying to kill the world, Frank.'

This man, Jon Santer, broke down to tears right in front of me. I remember feeling a hair of guilt that I had stolen from him. I saw him all—the rotting teeth, wiry gray hair, the red crucifix tattooed on his chest.

'Frank, I want you to come out there with me,' said Santer. 'I was thinking about just leaving this fucking mess here in Santa Fe to you. But what's the good there? Do you see where I'm going with all this? I'm fucking lonely, Frank. I miss my boy. I want you to come out and help me start again. My old girl, Mary, is waiting for us. I told her

I had to come back for you. And don't even worry—I'm real fucking good at it. Run. Stop. Run. Over the border and back. Hopefully, affect this precious world along the way.'

I stared at Ben on the ground and didn't say no fast enough. Before I knew it, I was on the back of the bummed-out Harley hauling to Phoenix. My last good memory is holding tight on to Santer's old ribs, smelling his greasy hair, and then all that black hell comes in. Holes and blackouts. Spots and clips of old blonde strippers and heat—so much heat in the low desert. I worked for Santer. Show me a calendar, and I can allot for the time—fourteen months—but piecing it together is a mess. Being a different man ain't enough. Because before that, I know I saw a man with his head taken off. A woman opened up with a hunting knife from her cunt up. Children at a barrel. I don't know my place in all that. I know a part of me was there.

Maddie put the window down as we drove past the southern mouth of the Grand Canyon. All the snow, dirt, and rock rested in the shadows of late-day sun. The sky was big and clear, and I could see dark formulas of storm clouds gathering south down Highway 89. Save for the radio at a whisper and Sean's quiet breathing as he fell in and out of sleep, we drove in silence. Maddie's cheeks were red and wind torn, and her busted lip had blackened up throughout the day. We were fifteen miles from Flagstaff when she finally spoke.

'I want to call Noni when we stop.'

Her eyes didn't move from the red cliffs and red land.

'You don't have to ask me,' I said. 'We're gonna stop and eat in Flagstaff. Call her there.'

'You're so kind, Frank.'

She mocked me with the last bit. Her hand was out the window, playing with the wind. I didn't say a word. I would eat crow and like it. I leaned back in my seat and held the steering wheel at the bottom with one hand. Maddie figured all it would take was a freezing night in Flagstaff for Noni to come get her. She would get away from me, threaten to call the police and run. It was all an open deal until we got back to Santa Fe.

The highway lights clipped on up and down the interstate as we hit Flagstaff city limits. The pink lamps put off fading yellow lines, and all the red and white lights from the other cars blinded me if I focused on them. My pupils grinded open and closed, trying to get a decent read through the windshield. I sprayed the glass down and turned on the wiper, but all that did was turn the whole picture into bright puddles of echoing light. This was the last bit of comedown off the Utah crank. My forehead beaded up with sweat one more time, and my shoulders and neck started aching from being locked up and high all day. Cold sweat emptied all over my body, and then my face dumped any blood that was there.

'Are you all right?' asked Maddie.

'I'm fine. Just need to eat something.'

My mouth was drying up quick. I grabbed Sean's warm bottle of soda from the backseat and drank it down.

'I can drive, Frank.'

My temples swelled, and my fiend came back with a vengeance. My hands got wet, and the car heated up like a toaster. I cracked my window and breathed in deep. The windshield broke into beams and lines. I checked the mirror to switch lanes and get off the highway, but with the Jew's fucking tint, all I could make out was a wall of dull lights.

'Fuck it.'

I swerved the car into the right lane. Brakes screeched, locking up behind us. Maddie white-knuckled the door handle—too scared to say a word. An exit with bright gas signs came barreling towards us. I bit on my tongue till I tasted blood, hoping the pain would sober me up to take the exit over eighty. I turned on the blinker, put both hands on the wheel, and threw the Benz onto the ramp.

'Where do you guys want to eat?' I asked.

'Just pull over, Frank.'

I clipped the rear tire making a Carrows parking lot and hurled the car into the first space I saw. I opened my door and wretched onto the pavement. Sean was awake in the backseat, but I couldn't turn to look because my head was spinning. I heard his voice but couldn't hear over my stomach throwing it all out.

'Don't worry, it's going to be all right,' said Maddie.

She got out and walked around the front of the car.

'Don't run,' I blurted, vomit leaking from my mouth.

She stooped down and held out a bottle of water.

'I'm not going to fucking run, Frank. Drink this.'

She helped me sit up and held the water to my face. I took a mouthful and spit it out.

'Keep drinking.'

She handed me the water, went back to the other side of the car, and got her purse.

'Come on, Sean,' she said.

This is God's land. It was made clear in the word. The Gospels were written in a desert just like this, and none of them had the benefit of peacock quills or india ink. They used lead pencils and dirty toilet paper, writing on the kief like the waitresses today on their smoke breaks. Even with my chest sore and broken heart failing with speed, I can see my story and piss-poor sorry song come from the same dry desert gutter.

Sean slid around the vinyl booth inside the Carrows. Now it was just the caffeine making him uneasy. All his sleeping in the car was nothing more than his young brain shutting down from trauma, swallowing down our whole stinking lot. Maddie sat next to him trying to keep it together. In the crap yellow light of the diner, we all looked cheap and worse. Maddie's hair was put back from her bruised face with a barrette, and I could see the streaks of blue dye pulled through her black hair. She didn't scowl or smile like she usually did, and her big eyes that were always just sex and secrets broke dull.

A busboy ran by and slid three small glasses of water onto the table. I drank the whole glass while Maddie lit up a cigarette. As soon as I set it back down, she used the empty glass as an ashtray.

'Sean, what do you want to eat?' asked Maddie.

'A cheeseburger and some fries. Can I get that, Frank?'

'Whatever you want,' I said.

A waitress walked over to our table. She was a timeless woman with foul hairspray and perfume. Thirty? Fifty? Her only tells were the glowing liver spots on her forearms. Her eye shadow and lipstick made her look young, but with the grease in the air or maybe just the dried sweat, her skin looked like sailing canvas under her orange uniform.

'You guys look tired. Where are you coming from?' she asked.

'Far away,' said Maddie.

'That's where I'm headed. You ready to order?' she asked.

'Two burgers and fries and—'

'Make it three,' I said.

'You want cheese, mushrooms?'

'Cheese on all of them,' I said.

'American, Swiss, cheddar—'

'American,' I said. 'And more water and a Coke. Do you have beer?'

'Yeah, we have beer till ten.'

'Two beers, then.'

'Budweiser, Bud Light, MGD, Miller?'

'Fuckin' a—surprise me.'

Maddie pushed Sean's menu to the center of the table. The waitress already hated us. She slammed the menus between the ketchup and salt and walked away.

'Be right back,' I said.

I walked through the restaurant looking for the bathroom. People glanced up and looked away. My legs felt heavy, and it was all I could do not to dry heave in the middle of the dining room. A plastic yellow Wet Floor sign was propped outside the bathroom. As I opened the door, my foot caught it, and I heard a Mexican curse me in Spanish. I went into a stall and rolled out a handful of toilet paper. I wet it, wiped my face, and threw my jacket over the top of the stall door. The door opened, and the same shit who cussed my back came in and tried to look busy. He checked the hand towels, wiped the sink next to me. I ran my wet hands through my hair, smelled them, and did it again. He eyed me hard, and I mad-dogged him right back till he left.

When I got back to the table, Maddie and Sean were both eating. I covered my fries in ketchup and cut my burger in half trying to stir up my appetite.

'How long are we going to stay in Phoenix?' asked Maddie.

Sean wasn't listening. He wolfed down the food with his eyes closed. This was the closest thing to a real meal he had had in a few days.

'Not long,' I said. 'I know you want to get back, and Ben—'

'Sean, slow down,' she said.

Maddie rolled a French fry in ketchup.

'Why? What are you thinking?' I asked.

She took another small bite from her cheeseburger and set it down.

'Nothing. I just heard you talking to Ben back at the motel.'

I tried to eat and drank the beer slow, hoping it would loosen me up. I felt the color come back to my face, and my hands quit with the sweat as soon as a bit of food hit my belly.

'Who's Santer?' asked Maddie.

'You don't know him.'

'Are we going to be safe? Me and Sean?'

Sean looked up from his plate, waiting for an answer.

'You'll be safe. We'll all be safe.'

'Can I get a milkshake?' asked Sean.

'Sure. Just get it to-go.'

I threw two twenties on the table, picked up the rest of my burger, and stuffed my face as I walked out. I didn't want to answer any more of Maddie's questions. She was poking me, checking my wits, seeing if I'd bite.

Outside was loud and cold. The little warmth of daylight had been killed off by a freezing wind. Towering white street lamps lit up the whole parking lot. They made the concrete look hard and sharp. Maddie pulled her jacket closed and trotted ahead to the car. Sean walked next to me backward, leaning into the gusts, arms outstretched at his sides.

'Open the doors!' Maddie shouted back.

I pulled the keys out of my jeans and pressed the unlock button.

'Let's go, Sean.'

I tucked my chin and jogged up to the car, but after a few feet, I noticed Sean wasn't with me. I stopped and turned around. He was standing in the middle of the parking lot, arms still out, head tilted up to the sky. His hood was pulled over his head, and in his winter jacket under all the lights, he looked half his size.

'Sean, what are you doing?' I called out. 'Let's go!'

He didn't move. He shifted his weight from one leg to the other, trying to stay warm. I walked back to him.

'Sean, it's freezing. We gotta go, man.'

'One sec.'

He looked straight up and mouthed out some words. His

eyes watered from the cold as his nose turned pink. He shut his eyes tight and pushed his hands together in front of his chest. He opened them back up and held his hand out to me.

'All right, we're ready,' he said.

'Good. What happened to your milkshake?'

'I put it on the ground. It's too cold.'

He squeezed my hand and ran the rest of the way, pulling me along. Maddie was in the passenger seat with her jacket buttoned to her throat and her collar turned up. She smiled as we got closer but caught herself and looked down. I put Sean in the backseat and got in.

'Sean, what were you doing out there?' Maddie asked.

'He dropped his milkshake,' I said.

'I didn't drop it. I was telling my dad not to worry. We'd be there soon.'

'You were praying?' said Maddie.

'No, I was just telling him.'

Phoenix is a lousy picture book, a horror show with a handful of words. I remember kids, lots of them. Teenage shits, probably Maddie's age and younger. They came in packs of three and four for Santer's cheeva. We stayed with Mary Kandi, an old girlfriend of Santer's who somehow never died or gave up. She was a junkie real estate agent, tall and skinny with teased-out blonde hair that fell like Big Bird's nest on her back. I always wanted to ask her age but I never did. Her eyes were always bright—hardwired high in love with Santer—but her face looked a worked-over forty and beaten.

Her house was a flophouse tweaker den. She'd carved up the home into two illegal units. She lived downstairs in the front. Every window was tinfoiled up from the inside. The carpet was stained all over, and there were two shitty electric guitars and an amp but no TV. She let us stay in the upstairs back unit for baggies of Burning J that Santer always traveled with. She would invite all her friends over— fags, hippies, biker folk—and they would go at it strong. Weeklong benders listening to Zeppelin then blaring computer shit. More than once, Santer promised to fix up a kitchen for all these tweakers, but he never got around to it.

The cheeva took a minute to get started. I remember sitting in Mary's kitchen on a dirty plastic table—fucking patio furniture— weighing out twenty and fifty baggies on a triple beam. I was so high on the cheeva, my teeth were shaking. Santer kissed me on the lips and said, 'I told you. Your little black god is having a good time, isn't he? Give him his due.'

I wanted to cry, but we both laughed instead. And then I remember sitting in the living room upstairs. It was smaller. Santer was never home. I was clipping on Dilaudids with one of those old, big cell phones next to me. I was giving directions to the kids, one after another, so they could come score. It's a mess of faces then— just a few of them at a time coming in, getting me high, and then leaving with their baggies. When they left, I'd stumble into the bathroom, punch my face with both hands so I could stay straight for the two minutes it took me to stash my end of the cash in the floor. Santer didn't care. He was taking off to Nogales for days at a time. I remember Mexican music, horns playing all around me. I was having at the cheeva stash more and more often. Then, Mary came over by herself. She was crying, saying 'spics stole her family. We spiked the meth with cheeva and lay on top of each other. She kissed on me with her tongue, and I scratched a scab off my shoulder and let my mouth fall open on her body.

The morning I left, I took an early bus out of Phoenix. Mary and Santer dropped me off at the Greyhound depot in the center of downtown. I remember standing in line, waiting to get on with three Mexican men and a white woman with a baby and another child next to her knee. I had on a leather jacket. I remember that because I was sweating even though there was just a hair of sun from the horizon. Santer thanked me and said, 'Funny how people change.'

I don't know why I was leaving and why Santer was staying. I don't even know the day. I just know when I got back to Santa Fe, Ben wasn't acting right. For a long time, he wouldn't leave me alone in the house and always watched me with one eye. I asked him one morning, 'What the fuck is the problem?' and he wrapped his arms around me and told me he was just glad I was back.

The 17 South took us out of Flagstaff and past Sedona. We drove another eighty miles in dark desert before the yellow highway lights gave way to the pink canopy of Phoenix. When we left the diner, Sean had tried his best to stay awake in the backseat, but eventually, the road noise overtook him, and he folded over. Maddie had been waking and straightening herself up in her seat. She'd wait until we passed at least two mileposts before she'd relax and let her head fall back down against the seatbelt. The closer we got to Phoenix, the more my nerves acted up. My anxiety kicked in the more I sobered. We headed south into the city. Mile by mile, strip malls gave way to long cookie-cutter business buildings—none of them taller than four stories, all brown and flat-faced with tinted windows. The whole city glowed bright. We passed football field car lots lit up by towering flood lamps. Brand-new vehicles pirouetted inside cathedral showrooms behind high walls of clean clear glass. Even on the side streets, the cement gleamed white like it was just poured that morning and had waited till the sun fell to show its true color. Maddie shifted in the passenger seat but didn't open her eyes. The right side of her top lip was still black and blue, but the swelling had gone down since morning. I hate to say it, but at the time, I really believed it would all just pass. I told myself she was young, and youth affords forgiveness and compassion. *Let her be,* I thought, *and she'll turn. She always does.*

Six red lights blinked on top of skyscrapers in downtown Phoenix. It was a predictable city, laid out like so many others: giant four-lane interstates coming from all the cardinals tangling in downtown. Five or six tall black buildings were the skyline, then a stadium, and a tower of sorts lit up in a different color. The downtown streets—save for the one with three or four bars—would be cleared clean by the pigs every night at eleven o'clock. They localized the scum to the south and let them loose on each other while they patrolled the border and made eyes at the whores. It's the same in Denver and Albuquerque. Salt Lake, at least, has their grand white god protecting all the land and underground tunnels—that's a kind of character.

When we were deep enough into the city, I exited off the freeway and put my window down halfway. I took a right at a light, then another left. Even in winter, desert heat rose out of the sewers, and all the downtown bums' piss and shit crawled out of the alleys. Mexicans and blacks, greasy Chinamen and Filipinos in their liquor stores—they all popped out of the storefronts. Marble walls gave way to older sun-bleached buildings and burglar bars.

Sean touched my shoulder. He was awake and smiling.

'Are we here?' he whispered.

'Yeah, we're here. How long have you been awake?'

'Awhile. Are we going to stay here tonight?'

'Probably. Your dad's not getting here till tomorrow.'

It was just getting past eight o'clock in the evening, and this whole side of the city was getting home from work. The noise of car stereos and drunks at bus stops poured through my open window. The smell of grease and charcoal from street grills made the air thick and heavy, even in the coming desert cold. The liquor billboards turned to Spanish. A few homeless with shopping carts milled down the middle of the street, pushing their booty of plastic bottles and tin cans. We stopped at a light, and a Mexican family pulled next to us in an old small Datsun. The man stared at the Mercedes hard, wanting all that came with the Benz. But he could barely see inside and expected anything but strung-out and broken. We drove another mile passing taquerias and closed-up tailor shops. I drove through a light and pulled the car into a Jack in the Box parking lot.

'Are we going to eat?' asked Sean.

Maddie sat up and took some deep breaths, trying to wake up.

'What are we doing?' she asked.

'I need to put you and Sean in a motel while I look up Santer.'

'Why? I thought we were heading home tonight.'

'We will. I just don't want to take you and Sean where I'm going, you get it?'

'I want to go home, Frank.'

'We will.'

'Are you lying to me? Don't lie.'

'I'm not lying, Maddie.'

She didn't have the energy to argue, but if I gave her some time, she would start laying in.

'You don't know where you're going, do you?' she said.

'I do. I do. I just don't want to take you or Sean there.'

'Can we get something to eat here?' asked Sean.

He stared glassy-eyed at the Jack in the Box. I started the car back up and pulled into the drive-through.

'Where are we going to get a room?' asked Maddie.

'I saw a motel a mile or so back.'

Maddie looked out the back window, now noticing the link of shit we were in.

'I don't like it here,' she said.

'I'm not driving to the other side of the city so you can feel comfortable, Maddie.'

The voice from the drive-through speaker blared into the car.

'Can I take your order?'

'Sean, what do you want?' I asked.

He was up on his knees in the backseat, scanning the menu.

'Leave me the gun, then,' said Maddie.

'I can't. I need it.'

'Are you ready to order?' the voice crackled.

'Sean?'

'I want fries and nuggets and a chocolate milkshake.'

'Then we're coming with you,' said Maddie.

'Can we get an order of chicken nuggets, fries, and a chocolate milkshake?' I said, leaning out the window.

'Large or small?'

'What?'

'Large or small on all of them?' the voice spat back.

'Large.'

'Please pull up to the window.'

I rolled the car ahead in the line.

'I can't take you with me, Maddie—'

'Then leave the fucking gun, Frank!'

Sean's face, which had been smiling—excited for the fast food—went blank and quiet. He looked at his hands, bit on his bottom lip, and immediately went back to avoiding my eyes in the rearview.

'All right, I'll leave it.'

When we pulled up to the window, a young black girl held out her hand.

'$6.96.'

I reached into my pocket and gave her a twenty.

'Ya'll want ketchup, salt, hot sauce?'

'Sean?' I asked.

'Ketchup, please.'

The girl grabbed handfuls of ketchup packets from the bins in front of her and handed me our bag through the window. I gave it to Sean, and we pulled back onto the main road and started heading back the way we came.

'Did they give you an extra straw, Sean?' asked Maddie.

'Yeah, there's one.'

She turned around and took it from his hand. She turned on the overhead light and picked up her purse from the floorboard. She went through it, making sure I saw her find the last of her stash in her change purse. She palmed the baggie into the front pocket of her jeans and pulled the straw from its paper sleeve. She needed to cut it in half.

Maddie felt the quick. She didn't care to wait. She didn't care about being a big sister-mother to Sean anymore. When we got to the motel—before I even got the room—she started work on that inch of crank. The East Indian inside the office didn't give two shits once he saw my money. He slid the bathroom key under the bulletproof window, and Maddie walked barefoot around the back of the building. Sean ate his French fries from the bag as we walked to the room. The asphalt was fresh in the parking lot, and the leftover gravel caught under our shoes. It kicked out from our feet after each step.

'Which one's our room?' asked Sean.

'3E.'

He ran ahead and walked down the line of green doors, calling out the numbers.

'1C, 1D, 1E—'

The steel door of the bathroom slammed shut behind us. I turned around. Maddie was walking fast from the bathroom, wiping her nose. She gave the key back to the desk clerk and went to the car and got her shoes from the passenger floorboard. She didn't bother to put them on and carried them with her purse in her hand.

'I found it!'

Sean stood next to the burglar-barred front window of the room. He ate the fries in handfuls and sipped the milkshake from a straw sticking out the top of the bag. When I unlocked the room, he slipped in and jumped right onto the bed. I searched for the light switch. Maddie stood in the doorway. All the light and street noise came in from behind her. Her face was lit up red and yellow from the motel's sign in the parking lot.

'Why don't we pull the car up to the room?' she asked.

I found the switch on the cord behind the bed and turned it on.

'Because I'm heading out as soon as you guys are settled.'

Maddie jumped onto the bed next to Sean.

'We're not settling down. Are we, Sean?'

She grabbed the takeout bag from him and took some of the fries.

'Hey, those are mine!'

'Learn to share,' said Maddie.

She shoved the bag back to him and got up. She ran her hands over the thick polyester cover of the bed and then turned on the bathroom light and stared at herself in the mirror. Her lip was one day healed, still sore. All her makeup was gone, and her usually pale freckles popped bright in the cheap light.

'I look like shit.'

I handed the TV remote to Sean. He turned it on and immediately started flipping through the channels.

'Frank, where's the gun?' asked Maddie.

I took the pistol out from under my shirt and put it on the bed. Sean glanced at it, feeling the weight of it sink into the mattress. Before I could stop her, Maddie grabbed the pistol and started to laugh. Her pupils were big and black. Her whole face peeled back from her teeth.

'You really are an old fucker, Frank.'

She held the revolver up to the light and made sure it was loaded before she put it in her handbag on top of the television. I counted out five hundred from our cash and handed the rest—just over six thousand—over to Maddie.

'Just in case,' I said. 'So you can get home.'

She took the money and flipped through it like a deck of cards.

'Maybe we'll order some movies or get a better fucking room at least.'

'This is the best they got,' I said.

'I'm not talking about here.'

'I'm not gonna be gone long.'

'Are you leaving the car?'

'I need the car, Maddie.'

I swallowed down and bit on my cheek, told myself everything would be fine. I'd seen her more smashed. I'd been more smashed, and everything worked out fine. She put the cash in her bag and handed me her cell phone.

'Call me if you need anything,' she said. 'Help or whatever.'

'You hold on to it,' I said.

Maddie pressed the phone into my hand and looked at Sean on the bed. She grabbed my belt and kissed me, sticking her tongue into my mouth. I grabbed her body even though I knew it was the crank making her want me.

'Let's go out to the car,' she said.

'We can't leave Sean in here.'

She pulled me to the bathroom and shut the door. She sat on

the toilet, unbuttoned my jeans, grabbed my cock, and spit on it. She sucked on me hard while she fingered herself and then stood up, dropped her pants, and bent over the edge of the tub. While I fucked her, she grunted and moaned quietly. The volume on the TV went down for a moment and then back up, louder. When I started to come, Maddie pulled away and turned back around. She looked at me with her big eyes, slapped my dick on her cheek and told me to come hard. My insides felt like they were melting with hate and sex. She knew it too. She knew she had my number no matter what the score.

Maddie wiped her face off with toilet paper and handed me a washcloth. She pulled her pants up and dug into her front pocket, looking for the baggie. She spilled a bump onto the top of her index finger and snorted it.

'You can take the rest with you,' she said. 'I don't need any more for tonight.'

She wiped her mouth one more time before she went back into the room and left the meth on the counter of the sink. There was enough to keep me going for the rest of the night. I grabbed it, tried to flush it. I held it over the open toilet but couldn't let go. I folded it back up and stuck it in my pocket. I told myself Maddie was already too high, and I couldn't leave it here with Sean. When I went back into the room, Maddie was in the bed with her back against the headboard. Sean lay next to her watching TV and eating his chicken nuggets.

'How long are you going to be?' she asked.

I looked at the clock. It was already past nine. I threw the key onto the bed.

'I want to be back before the sun starts in. Lock the door.'

I had to see for myself. I wasn't going to take Maddie and Sean to Mary's house until I knew it was safe. I got in the Benz and drove west for twenty minutes. I turned on streets that I didn't remember, but somehow knew I was going the right way. Like a crevice in a flood, I only had to keep still, not flail, stay awake. Short palm trees stood guard in stone-covered front yards. Pitbulls dragged laughing children down empty streets. Cinder block fences dragged on and on, every other brick stained with black, purple, crossed-out gang scripts. I knew I should be speeding, happy and excited my brother, Ben, was safe and only a day away, but when I turned off Thomas Road, my mouth went dry and my stomach wretched. I didn't know if it was my fiend spiking with the city's smog air or that I was so close to Santer and every ground-out cheeva junkie that I served on this side of hell. I parked a block down from Mary Kandi's two-story tweaker den, cracked my window, and watched.

The house was smaller than I remembered. The upstairs where I stayed wasn't an apartment, but a half-assed addition that looked like a failing cardboard box on top of the garage. Every window was still dark, but not blacked-out like before with the tinfoil. The two in the kitchen on the first floor had glowing yellow drapes. An old long Buick that I didn't recognize sat in the driveway, and there were another three cars in front parked on the street. While I sat there, two sets of people came out—a white guy by himself and two black teenagers wearing basketball jerseys and potato sack jeans. No one looked familiar. I didn't see Mary, Jon, or Ben. The whole time, a skinny teenage white girl stood in front of the house under a streetlamp smoking a cigarette looking back and forth down the street. Her shorts were cut just below her ass, and even though it was getting cold, she wore a thin-strapped tank top that made her tits look like small fists under her shirt. Just as I was about to pull forward, I heard a Harley spitting and rumbling close. I slouched down in my seat and kept one eye on the passenger-side mirror and another on the girl.

In the rearview, a lone shaking headlight tore towards the house. My palms were wet, and I couldn't tell you why. I felt like at any moment the sky would start falling and the Benz would be crushed, and they'd be tearing off my arms with the Jaws of Life. The Harley slowed as it got closer. The girl flicked her cigarette into the street and casually raised her hand to her waist like she wasn't just chewing through smokes and spinning her head around for the bike. I pushed myself up so I could see over the dashboard. The Harley parked in front of the house and died with a pop. It was Jon's bike. The gas tank had been freshly painted with high-gloss black paint, but everything down to the rusted flaking ape hangers was the same. From the back, the rider was skinny, small-shouldered just like Jon. I watched him throw his legs easy off the bike just like the old man. I was fighting it, not wanting to believe I was staring at Santer. I couldn't believe I was back so close—right there. But then he pulled off his helmet, and my heart jumped. In the dark, I couldn't see his face, but his hair was cut short and clean to show off those black tumors—that branded *MT* raised clear on the back of his neck. I sat up, swallowed my willies down, and put my hand on the key, ready to start up the Benz.

Santer went to the girl in front of the house. She tried to throw her arms around him, but he pushed her off, grabbed the back of her head. The girl screamed, yelled something I couldn't understand, and he slapped her hard across the face over and over until she crumpled to the ground. He let go, laughed as the front door swung open. Booming music carried down the street. A black man ran out shouting. He pushed Santer back and pulled the girl up by her arm. I let go of the key and shrank bank down in the seat. The music rumbled, a winter desert earthquake rocking my shaking chest. Until I saw Ben, I wasn't going to move. I wasn't going to bring Maddie or Sean close to that place. I wanted guarantees that I wouldn't end up fighting for their lives again.

felt naked. I wished for my gun. For three hours, I watched men go in and out of Mary's old tweaker den without a glimpse of Ben. I called him twice from Maddie's phone but got no answer while younger guys in twos and threes and older men by themselves came in and out. When they left, all their eyes flashed up and down the street. They adjusted their belts, wiped at their faces, and trotted to their cars, running away from their favorite sin. The house may have been the same, but they weren't running the cheeva or any more crank. It was a whorehouse. The little white girl in the front was the eyes and cashier. She took the money before the johns could go inside. On the top of every hour, an older black girl—maybe in her thirties—came out talking loud on a cell phone. She wore a tight red stripper dress that barely covered her ass and exploded her tits. Every time, she yelled on the phone, shouting in ghetto tongue, and then broke into a strained crocodile laugh. She was running things, didn't seem to give a shit, because when the little white girl handed her money, she counted it out on the street daring any cop or street banger in the neighborhood.

I waited, but Santer never came out. I was nodding off in my seat. My head snapped every very few minutes begging me to let it go. I rubbed on my pocket with the crank. Just a fingernail would get me right. I cracked my head left and right, sat up straight, and started running through reasons why I shouldn't get high. *Because I beat*

on Maddie. Because I was in a stolen car. Because I was trying to kick.
Because I had to look out for Sean.

Just as I reached into my pocket, another john, an older white
guy in a Chrysler, pulled up to the front of the house and honked.
The white girl leaned in through the window and then went to the
front door. After a second, the black girl in charge came out, but now
she was in a tight skirt to her knees, a red leather jacket, and a low-
cut white blouse. She worked her angle from the passenger window.
She pulled the top of her shirt down and showed off one of her huge
breasts. There was just enough light I could see the shadow of his
hand reach over and squeeze her naked tit.

I started up the car as the black woman climbed into the front
seat of the Chrysler. As soon as she got in, the john tried to grab on
her again, but she pushed him back and pointed down the street. They
drove slow. I followed. They got back onto the main road and took
a quick right down another side street. The car was a couple blocks
ahead, but I didn't try to catch them. I lay back and watched them take
a left at a stop sign. For a minute I thought I lost them—I took the same
left and sped past an empty office complex and a block of two-story
white stucco apartments, looking for them on both sides of the street. I
was almost to another light—ready to slap myself—when I spotted the
Chrysler parked in the far corner of a supermarket's back lot.

I turned off the Benz's lights, slowly pulled into the lot, and
parked barely three cars away. I rubbed my eyes, watched them
knead smut in the shadows. The john licked on the black girl's chest.
Again, he grabbed her hard, and again, she stopped and pushed him
off. After that, he sat back and let the whore work his pants. She

could do it in her sleep—getting his cock hard, the zipper with her teeth. She let him grab the back of her head while he stared out, cursing and asking for more. I got out of the Benz, pulled my belt from my pants, and wrapped it around my right fist. I crouched down and double-stepped to the trunk of Chrysler. The windows were down. She groaned with him in her mouth, and he just kept saying,

'Yes . . . Fuck . . . Yes . . .'

I stood up and walked straight to the driver's door. Before he caught my shadow, I punched the john across his jaw with my wrapped hand. His cheek felt like a ham, and then his terror broke when he realized he was getting rolled.

'Oh shit! Oh shit! What the fuck?!'

I punched him again. He scrambled, bucking the girl off his lap. I put the lock down on the door and held my hand over the latch.

'Shit! Please, whatever you want!' he yelled.

He pulled out his wallet and started pulling out cash.

'Don't give him that money,' said the girl. 'That's my fucking money.'

He threw the cash out the window onto my feet. I leaned down and looked into the car. The john's dick was still out of his pants. The black girl pulled a cigarette butt out of the ashtray and lit up. If she was scared, she didn't let on.

'You want to finish this trick for me, motherfucker?' she said to me.

She smiled. Her face was fat, and some of her teeth were jacked-up and crooked. Her bright purple lipstick crusted the outside of her lips and stained the top half of her gums.

'We need to talk,' I said.

She looked at me, laughed loud.

'You kidding, right? You must be fucking with me with your belt around your fucking hand.'

She kept on laughing and flicked the cigarette out the window.

'Let's go for a ride,' I said.

'You pulled all this shit, and you just a horny motherfucker looking for play?!'

The john pulled up his pants. He was calming down. He rubbed his jaw and started blabbing.

'Why did you hit me, asshole?' he asked. 'What the fuck's wrong with you?'

He examined his face in the rearview mirror. The black girl rubbed on his crotch.

'Don't worry, baby. I'm gonna finish you up.'

She kept talking while her right hand went down her leg by the door. Her eyes didn't break with mine.

'You think I'm just some crackhead nigger ho, don't you?! I can see it on your fucking face—I ain't going nowhere.'

Her hand was moving around, searching for something at her feet. I walked fast around the front of the car to her side.

'Oh, hell no!' she yelled. 'What the fuck you think you gonna do? What?!'

I yanked her door open. She fumbled with a pocket .25 on the side of her seat. I didn't think and stomped her hand until she dropped it on the ground. Her body folded over her forearm, and she grabbed onto her waist, screaming and trying to catch her breath. I grabbed the back of her neck and threw her onto the ground. The john's mouth dropped open. I leaned into the car and pulled the keys from the ignition.

'You broke my arm, motherfucker!' she screamed.

The girl was on her knees, cradling her right wrist with her body. She cried both from the pain and her mounting rage.

I grabbed her face and started the push.

'What's your business with Santer?'

'What?!' she yelled. 'What the hell you talking about?'

'Back at the house—what are you into with Santer?'

'I ain't telling you shit, you punk ass. Do you know who I am? I can get you killed yesterday—'

'I got money,' I said.

She stopped—her face changed when I said *money*. I picked her .25 off the ground and crotched it at my waist. The girl sat up on the ground and extended her right arm back and forth, checking to see if it still worked.

'We can talk about whatever the fuck you want, but you're gonna *pay me*, motherfucker.'

I reached into my pocket and flipped my five hundred onto the ground. She picked it up, stuffed it down the front of her shirt, and looked me in the eye.

'Real money, motherfucker,' she said. 'You wanna talk about Santer? You pay me Santer money, ya' feel me?'

The girl stood up, straightened her skirt, and grabbed her purse from the seat of the john's car.

'You're going with him?!' said the john, stunned. 'I thought you said—'

'I didn't say shit. You know where I stay,' said the girl.

She slammed the door, and I threw his car keys through the open window. He started the car quick but then remembered his cash was still on the cement. He got out and dropped to a knee to pick it all up.

'My brother-in-law is a cop,' he said.

He jumped back in and sped down the back alley of the super-market. His whole car bounced and shook like his terror had infected the engine, the shocks, and rubber. The girl walked behind me. Her heels snapped across the cement like she was walking on nails.

'You owe me for the trick, my arm, and so I don't call the cops,' she said.

'What's that gonna cost?'

'Two thousand to start and then it's up to you. What you wanna know?'

'I don't have that kind of money on me. Get in the car.'

I unraveled the belt from my hand and threaded it back on my waist. I heard everything again: the traffic from the busy intersection, my own boots against the ground, the slow air even—it funneled into my ears in a steady blank whirr. When I unlocked the Benz, the girl checked the backseat before she got in.

'You act like a fucking pig, you know that?' she said. 'You ain't some crazy po-po, are you? Breakin' hos down and shit for their cash?'

I shoved her pistol back to her across the roof of the Benz and opened the door.

'I ain't no cop.'

'Fuck you, anyway. Close enough. You're gonna pay me for this. Believe that.'

I pulled out of the back lot, took a left at the light, and started heading back to the motel. She turned the visor mirror down and checked her makeup.

'Do I look all torn up?' she asked.

'You look fine.'

'Well, I didn't ask that. I asked if I looked all torn up—'

'How do you know Santer?' I asked.

She reached over and grabbed at my cock. I pushed her hand away.

'Money makes this mouth open, baby,' she said.

She shut the mirror and slouched back into the seat. We drove back to the motel in silence. After every block, the rush of rolling the whore and her dumb-ass john wore off a bit more. I was back where I started, my head getting heavy, eyes wanting to close. I rubbed on the crank in my pocket and watched the gas station lights, liquor store signs, and dark churches melt into one long string of empty intersections and black street. I sat up, forced myself awake. There were bad ghosts in that old tweaker den. I'd seen them myself. Ben thought it was going to be so easy, but it was all adding up like I knew it would, like gypsy math—no straight lines, not a thing made sense.

'What the fuck happened up here?' said the girl.

Red and blue lights bounced off the dark strip mall across from the motel. My blood went cold. Spit collected in my mouth. I sped up and drove past the motel and tried to catch as much as I could—two cop cars flashed their sirens with their doors swung open, the front door of our room opened wide, the lights on inside. I saw the East Indian manager standing in the parking lot with his arms crossed, shaking his head, trying just like me to make sense of all the sights and sounds.

The whore ate street tacos and drank Big Red from a takeout cup. She was sitting on top of a blue plastic table with her legs crossed, picking around the onions and cilantro on the paper plate in her lap. She only wanted the charred chicken with bits of the shredded cheese. I sat next to her with Maddie's and the Jew's cell phones in front of me. I could see the motel parking lot two blocks away. I waited for the cops. I prayed for them to leave.

'What you think happened?' she asked.

'I don't know,' I mumbled back.

I was lying. My mind clipped over and over, wasted from no sleep. All I saw was lousy draws for Maddie and Sean. I was sure Marcus had caught on, that he'd walked in on Ben hanging up the phone. Goldstein, his ear held together with crazy glue, beat Ben and strung him up in one motion. And after maybe three minutes of the Jew's knife at his throat, Ben spilled our story like I knew he would. Then, Marcus did what he promised, used the entire Phoenix police force to get back his grandson.

'I used to live here,' I said.

The girl sucked down the last of her soda and kept sucking until the last drops gave way to drawing air.

'How's that?' she asked. 'Where'd you stay? Gimme one of them squares.'

I slid the box of Parliaments across the table.

'In your house. I stayed with a bunch of tweakers in that house.'

As soon as I said it, the girl sat forward and pinched a lock of her hair nervous, not knowing what to do with her hands. She pulled it in front of her face and examined the end. Whatever came out of her mouth next was going to be a lie.

'I think you got the wrong house, player. That's why I don't fuck with that crystal. Weed don't be working you over like that.'

'Give it a sec,' I said.

I walked from under the awning of the taco stand and stared down at the motel parking lot. The cops were still parked, but they had turned off their siren lights.

'Do you know Ben?' I asked.

'Who?'

'Ben Shenk, you know that name?'

The black girl set down her half-eaten plate of tacos and wiped her hands with a paper napkin. She opened up the top of the Styrofoam cup and smiled, sucking on some pieces of ice.

'Money. I tell you everything for that money.'

She wiped her hands again, winked at me, and lit up the cigarette next to her.

'You don't got any menthols?' she asked.

I rubbed the back of my neck and felt a chill on my skin. My hands were freezing. The night was giving way to the desert cold. Snow would dust Phoenix before morning. I rolled my lips together and feared all my thoughts—Maddie being gunned down with that pistol in her hand. I saw Sean, but he wasn't crying or screaming. His head was lowered while police walked him to the back of a cruiser and set him to tears behind a plexiglass window and black diamond fencing.

'Them pigs are rolling.'

Down the street, the two police cars pulled out of the parking lot. Their sirens flipped on in unison as they accelerated past us.

'I need to borrow your gun,' I said. 'You can put it on my tab.'

'Don't be going crazy,' she said, handing over her .25. 'Them pigs will shoot you up out here.'

'I'm gonna find out what happened. I'll get the cash and be right back.'

I picked up the phones off the table and got in the car. I floored the Mercedes down the two blocks and parked the car at the back of the motel's office. I got out and walked around the building to the window. The East Indian was packing up a shoulder bag getting ready to leave. When I knocked on the window, his eyes went wide.

'What happened to you?' he asked. 'Where did you go?'

'What happened?'

'The boy. He came to the window. The girl was sick. Very, very sick. I had to call the ambulance for her. I didn't know what to do. She was sick.'

'Where's the boy?' I asked.

'The police. They took him.'

'Where?'

'Is he your son?'

'What was wrong with her?'

'She wasn't moving. I had to call. I didn't know what to do,' said the man.

'Is the room open?'

'No, police said to lock it. They will be back very soon.'

'Then I need you to open it now.'

'I can't. The police, they said . . . Just wait. The other manager is coming. He's the owner. I have to leave. My shift is over. I'll leave a note.'

'I'm sorry,' I said. 'I don't have the time.'

I walked back around the office and crouched down behind the Benz. The steel door of the office unlocked from the inside, and the East Indian came out with his bag slung to his back. I waited until he shut the door, pulled out his keys, and started fishing through the huge ring for the right one. I stepped to him, yanked down hard on his bag, and sent him and all his papers and books onto the asphalt. As he turned to me, I whipped across his face with the pistol. He fell back, covering his eyes. I grabbed him by the back of his shirt and pulled him up.

'Walk,' I said.

He held his head and breathed loud through his nose. He tried to turn around again, but I pushed him forward towards the room.

'I . . . I . . . Wh . . . Why . . . Why can't you wait?' he stammered.

I pushed him into the door.

'Open it.'

'My head—'

I stabbed the gun under his ribs. His right hand was covered in blood. He kept taking his hand back and forth from his face. He didn't believe he was bleeding. I grabbed him by his shoulder and turned him around.

'I have to get my things,' I said. 'Open the room, and I'll leave.'

He looked more confused than scared, like he didn't understand what I was saying. Sweat collected at his temples. He dropped his bloody hand from his forehead and sorted through the keys. When he opened the door, I pushed him inside.

'Sit down and don't move.'

The sheets were pulled back. A pool of orange vomit soaked into the center of the bed. The pillows were thrown on the floor, and Sean's bag of Jack in the Box was spilled out on the ground. I looked in the bathroom for Maddie's bag, knowing it wasn't going to be there. Vomit covered the base of the toilet and the seat. The light was still on, and the fan ran loud, clicking and popping in the ceiling. I took a clean towel from the rack and threw it to the East Indian. He sat straight up on the edge of the bed, his hand still at his head. He wiped his face with the towel, smearing blood down his right cheek. Now I could see the three-inch gash on his hairline. Blood kept collecting in it like an ant-sized trough before it fell in fat drops.

'Was she awake when the ambulance came?' I asked.

He closed his eyes, shook his head back and forth like he was trying to think of the right word.

'No.'

They kept their word. Before I could make the eight steps back to the Benz, the police pulled back into the motel. They shut their sirens off, and only one of them pulled a gun on me. They weren't scared. The cop didn't yell, and I didn't fight. I threw the whore's .25 out and let him zip-tie my wrists and put me facedown onto that fresh asphalt. The other cop, a stocky white woman, kept one hand on her piece until she had the small pistol in the other. She was the one who frisked me and stood me up like I was some child caught in the act.

'Do you have anything else on you?' she asked.

'In my front pocket.'

She reached deep into my jeans and pulled out the last of the New Year's stash.

'Any more weapons? Knives? Guns?'

I shook my head and let her walk me to the back of her cruiser.

'You high?' she asked.

'I'm tired is what—I don't even know.'

She opened the back door of her cruiser and put me in. The other cop, a fatter younger Mexican, had all the doors open on the Benz. He was going through the interior with a flashlight but was trying not to bend down. He held on to the roof with one hand and flipped the light back and forth around the inside of the car while the lady cop talked to the East Indian night manager by the

WALLY RUDOLPH

open door of the motel room. I couldn't hear a word. I blinked my eyes over and over. The East Indian was still holding the bloody washcloth to his forehead while he told the story. The lady looked at me through the front windshield with her hands at her waist. An ambulance pulled up silently with just its lights flashing. Everyone was quiet because of the hour of the night.

It took me a couple of months after I got back from Phoenix to start sleeping straight through the night. I had brought back one white envelope half-filled with cheeva smack, but I was taking to it less and less. No one wanted it. Even when I offered it up to strangers in the house, they all waved me away and situated with Ben and that Los Alamos coke. It was fall 1997. Ben had been living with me for close to four years and was finally getting used to life without Sean. He cried, usually just the few hours after he'd seen his boy. He would tear up over nothing. No specific activity caused it. He was just poor and sad his son wasn't with him every day.

The night I met Maddie in Española, I felt clear and good. I met Ben in purple dusk at the Texaco just north of town. I left my truck on the edge of an arroyo behind the station, and we drove the Saab for forty-five minutes with the top down. I didn't ask where we were going or why. I remember touching the air vent of the car and feeling a little bit of heat coming out. I wished I could see the vapor get sucked away by the cool March air, like the trail of a jet plane or thick pipe smoke.

137

We parked at the bottom of a hill and walked ten minutes in the dark. There were cars and trucks lined up on one side of the dirt road. I was concentrating on the ground in front of me while my eyes adjusted. Then I heard the sound of warm guitars. Ben was ten yards ahead. He was shaking hands and laughing with two people in front of a two-story house. All the lights were on in just about every room, and the yellow lit up a clear path onto the rocks in front of me. Behind me, I could make out the first few lights of Santa Fe. I drank from a dollar bottle of Beam, spit, and walked up to Ben. He was eating a handful of mushroom caps. I don't recall the names of the two hippies he was talking to, a young smiling girl and boy with matching dreadlocks. Ben held out his hand and offered me some of the mushrooms. I chewed them fast and washed them down with a mouthful of bourbon. There was dancing inside, and I was laughing and talking with one of the guitar players, an older man with tied-up gray hair and an eye patch. He said, 'You're kind.'

That's when I saw Maddie for the first time. Her hair was bright electric blue, and it matched the cheap leather jacket she was wearing. She was with two other girls. They all looked young, angry, and bored. They chain-smoked cigarettes and looked back and forth around the room, trading on a jug of blush wine. Maddie made eyes at me, and it was done. We walked into black, past the lights of the backyard. I carried a bottle of vodka, and she peeled a tangerine and dropped the skin on the ground. The mushrooms made it so I could see clearly in the dark. A purple moon, purple dirt, and all the rocks were cratered on their faces, even the smallest. Before we kissed,

Maddie took off her jacket and shirt and stared at me naked until I was quiet. Both our faces tasted like sugar, and our skin was plastic bags stretched over bloody muscle fever.

I slid around the hard plastic backseat whenever the lady cop turned the car. I realized I had only ever known a few things—clouds act as they look, dirt stains with pressure, a handful of moments does not add up to a life. I had lost years because of whatever dope I was on. My body was just broke, and now Maddie was near dead, and Sean was gone. The billy goat had his fill, I believed. I would leave this place all jacked-up when it was over. A baby walking out a window, just a fucking mishap.

The county line put me in Phoenix's west-side police station. The building was new, lit with white and pink lights. Cacti and small skeletal bushes surrounded the entrance. Cops working that late didn't feel like doing a thing besides sitting on their asses and taking shift naps in the empty holding cells. All of them stank like cologne and sweat, the whole lot all local and country.

The woman handed me over to a shorter white cop with a red-head buzz cut.

'Is he part of this motel mess?' the redhead asked.

'Looks like it. The girl's boyfriend, I think.'

'He say anything?'

'No, he's been nodding out for the past hour.'

'Is he high?'

'Pissed himself in my car.'

'How am I putting him in?'

'We're still adding it up,' said the lady. 'I'm waiting for Steve to get back. He's going over the car. Get his blood and stick him in holding. Let him sleep it off.'

'How much longer you on?' asked the redhead.

'As long as it takes to push this shit through.'

'Stop by before you leave.'

The redhead winked at the lady before he took me by the elbow and walked me into an orange room. He sat me in a chair and walked over to a white metal cabinet.

'Don't fuck with me, all right? And we'll be done with this quick,' he said.

He put on a pair of surgical gloves and pulled out a white plastic box to get a blood sample.

'I'm going to put some real cuffs on you now,' he said, cutting the zip-tie off my wrist. 'Put your arms in front of you.'

I held my wrists out. I smelled pine cleaner and burned toast. I looked down on my pants and saw the wet piss stain on my crotch and legs. I didn't remember sleeping in the police car. I didn't remember wetting myself. My eyes burned. The overhead lights bounced off the orange paint on the walls. I heard the hum of the fixtures getting louder and louder.

'Don't pass out on me, amigo. We're almost done.'

The middle knuckles on my right hand were swollen up and red, but I didn't feel them or the right side of my face. The longer I stared at them, the more I felt like collapsing.

'What are you on right now?'

My jaw clenched, and my head fell back.

'Hey, buddy!' he yelled. 'What are you on? What are you coming off of?'

My eyes shut, and my body fell off the chair. My chest warmed, and when my head hit the cold floor, I felt the grit of dirt press into my cheek. I didn't hear anything, not even my heaving breath. The cop took the blood sample and then left me on the floor to get help.

I was in the tops of Colorado pines with an orange sun beating down on me. I was warm and tired. Gusts of cool air blew into my face. A shadow moved me into the middle of the sky, and my head was resting on a large breast. My back was strong again, and I mumbled words in Spanish. Straight above me, there were small black birds really far away. I remember only the end of what I said.

Copper was getting worked. A ball-peen hammer. A thin sheet of copper. I opened my eyes. White speckled linoleum stretched towards an olive steel door with a window the size of a big book. Above me, the ceiling was painted shiny mustard yellow except for around the broken mount of the long fluorescent light. I was under a gray blanket that felt like wall insulation. My legs and crotch were warm and wet. My face was greasy with oil. I threw the blanket off my body, and my right arm got tugged back by an IV drip hanging from a chain locked to the wall.

Two cops walked past the window. One of them glanced over at me and motioned to another who I couldn't see. The pinging quieted in my head. I poured a cup of water from a plastic pitcher next to my bed and drank it down. I didn't know how long I had been out. I didn't know what day it was, and there weren't any windows to the outside. At the worst, I figured I was in the larger county jail in downtown Phoenix. They would end up processing me through and ship me out until my court date. I got up and tried to walk towards the window. I only made it two steps before my legs gave out, and I was on the ground. A loud beep came from a speaker in the ceiling.

'Take it easy, champ. Just get back into bed. Somebody's coming down to take a look at you.'

I pushed myself up onto my knees and slowly got back to my

feet. Outside, I could see a cop behind a desk of security monitors in the center of the room.

'Where am I?' I asked out loud.

The cop at the security desk shook his head no and mouthed out, *Get back.* He leaned forward and spoke into a metal microphone in front of him. The speaker beeped again.

'Just take it easy, buddy. Go ahead and get back into bed. Someone's coming down.'

The little I said had winded me. I was lightheaded, trying to catch my breath. I sat on the bed wanting to pour another cup of water, but my body just fell over to its side. I rolled onto my back. Everything tumbled. I put work on that black girl and her john. I downed the motel's night manager. I had that bit of stash, and they arrested me, drove me to the station. And Maddie and Sean—I didn't know.

The door unlocked and the cop from the desk came in. Behind him, a young-looking EMT, a Mexican girl not much older than Maddie, stood waiting outside the door. The cop was tall, built like a refrigerator, huge thick arms and a barrel chest. His brown hair was short like the rest of them, and his mustache was clipped into handlebars like an old-timer. He walked in first and closed the door behind him.

'How you feeling, buddy?' he asked.

I moved my hand away from my forehead and eyed him up and down from my bed.

'Look, I'm not dealing with any of that shit, so speak the fuck up,' he said. 'They sent this girl down to look at you. I need to know if you're in charge of your fucking faculties right now.'

I ignored him, kept my eyes on the ceiling.

'Get fucked then, son. I'll send her back up. I'm not wasting her time.'

He turned and opened the door.

'I'm all right,' I said.

'Are you going to try any bullshit?'

'No.'

'You sure? Because your attitude is saying different—'

The girl knocked on the window and motioned to her watch.

'I won't try anything,' I said.

'God bless you then.'

He opened the door and let the girl in. She walked in fast, put her kit down next to the bed, and opened it up. She checked my pulse and pulled out a new IV bag while the cop kept watch at the door.

'How are you feeling?' she asked.

'Weak. I tried to get up, but I didn't make it.'

'That's understandable, considering . . .'

'Considering what?'

'Your stroke.'

My mouth went dry. I swallowed over and over, trying to wet my tongue. The paramedic must have thought I was gonna check out again because she stopped what she was doing and looked me in the eye.

'Don't worry, it's gonna be okay,' she said. 'It was minor. We got to you early enough. You just need to stay on the drip and *rest*.'

'Okay, okay—do you know where the girl from the motel is?' I asked.

The paramedic ignored the question and started changing out the IV.

'Her full name is Madelyne Nicole. She would be at the hospital . . .'

She glanced over her shoulder, checking to see if the cop was listening, and then pulled out a syringe and a bottle of medicine.

'Do you know about the kid?' I asked. 'Anything, please—'

She spoke low and fast as she ripped open the package of the syringe.

'I don't know about the boy. Your girlfriend, the girl . . . She wasn't well.'

I watched her draw a dose into the syringe. My stomach turned again, and I felt the start of the spins.

'She lost a lot of blood, so I don't know—'

'How long was I out?'

She flicked the needle in the air. Clear liquid spat up and landed on the small of her hand.

'Two days—this should help with the aches.'

With one hand, she injected the painkiller into my arm and wiped the spot with a swab.

'I'll tell them to get you something,' she said. 'You need to eat.'

She quickly picked up all her gear and closed her kit. I grabbed her by the arm.

'Where am I?'

'Hey!' said the cop, dropping his arms from his chest. 'Let go of her, buddy.'

'Where the fuck am I?!'

The cop whipped out his baton and raised it up. I let go and lay back down on the bed.

'Get your rest,' she said.

The cop locked the door behind them. I could feel the painkiller starting to kick, but my chest still caved. I didn't want to believe a damn thing. Maddie, close to dead? Sean, I didn't even know. I felt a sob in my throat. The speaker beeped in the ceiling.

'So I prayed, but you never showed.'

I sat up, my heart jumping, convulsing like I'd dropped it in cooking oil.

'You alive in there, Frank?'

Outside, Ben leaned into the microphone at the security table. He was clean, fresh shaven. The bridge of his nose was swollen, black and blue spread out under his eyes. His hair was slicked back behind his ears, and he was wearing a gray suit, pressed perfect, starched stiff. He sipped from a paper cup of coffee and tapped at an unopened fried pie in front of him.

'There you are,' he said. 'Thank God. I've been sitting out here all day. The coffee's shit. The food's shit. I don't know how these people do it.'

'What the fuck's going on?' I asked. 'Where's Maddie?'

Ben picked up the pie and ripped it open with his teeth. Crumbs burst in every direction, dusting his face and thick black tie. He brushed himself off and mouthed out, *Whoops,* before he leaned back into the microphone.

'Can you believe this? I bought this getup so I looked regular. So they wouldn't lock me up with you—fuckin' a.'

I swung my legs out to the floor and pushed myself up to my feet. I stumbled, barely made it to the door, and held myself up on the wall.

'Ben, fucking answer me,' I said through the window.

He pushed the pie from in front of him and stared into the microphone. He couldn't look me in the eye.

'You fucked up, Frank. Why didn't you call?'

'I did call. Twice. I waited outside Mary's, but you weren't there.'

'I got there in the morning, asshole—apparently too late for you because you went ape shit and beat down that motel manager. He was a fucking college student, Frank. You're lucky you didn't kill him.'

'Where's Maddie, Ben?'

'Maddie's fine. I got her into a hospital—best doctors in the state.'

'What happened?'

'What do you think happened? She fucking OD'd.'

'Bullshit.'

'You want me to show you her fucking charts, Frank?! She was unconscious when the ambulance arrived. How could you leave Sean with her? *With a fucking gun?*'

I rested my head on my arm, closed my eyes. He was right, and I knew it. I shouldn't have left. When I was walking out the door, I knew I shouldn't have been going anywhere. My throat tightened. I swallowed down my tears, trying to keep it together. The speaker beeped again.

'Sean's fine, by the way,' said Ben. 'Thanks for fucking asking.'

'I'm sorry, Ben. I just thought—'

'No, you didn't, Frank. You didn't think. That's the one thing you didn't do. All you had to do was go to the house, and now my fucking hands are tied—Marcus and Ali got here last night.'

'You can still go. I was scared, Ben, you have to understand. I couldn't take Maddie and Sean over there. Santer beat this girl down—'

'Like you beat that fucking kid, Frank?! Like you shot off Goldstein's ear? You're no fucking saint, crazy.'

Ben sat back, loosened his tie from his throat, and rubbed at his brow. He took a deep breath before he leaned back into the microphone.

'I'm not going anywhere. Sean's not going anywhere. Marcus is pressing charges on you, Frank—kidnapping across state lines. He wanted Maddie in jail too, but I begged. *I had to beg him, Frank*, just to let off that.'

I couldn't stand it. It was all too much, too fast. My arm folded under my weight. I dropped to the ground and pushed myself up against the door.

'Marcus is sending you up, brother. I got you a lawyer—a good one. He should be coming down. But I'm gonna need money. And you gotta tell me what you want to do about Maddie. I can cover some of the hospital, but Marcus ain't turned back on the faucet, if you what I mean.'

'Give her everything,' I said.

'What? I can't hear you.'

I grit my teeth, bore down, and with both arms, pulled myself up to my feet.

'Give her everything,' I said again. 'Everything from the house—all the Aspen cash is in the garage, you know where.'

'How much you got in there?'

'Enough. Make sure she's taken care of and once she's better, give her the rest—*all of it, Ben*.'

'Nothing for my troubles?' he asked, smiling.

'Fuck off.'

We stared at each other, nobody knowing what to say next. After a moment, Ben smiled, leaned back into the microphone.

'Look at the bright side, Frank,' he said. 'Everyone's getting what they wanted.'

'How the fuck you figure that?'

'After all this, Marcus said he's going to back off with the guardianship papers as long as I clean up. Maddie's gonna be taken care of. And you're gonna kick in here whether you like it or not.'

My heart split, cracked open. A hopeless black spread through my insides. Ben pushed back from the table and walked over. He put his hand on the window, and I did the same.

'Tell Maddie I love her, Okay? You tell her that.'

'We're gonna get you better, Frank. Then we'll get you out. I promise,' said Ben, his voice cracking behind the glass.

Tears fell down both our faces. I pressed my head to the window and felt Ben tapping at the glass.

'I'm sorry, Ben.'

'Me too, Frank. Me too.'

Maddie drank bleach to thin her blood, she said. I caught her in the act a few days after we met. It was our first proper date. I tried to stay clean the day before but ended up falling for a plate of blow with Ben in the back of an art gallery off Canyon Road. I slept an hour and bought some expensive cologne and a bottle of expensive perfume to give to Maddie, thinking she'd just smell it and be mine. She didn't notice. She was too embarrassed I had caught her with the gallon of Jewel-Osco bleach, a pint glass, and a jug of distilled water. I asked if I could watch. Then she poured a capful of bleach into the glass and filled the rest with water and went to the bathroom.

'I always gag. I don't want you to see that,' she said, closing the door.

I sat in the living room of her tiny apartment watching her fat gray and white cat clean himself while she dry-heaved in the bathroom. She came out with her hair tied back, lip gloss on, and no other makeup. For the first time, I saw her freckles and short legs. We walked to the Cross of the Martyrs and watched the sun fall. We smoked cigarettes, and she said she wanted to get back in with Jesus.

Once I met Maddie, I didn't think of Phoenix. Ben never spoke of it, and the terrors and screams died off when I realized Santer was never going to call. I knew plenty of junkies who barely remembered where and when they were born, so me losing a year on the cheeva seemed square. I took a job at the El Paseo bar downtown. I knew the bar owner there—an Irish ex-model who ended up in Santa Fe after a divorce. She was pretty and knew it and could barely stand me. I told her I needed a hand not so much for the money, but to try and keep my nose clean, remember how to walk and talk regular-like. She let me wash glasses and work with a short-bearded prick named Larry. One night, I cut him with a paring knife and said it was an accident. I would have done it again, but they fired me.

Maddie and I didn't talk much at first, and I tried my best not to let her see me on any speed. We only had sex when we were drunk and high. Maddie kept all her hair unkept, so her pussy always looked fat and swollen in her underwear. After we finished, I would cough and drink whatever liquor she had around. I took showers with my arm against the wall. When I puked up blood, she would drive me to the only free clinic in town. The doctor there knew Ben and I were eating too much coke. He always winked and told me to stay away from spicy food and get checked for AIDS every six months. I knew I couldn't go straight, but for the first time, Maddie was an appealing angle. I thought that was enough. I didn't know about my lot. I didn't know people had lots. I didn't know that when you tempt fate, you're only itching on little brother doom.

After Ben left, I stared into the corners of the cell for hours. I pissed at the door and hoped one of the cops would see. I wanted them to bust in and lay a beating, but they just let the piss dry and watched me fall in and out of sleep.

I don't know how long it had been when the same cop who had been watching all the monitors knocked on the door and held up a tray of food. He unlocked the door and set the tray on the end of the bed.

'How are you feeling?' he asked.

'Better.'

'You getting your strength back?'

'Feels that way. What time is it?'

'Eight.'

'Morning or night?'

'Man, you've done a number to yourself. It's eight o'clock PM— nighttime.'

'What are you doing with me?' I asked.

'To be honest, I'm not quite sure. We're waiting for a call.'

'From who? Marcus?'

'No . . . Is that your friend who was here?'

The man didn't know who he was swimming with. He waited for me to answer, but I just sat up and took a bite of the bologna sandwich.

'We're waiting for a call from the judge in Phoenix, but I'd say it's not coming today by the looks of it. Who's Marcus?'

'Nothing good.'

'What's that make you?' asked the cop.

'Why are you here?'

'My shift's ending. I'm making sure I don't have to come back up here once I'm home.'

'Wait, aren't I in county jail?'

'You're in Lewis, son.'

'Lewis what?'

'Lewis State Penitentiary—that's what I'm saying. It's a hike for me. I get home, get comfortable, then I get a call, and it takes me forty-five minutes on a good day.'

My guts started moving. Marcus put a fix on me.

'How'd I get here?' I asked.

'They rolled your ass in. You were out cold.'

I felt sick and nauseous all over again. My legs shook even though I wasn't standing. Sweat dropped down my back.

'I know *that*,' I said. 'How'd I end up here with no fucking arraignment?'

'We got the paperwork out there. You can read it,' said the guard, motioning outside. 'You conked out in transit.'

'What?'

'That's what they said.'

'What the fuck are you talking about?'

'Your paperwork. The two cops who brought you in. You went out in transit, after your sentencing. God bless you, you've done a number.'

My body went cold. My ears warmed. My face flushed with blood.

'Don't do it. I know that face,' said the guard, pointing to his baton. '*I will hurt you.* You don't want that the way you are.'

The more the shock set in, the more I stopped thinking. Same feeling after a car wreck—real clear, real empty.

'That's what I'm saying—I don't know what's going on with you. At some point, we have to do a full intake. Get you a jumpsuit and shoes and all that. Otherwise, you're making my job hell with all the extra paperwork. Until you're state property, you bite my ass.'

I nodded my head but couldn't get out any words.

'I'll have them bring some more food down. I know you need it. God bless. Evening.'

He unlocked the door and walked out. For another hour, I watched him while he waited for another guard to show up. He got the desk in order, threw garbage away, and went over two clipboards side by side with a pen. I believed that old-man Marcus only had two or three plays and they all involved that big-headed Jew. I didn't fucking think. Just like Ben said, *I didn't fucking think.* Ben told me his father was sending me up, and here I was—sight like a moth—thinking Marcus was going to play me out by the rules. The man had turned me completely sideways, had me eating shit in my sleep like frosting in a dream.

It ain't news to most, but if you're rich enough, truth isn't nothing but a Ferris wheel. For the down-and-out, the same truth—life, money, your poor little heart—is a horned mongrel, a scat-eating crossbreed of fact and fate. Let the prestigious laugh me off when I'm dead. All they ever see is glory muzzled by thousand-dollar bills. For the rest of us—Mexican to marine—get used to eating the pavement well after your fill. And when we start to grin at the outset of what seems a tolerable fair shake, don't forget who you are.

It's the way Ben said it would be. We were headed to the Chimayo chapel.

'We're just screwy thieves, Frankie. We'll get our due. I just don't want Sean to be there when I get mine.'

Barely a year ago, Ben reached a resolve. I saw it myself. Marcus could kiss on Ali in front of him—brush her ass, nibble her neck—but Ben wouldn't go batty and jump for his old man's throat. He didn't want to give them that anymore and didn't want Sean to see him hopped up, spitting red. He stopped sleeping in the garage, put some framed pictures in his room at my house. He opened the blinds and stopped believing in most everything good. His calm came with a price. It ate him up holding everything back. He would give up at the end of every day and numb out, putting a hurt on himself before bed. If anything, Ben saw before I did that we had been playing like heavies for too long. We never set out to drum up fear and ruin. They just seemed to latch on to us the way poor children surround you in poor country streets—the way it plays on television. When Ali and Marcus allowed it, Ben picked up Sean on the weekends. Sean didn't go to the holistic school or get taught by Goldstein anymore. Marcus had hired a private tutor with the job of fast-tracking the kid into a prep school back East. He had done the same thing with Ben. Ben said his father came from the kind of nothing that soured most.

Turns out Marcus's father, Ben's grandfather, was a raging drunk. He mellowed quickly once his body was worthless, but before that, he was a true tyrant. He broke his kin down in eerie beatings, lining up his wife and children in order of age and walking down the line slapping faces, chopping necks, and for the smallest, stern kicks to the ground. Marcus was the middle child and the only one that stayed once his father couldn't care for himself. When the youngest child turned ten, his mother ran off and never sent a word. One by one, the family broke apart.

'I only met my grandfather a couple of times, but I could tell he was sick inside and out,' Ben said. 'He could barely walk, but he ran Marcus around like a housemaid. The fucker was poison, through and through.'

Ben wasn't lying. I wondered if he saw it clear how I did: his grandfather, Marcus, even Ben—probably going back to some dirt-bag clan—got a shittiness beat into their blood that couldn't stand its own likeness. I hoped, wished Ben was different. But in truth, he was just more inspired with the ways he hurt Sean.

They shut the lights off, but I didn't sleep. A couple hours earlier, by what I figured, the bull-looking guard who had dropped off my food waved to me one last time before he left. He seemed as good as they come in this place. A black guard took post at the desk for the overnight shift. He was younger, swollen up with muscles and a shaved head. He didn't look a spit my way. He just sat down and slowly made his way through a stack of magazines. He gave a 'lights out,' flipped a switch on the board in front of him, then turned on a desk lamp and kept on reading, studying each picture in his magazine page by page.

The shot of painkiller the EMT had given me that morning was wearing out. All my aches and sore spots warmed up until my back and sides were hot with pain. I rubbed on my lower back and flipped around on the cot, trying to take off some pressure. I kept my eyes closed and chalked up schemes to get out. They all stank of bullshit and worse. I was still weak. I thought my body would come back around after some food. I kept forgetting I'd been out for two days, had a fucking stroke. If Ben hadn't shown up, I wouldn't believe it. I'd felt worse, seen worse, done worse, and kicked off broken hands and rich stranglers of dope like a pair of hand-me-down boots. All I could think was there was a part of me that wanted to quit. Since the New Year, a part of me had worked the odds and didn't see a way to come out ahead. The same part was happy being locked away in my sweaty, filthy clothes with nothing in sight. Here was a pardon for failure. I could walk up to Maddie's parents without a wink and tell them I was behind lock and key with a good Christian ushering me around. Her family would probably take me in. They'd wrap their arms around me and keep me close for the rest of our lives.

A man started yelling in another cell. His words muffled in the walls and barely carried through the thick glass window. He was angry and ranting. The black guard pulled his baton from his belt. He walked across to a cell I couldn't see. The yelling got quiet for a moment but then started up again louder. The cell door opened, and the yelling got frantic and high-pitched. I heard two clear *fuck yous* from the prisoner before his voice was just screams getting beat down. Made-up prayers rushed my mind the longer it went on. They all started, *Dear God, help me,* but then I lost my way in the words. Each time the man screamed, I had to start over.

The guard walked back to the desk with his shirt untucked. He pushed his magazine aside and turned on the microphone. The man still wailed in his cell, but not loud enough to drown out the electronic tone from the ceiling.

'Everyone needs to quit the shit tonight.'

The guard's voice was raspy, like he needed to cough.

'I'll drag all your asses out and fuck you up. Now, shut the fuck up and sleep.'

He said the last bit like he was begging for a favor. He slid his baton back into his belt and sat down at the desk. He pulled a raggedy bandanna from the pocket of his pants and wiped his mouth. He didn't care for his work. He didn't get off giving all that hurt. He wanted a quiet shift reading magazines, watching the clock. He wasn't scared or angry. His hands weren't swollen. His body still had living.

Let me tell you, when I heard the screams from that sorry piece, I turned onto my side and put my hand on the wall. I felt the slick paint in the pores of the cinder blocks, and my heart dropped and dropped. I saw it plain. I said it plain. *I was wrong. I was so, so wrong. I can't lie or hide. Dear God, help me, I don't know what to say. I was born in 1961 and am barely six feet tall—*

A short white guard with fresh coffee on his breath came in the cell and stood me up. He cuffed my hands, walked me out, and told me to stay put while he rolled the IV out from my cell and set it next to the guard desk. I didn't see when the night guard left. It must have been close to morning when my eyes gave in and closed tight. For the first time in I don't know how long, I rested without a fix or fiend slapping at my back.

No, I didn't say a word while I stood naked in front of the good giant Christian in another locked cement room. He peered close at my dick, balls, and asshole. He took my clothes, boots, and belt and logged them on a clipboard before he balled-up the whole mess into a black trash bag. He was quiet. He didn't mention God. I tried to cut up about it.

'Guess I don't have to ask if you've ever seen a grown man naked,' I said.

'What?'

'From the movie.'

His head was down in his clipboard. He pushed an orange jumpsuit towards me and made me put it on so he could make sure it fit.

'There's a drawstring at the waist if they're too big,' he said.

'I saw that.'

He set his clipboard next to the garbage bag and handed me a slate board with my number.

'Stand over there, Frank. You know the drill.'

I walked across the room and stood behind a blue line painted on the ground.

'Hold it up to your chin . . . Now, turn . . . Other side . . . We're done.'

I gave him back the board, and he set it on the desk.

'We got the call from the Phoenix judge this morning—'

'I figured as much.'

'I don't know if I'd be as cool and calm if I were in your shoes.'

'You'd be surprised,' I said.

'They want me to break a few amount of rules for you, which I usually don't mind doing.'

He picked up the clipboard and scanned it again.

'Just seems a bit excessive is all,' he said.

'I've seen—'

'Just be quiet for a minute, all right, and listen real close to the question I'm about to ask you. Because I'm throwing you a bone here in the hopes that the system will catch this and sort it all out.'

'You don't gotta do all that—'

'Just listen, damnit . . . *How are you feeling?* Keep in mind, I can afford you a couple more days in the sick tank if you're not up for it.'

'For what?' I asked.

'General pop. I'm supposed to stick you in E wing. You don't want to go to E wing, Frank.'

'What about my lawyer?' I asked. 'Did you hear from him?'

'Just the Judge, Frank. Not one lawyer. They want me lose you in here, understand?'

I wanted to scream, bum-rush the bull Christian and rip at his eyes, yelling, 'Marcus Shenk!' I wanted to break my foot on the walls, crack my fists on the door, tear at the room like a lame horse making my final point in vain. But then I thought of how many times Ben told me he bit through his cheek—how many times blood soaked his tongue while he watched Marcus lick on Ali's neck. I snapped my fingers, clapped my hands, and told another funny to swallow it down.

'I don't think I've gotten my appetite back just yet. My legs are still shaky, and I can't hold down anything but water, and my cancer has been flaring up—'

'All right, all right,' said the guard, smiling. 'For your sake, I hope you have your affairs in order.'

He banged on the door twice, and the short little guard opened it up.

'Take him down to the showers and then back up to medical. He ain't up for shit yet.'

I gave the Christian a nod as I left. The little man walked me through the maze of the prison and watched me as I washed in the empty showers. He walked me back to my cell and locked me up, blank-eyed and pissed the whole time.

The next few hours, I sat up and lay down over and over. When I was on my back, my legs cramped up on me, so I'd get back up, throw them off the bed, and walk the four steps to my door, IV tugging on my arm, and then lie back down. My fiend was still hankering, but it wasn't the same. I was so upside down, I wasn't sure if my nerves were shot from wanting a fix or from thinking, *You're getting worked, huh? Real good.* By the time the short guard brought me food, my palms were red and scratched from digging my nails into my skin. I stuffed my face with white-bread bologna and cheese until I couldn't chew. For as long as I was locked up, I was the queen of something less. Marcus Shenk had stuck me in one of his cupboards hoping I'd gnaw on myself and bleed out. I knew I had only a few more hours alone. The jail was all new and fixed up on this end like a concrete hotel, but if they put me out with the rest of them, I'd have my hands full with blacks, Mexicans, and stringy-haired white folk. Every single one murder-ready, eyeing each other with horny, junked-out eyes.

I proposed to Maddie lying on my back outside the St. Francis Cathedral in downtown Santa Fe. I was worked up on Alamos white, and she'd just finished a plastic flask of Southern Comfort. We'd been trying to make our way back to the pickup, but I couldn't remember where I parked. Maddie carried a brown paper bag filled with gas station fried burritos. As we walked, the bag got shiny and thin from all the oil. I know I wasn't thinking straight. I caught the eyes of a taxi driver. He shook his head when he looked at us. Maddie said I was just walking down the street and then took off after the cab in a dead sprint, shaking my arms in the air like I was King Kong. I don't remember, but I believe it.

We'd been downtown because I had to meet a particular piece of shit who ran one of the Canyon Road galleries. I won't even give a name. I met him at my stint at the El Paseo bar. We called him Back-wash because the shit would noodle his way up to people and finish their drinks. He was a cheap bastard and nothing else. He was tall and flashy with thinning blonde hair, but damn it if he didn't have handfuls of white snowflake coke.

Maddie and I walked into his gallery just before sunset. The whole city was lit up orange, and all the tourists were drinking box wine despite their sweating. Backwash gave me an ounce of blow, and before I reached for my money, I went to the gallery's tiny backyard and stuffed up my nose till I looked like I'd been fumbling donuts. When I got back, he tried to raise the price on me, and I knocked the air out of him. He got quiet and rolled back four hundred-dollar bills in my direction. I was feeling fine and high so I took Maddie to the old Walgreens down there in the Plaza. I bought four flasks of Beam, and she got that So Co and a package of long red licorice. We just walked with the rest of the tourists trying to slip by and breathe the cool clean air. It didn't take long for the bourbon to get a hold of me, and Maddie left me at the Catamount bar while she walked to the gas station for the burritos. I sat down in the middle of the bar between two tall white men and put in work until the bartender cut me off. Maddie came back at the right time because I had lost all my cares and was grabbing at the bottles behind the bar. The poor barkeep didn't want any of it.

We walked in circles up and down the side streets. We talked about selling pig leather belts with tin buckles painted turquoise. We were missionaries. The walk seemed to go on for days. We counted signs and listened to our boots hit the cobbled bricks. Then everything got worse. I couldn't remember where I parked the truck. I knew I was stupid, and the fact I couldn't find the truck shook all of me. I felt inadequate. I wanted to love this girl.

'Is this enough for you?' I asked Maddie.

'What?'

'All this. Have you had enough?'

'We haven't even gotten to the good part—you know that, Frank.'

'I'll love you then. Forever.'

'Be honest and marry me,' she said.

We kissed, and she helped me up from the grass in front of the cathedral. And then like that, we found the truck real quick—like the whole time we just had to be lost. I repeated the story to myself over and over trying to remember how she walked in front of me that night, how she smiled, bit her lip, when we picked out her ring the next day. There's no sense to it, but I wanted to remember it right so I'd have it all—so I could forget it—because the whole pretty picture was gone.

The shift change was happening again. The Christian talked to the black guard at the desk. The Christian looked my way as he walked out of sight, and I thought he was gone for the day. An hour or so later, a couple knocks came at the door, and he walked in wearing his regular clothes—jeans, clean white sneakers, and a Cardinals T-shirt.

'You got a visitor.'

'How's that?' I asked.

'There's a girl with a kid. I guess she's been here all day. I wouldn't have known if I didn't hear two of the guys joking about it in the locker room. I haven't checked you in, so you don't come up on the screens. They thought the girl was crazy, looking for a ghost.'

'You gonna let me talk to her?' I asked.

'I can't.'

'Well, get fucked. The shit is worthless to me.'

'Get up,' he said.

'I told you to move on.'

He ducked his head out the cell door and then closed it behind him.

'Get up!'

He yanked me off my back by the front of my shirt and jacked me twice in the face. I swung, ripped the IV from my arm, and caught him hard in the temple. His face flushed, his eyes turned to lotto balls, and he threw me to the ground. The black guard was yelling and banging on the cell door. But by the time he opened the door, the Christian had me face-first on the floor with his knee in my neck.

'You all right?!' the other guard asked.

'Don't give them an inch. Isn't that what I always say? Get your ass up!'

The Christian pulled me up to my feet.

'Give me your cuffs.'

'I can take him. Go home,' said the black guard.

'I want this motherfucker for myself.'

The black guard handed the Christian the cuffs, and he pulled my arms back and locked them up.

'Go read your magazines, Derone. I'm about to baptize this son of a bitch.'

thanked God for my health—the time seemed right. I'll give it to him—when the Good Guard of God got moving, he had bricks for fucking hands. Half my head felt caved in, and it swelled like a big red blinking light. The guard was still sucking air and cursing to himself while he walked me down another set of hallways that I hadn't seen my first time out. There wasn't a soul back there. It looked like this part of the lockup was still under some work. He walked me into an empty unpainted room and cuffed me to a table bolted to the floor.

'Some of the guys come back here and get high,' he said. 'They think I don't know. Wait here and keep quiet.'

I pet at the right side of my face, trying to see how bad he busted me up. My whole eye was tight—bloated with pain. I leaned back in the chair as far as I could and took a deep breath. The air smelled like fresh sawdust and paint. I noticed then I had only smelled my own stink and shit for two days. Without a mirror, I figured my face hurt worse than it looked. I tasted blood, but all the stinging was calming my nerves while I waited.

The Christian brought in Noni and baby Margaret and sat them down on the other side of the table. The baby was bundled up in her winter jacket, and Noni was wearing a T-shirt and carrying a black jean jacket just like Maddie's. She looked tired, like she'd had enough.

The guard set a cup of coffee in front of her and then waited just outside the door. Noni stared into the cup, rolled it back and forth in her hands.

'Maddie made me come over here,' she said.

'You didn't have to.'

Noni looked up from her hands, scorning me like I'd just spit at her face. As she took a sip of coffee, I reached out to touch the baby, but Noni pulled her away and put Margaret on her lap.

'Maddie wanted me to come over here and check on you,' she said again.

'I was a little torn up, but I'm fine now.'

'Where's Sean?' she asked.

'Marcus has him. How's Maddie?'

'Marcus has Sean? What happened, Frank?'

Margaret watched Noni as she talked. When her mother got angry, her little face frowned up. Noni picked her up and held her. She tried to talk quiet, put it all together, hold it all back.

'That's what I keep asking myself,' she said. '*What happened?* I thought you all were going back to Santa Fe.'

'We were. Things didn't work out. How's Maddie?'

Noni squinted at me, cocked her head to the side like I was speaking a different language.

'She almost died, Frank.'

'I know.'

'And that's it? You're done?' she asked, leaning in.

'She's gonna be all right. Ben's got it covered.'

'You're a piece of shit, you know that?'

Noni caught herself and stopped speaking. She looked at the door nervously, checking to see if the guard was in earshot.

'This whole thing is so fucked up. You should have told her. How could you bring her here?'

'What?' I asked. 'What are you talking about, Noni? I'm not doing anything now. Look where the fuck I am.'

'You have to get out,' she said.

'That's not happening,' I said, laughing.

I didn't even know what we were talking about anymore. Noni's face was flushing red every time she opened her mouth, panting with every word.

'Noni, calm down. Marcus worked his angle,' I said. 'It's done. I'm fucked. Maddie's safe. He's not gonna touch her.'

Noni didn't seem surprised by any of it—that, or she wasn't listening to what I was saying.

'Some lady came looking on Maddie with a black girl,' she said.

'So—what did they want?'

'She came and talked to Maddie yesterday. Maddie wouldn't say what it was all about. I wasn't going to come here—Maddie made me.'

'You keep saying that. What'd the lady have to say? Was she from the hospital?'

'I told her you were a piece of shit for leaving her at that motel—'

'Noni, what did the lady say?'

'I don't know. The black girl looked like trash. She was fat. The lady was old—like sixty. She had blonde curly hair. She said she was a friend of yours. She knew all about you.'

'Wait a minute . . . Who was this?'

Noni zipped up Margaret's jacket and pulled the kid's pink winter hat over her ears. She checked the door again and then leaned in and spoke low so the Christian wouldn't hear.

'Maddie said to tell you, the lady wants her piece of Burning J.'

'Noni, I don't even know what the hell you're talking about anymore.'

But I did, and I wanted her to leave. I wanted her to get right up with Margaret and leave because I knew there was another end coming.

'She said she's going to take it out of Maddie, Frank. Square up on her end. Maddie isn't acting right. She's terrified . . . Are they going to kill her?'

I felt a frog in my throat the size of a shoe. I was breaking down the mess, and all of it was turning around on me. Sweat poured from my body.

'Where's Maddie?' I asked.

'Phoenix Memorial. What the fuck is going on, Frank? Why did you bring her here?'

'Go back there and don't you leave, Noni. You stay right next to her.'

Noni got up, put on her jacket.

'Are you listening to me?' I asked.

'Yes.'

'As soon as Maddie is good enough, get her back to Denver. You hear me?'

Noni picked up Margaret and put her on her hip. The baby clutched at her mother, her tiny knuckles turning just the start of white. The guard stepped back in and stood inside the door.

'I'm hearing some bodies move on the other end.'

'Okay, okay,' said Noni. 'We're ready.'

I listened to the clicks and echoes of their footsteps as he guided Noni out. The slap of a metal door meant they were gone, and all that was left was ringing steel and the same smell of sawdust and paint. My legs shook underneath the table. I thought of Maddie in a hospital bed, Santer's old meth whore at her throat.

'... Cursed shit ...'

I don't think Santer ever quit cooking is the point, no matter his said desires to end the legacy of Burning J. I know he never quit off the crank. He kept tweakin' and left me in that apartment with all that dirt heroin. I never made a peep because I was getting a king's end—so much my cash jammed the plumbing on the second floor. I know his work with the true Mexicans had him back and forth from Nogales. Grand Madre had him set up a kitchen in exchange for her daughter's hand. He called them his *familia perdió*. He bought a video camera and started carrying a creased Polaroid of him with the whole family on some Mexican beach. I remember the picture because when he first showed it to me, I didn't recognize him. He was tan, wore a straw sombrero, and the youngest baby boy was laughing in his arms. Santer was smiling too. Under that sun, in front of that ocean, he looked changed.

I don't know if he ever married the girl, but he was trying to teach her English. He bought an old tape deck and a bunch of used cassette lessons and told her to learn her studies. Every time he went down there, he stayed longer. He'd bring back papier-mâché death masks filled with cheeva and go back down with bags of clothing and tiny shoes for the youngest. At some point, things started to sour—I don't know why. The phone in the apartment rang all the time with collect international calls. Santer would answer them, go to the bathroom, and I'd hear him yelling then pleading in shitty broken Spanish. Nine times out of ten, he'd hang up the phone, grab his jacket, and tear over the border on his shit Harley. Three or nine days later, he'd show up saying his dead son, Jon Jr., had given him a second chance and blessed him with the family of Mexicans. He got PRIMER PADRE tattoed around his neck and started showing me videos of all his latest trips. Sometimes he rode the daughter, her skin shining like caramel when she sweat. Other times, her mother, the Grand Madre, rimmed him clean. He held the camera between his legs and the sixty-year-old smiled and lapped at his balls like a gutter cat.

And there was that night. I tried to never think on it. That man got his head torn off and that woman gutted with a cheap old bowie. None of it made sense. I was there. I put hurt on people, and Santer was there, and he was . . . He was cursing and turning his face up into a car's headlamps. It could've been two motorbikes, though. He'd been angry. So angry. He told me to get good and high.

'Get growling for me, Frank,' he said. 'I told them to let it alone, but English or Spanish—the shit don't change. People get greedy. First thing they lose is respect.'

He told me to shoot the whole mess of them. The Grand Madre

was there, bleeding out in front of them, and he told me to gun them down—the three kids. I don't see their faces—only Santer's. And my arms feel huge with this cannon in my hands. Like I had legs coming out of my shoulders and just a blur for a face.

The Christian walked me slowly back through the hallways of the renovated wing. He flipped his pocket flashlight into the empty rooms. In some of them, he stopped and ducked his head in to examine the walls and ceilings.

'This is all supposed to be administration. Offices and shit,' he said. 'But I don't know what they need with all this space.'

I shoved my feet forward, step by step. I didn't want to go back to the sick wing. I didn't want to go back to any wing of this prison.

'That girl looked real shook-up when she left,' he said.

All that wishing to be a faceless stump inside there seemed real dumb and local after all Noni had let on. When we got to the end of one of the better-lit hallways, I stopped and turned around to the guard.

'You mind me asking your name?' I said.

The guard looked at me, genuinely surprised.

'Please don't tell me you can't read. It's right there on my name tag on my uniform.'

'I can read, but you ain't in your damn uniform, are you?'

He looked down at his clothes like he just remembered himself.

'Ethan. John Ethan. That's my name. Sergeant, if you want to know.'

'I didn't ask all that.'

'Well, now you know.'

We walked a few more steps before he grabbed my shoulder and stopped me.

'You mind *me* asking *you* a question?'

'Shoot.'

'Was that your daughter back there?'

'No, she ain't mine a bit.'

I turned around and kept on down the hall.

'That's what I thought. She didn't much look like you.'

'I care for her. She's probably as close as I'll ever get to having my own.'

'Then she's a blessing.'

We got to the door that went back into the guts of the prison. John Ethan stepped in front of me and peeked through the small window.

'I don't know why I'm so jumpy. No one hardly comes back here. I'm going to have to cuff you up again.'

'What'd you mean by that?' I asked.

'I can't have you just walking around like a free man, Frank. Come on, now.'

'No, what'd you mean by the 'blessing' bit?'

'You really want to know?'

'I'm fucking asking, aren't I? It's not some fucking secret, is it?'

'You don't have to curse at me, Frank. That's half the fucking problem right there.'

'Get fucked then.'

I turned around, waiting for the cuffs. John Ethan clicked them on tight.

'You ready?' he asked.

'Let's go.'

I turned to the door, but he grabbed me by the shoulder and hit me hard with I don't know what across my face. I started falling, but he held me by an arm and pushed me against the wall.

'Don't think anything of it, Frank. I have to lay a few ones on you for this to work.'

'What the fuck did you hit me with?!'

He held up a blackjack from his back pocket.

'I'm big, but I ain't stupid.'

He started to laugh. The other side of my face tensed up, getting red and hot.

'Country piece of shit,' I said.

He dropped me to the ground and kicked the air out of me. I was spitting, wheezing.

'Like I said—that's half your fucking problem. That kid's a fucking blessing to a sack of shit like you because she gets your hateful little brain thinking of something other than yourself. I never get over all you pieces of shit that come through here thinking you got it the worst. You know who's got it the worst, Frank?! All those people you hurt! The good and the bad . . .'

He was worked up now. Red in the face and breathing heavy again. He kicked me in the gut and was going for another but stopped himself.

'Read the fucking Bible, why don't you?!' he shouted. 'Quit being a fucking asshole while I throw you a bone. You haven't even said thank you, you piece of shit. I could be at fucking home!'

I slid around on the ground, got my feet underneath me, and pushed myself against the wall.

'Thank you,' I said. 'Thank you.'

My chest tightened up and tears ran down my face. My throat

closed on me. I wanted to tell this man everything, but I just cried. Nothing I was thinking made sense. I hated that jail. I hated John. I hated that I hurt everything that I loved even when I was locked up far away. I hated myself, every single part of me. John waited as long as he could and let me have my time falling apart.

'Look at me, Frank.'

I wiped my eyes into my shoulder and looked into John's shining sweaty face.

'I won't lie to you. This place is a square of hell. I don't know what got you here or who's screwing who to keep you here. But whoever or whatever it is, God has a plan for you, friend. He brought you right here and right now for a reason—'

'Fuck you and your God bullshit, John.'

Before I could blink, he slapped me across the face with an open hand.

'Don't you curse my God. You save that shit for everyone else, but don't you curse him in front of me.'

My whole face burned, stinging like I'd just eaten fire. My cheeks swelled. Blood dripped from my right eye.

'I'm going to pray for you, Frank. Right now. And before you start spitting and swearing, you think real hard on what you got here and how bad you want something better. I've been there, Frank. I know where you're at.'

He closed his eyes and kept his hand on my shoulder while he spoke from a deep voice that carried through the empty walls like a moan of thunder.

'Dear Lord, please help Frank find his way. Help him open his heart to your son, Jesus Christ, our savior. Help him see your light and experience your unbounding greatness and compassion as you have with me. Help him is what I ask in your name. Amen.'

And like that, he opened his eyes and smiled. I didn't know what to say, so I curled up my ripped-up face and tried to smile back. He pulled me up and unlocked the door. John Ethan was pleased with himself. He didn't know anything but the truth of God. He felt it deep before his bones, before his heart, and behind his blood. I wished and hoped and prayed that it was all that easy. I wanted to smile and believe that this brick-house Christian made my quick turn. Yet, by my count, life was nothing but a terrifying staring contest with fate. All anybody can do is hope not to blink and lose it all.

Even after all my crying, I wasn't going to be resting. My beaten cheeks and chest would keep me up, and if they didn't, Noni had given me enough worry for the entire night. When John Ethan got me back in my cell, he gave one last 'God bless, Frank,' before he locked the door and left me on the crap mattress. I wiped my face on the bottom of my shirt. I ate John Ethan's words. I wasn't going to let Maddie and Sean take my share of hurt anymore. I owed them both. I prayed to everything everywhere to let me set it right. Make it all square.

never worked for dead men. There were plenty of offers. I watched them come and go. Twenty-two-year-old bump dealers who put away for years for a kilo of cocaine. I gave them time and watched them get rolled by Mexican and black bangers—kids too, swollen up from push-ups and chest checks, babies just wanting to cut their teeth with .22 pistols and stolen hunting knives, little butchers. I wasn't better than any of them. My money wasn't cleaner, and my hands got just as dirty. I worked with old-timers like Santer and Aspen. I won't fool around and say they worked from any more lauded dignity. I liked knowing my place. The geezers always had the drop. By the time I came around, their fears and suspicions were well beyond paranoia. The rest of the world called them lunatics for making every deal personal over straight razors. I took to it. I subscribed to it. I never took the shorts of playing calm. I am not studied. I played in the shit. Loonies had bought me thirty-seven years on this earth.

I wanted a quiet night and cornered some luck. The screamer who had been raising hell the night before was keeping quiet. The only sound was the water pressure groaning in the ceiling and the walls. Both sides of my face were busted stiff from John Ethan's beating. I was thankful he'd only

stomped me once in my chest because my breath was catching a
sharp pain when I inhaled too fast or too deep.

For four hours, I watched the black guard at his desk. He drank
from a tall cup of coffee and worked his way through another stack
of magazines. When he put on his jacket and turned off the lamp, I
took my shirt off and laid it on the bed. I thought of Aspen burning
his cash—how I'd catch him staring up into the sun smelling the air
before he poured diesel on his fortunes. He was greasing the altar,
putting up his goats. His last message, like he said, was in dynamite.
My fortunes lay in mercury and glass.

I stood on top of my bed and worked my fingertips under the
metal lip of the busted light fixture in the ceiling. The fluorescents
had been installed flush. To get to the lamps, I needed to bend the
metal collar straight down. I kept one eye on the door as I worked
my hand in enough to get a grip. Once I did, I let my weight out slow
and pulled my legs up so I was hanging from one hand. I took a
breath, yanked down hard. Two of the fixture's screw sinks popped
out from the concrete. I let go, checked on the black guard again. He
was sitting in his chair asleep with his arms crossed at his chest. I
figured I didn't have any longer than twenty or thirty minutes before
another showed up for the morning shift—that one was sharper
than he looked. He'd go checking in on the whole tank as soon as
he showed up.

I put both hands into the fixture and pulled down with all my
weight. The left side of the collar came loose, exposing the two fluorescent tubes inside. I took out the one closest to me, set it on the
bedsheet, and gathered the corners. I tapped the sack on the ground.

The lamp burst with a pop. I sifted through the pieces on the sheet looking for a shard big enough to do the work. I picked out a piece the length of my hand and used another to tear the sleeve of my shirt. I ripped off a long orange strip from my jumpsuit and wrapped it under my left armpit as tight as I could. I didn't stop and think. I kept Maddie and Sean in my head and cut lengthwise up my left forearm with the big piece of glass. I stuffed my mouth with the shreds of jumpsuit before I made the cut deep into my wrist. Blood came in a slow steady flow, forming a fist-sized pool on the ground. I sat on the bed, my right hand tight on the tourniquet.

Something scratched at my heart like fishhooks on a tin can. My anxieties and fears that had been ambling at a drunk's pace caught steam again. I was tired of playing the dummy grift. I had to pay in. I watched the blood drop from my arm in fat drops—four and six at a time. The pool on the mattress was soaking through and grew to the size of a dinner plate. I breathed slow and forced myself to stay upright. When the other fluorescent clipped on in the ceiling, I started my count loud, trying to shirk the faint.

'Ten, twenty, thirty, forty, fifty—'

I pushed myself up to my feet and peeked again out the window. The black guard was standing behind his desk, talking to the short motherfucker across the room.

'Eighty, ninety, hundred. Ten, twenty, thirty—'

The black guard's eyes followed the short man to each cell. He laughed, looked down, and then flipped a switch on the board.

'Seventy, eighty, ninety—'

When his gaze turned to the doors down from my cell, I stepped back and let out the knot from underneath my arm. My breath caught in my chest. Blood poured full now. It was well more than I thought. My legs buckled. My knees hit the ground. I tried to keep the numbers.

'Forty, fifty, sixty, seventy—'

My cell door unlocked. The black guard's raspy laughter boomed in. I stared at the single light above me and felt my mouth opening and closing. The short guard screamed into the room. Yes, I was scared. I didn't hear what he said. I was desperate. I was losing the count. They moved me fast. The gurney shook across the pavement. My eyes rattled back and forth. My chest heaved up and down. Over and over, it filled taut with air then collapsed in short bursts. The two guards ran next to me like cartoons, their eyes popping out of their faces and their mouths moving like they were yelling nonsense. The world was wide, loud, and fast like a grocery cart going down a hill.

The belly of the short guard's uniform was soaked with my blood. I kept trying to look down at my left arm, but every time I got my head up, the gurney kicked up and threw me back flat. A cuff tightened on my right wrist before they collapsed the gurney and put me in an ambulance. I saw the same lady paramedic who helped me before. She was talking directly into my face. Her spit hit below my eye. She was saying my name, and I was talking too, but my voice sounded like I was underwater. I felt a heat deep inside my body, like a warm finger put up my ass. Then there were red, white, and orange lights. Panic came in waves. I was scared I cut too deep and too long. I saw Marcus's cheeks and Mary's thin wrists. A chain hit a floor. Heavy rain slapping on a windshield, but it could have been anything.

I stopped seeing and hearing then–that's a confession by itself. None of the spectres came, not one Cadillac. If my compass was boxed for salvation, this wasn't it. I remembered smoking Canadian cigarettes dipped in formaldehyde when I poached my first high. I laced them up on my own in the garage and let them dry in a used mayonnaise jar half-filled with screws. I hotboxed them little burners all by myself. I saw stars and floated in car exhaust. I walked down the street and renamed two cats. I made them brooches out of trash. I was twelve and a half and wicked to the hilt. The cats were cowboys, Pine Sol and Snaps. I carried them back home. That afternoon, I was scared when I fell asleep. I knew I wasn't going to wake up in the morning.

My mouth was so dry, it was hard to move my tongue. When I reached for a plastic cup of water on the rolling table next to me, an alarm started going off. It wasn't four seconds before I heard boots coming down the hallway and in walked John Ethan in full uniform.

'Frank?'

He watched me fight with my left arm. It wasn't working. From the elbow down was just blank. I watched the hand move, almost close, and then stop.

'Let me help,' he said.

He came over, held the cup to my face, and I drank it all down. He filled the cup back up from a sweating pitcher and left it sitting on the table in front of me.

'Doctor says you did a little bit of nerve damage with your stunt. That's probably why your arm isn't responding so well . . . and you're doped to the ceiling.'

'News to me.'

I could feel my mouth drying out again as each moment passed.

'Were you trying to break out on me, Frank?'

'What about them straws?' I asked.

'I'm just saying, you know how this plays out if you're bent on escape.'

John Ethan tapped his pistol at his belt and nodded his head at me like the assured ass he was.

'We've never lost a prisoner,' he said, proudly.

'I forgot they give you men firearms on the outside.'

'Don't fuck with me, Frank. I'm begging you.'

'I'm just thirsty as all hell.'

'I'll see about the straws.'

He started out the door but turned back, tapped his ear, and smiled.

'I'm not far.'

I should have figured the good Christian would have handled me so personal. He wasn't going to let me shit out of earshot. I flicked the sensor off my finger and listened to the beeping drone until it stopped. A crafty man would have turned on one of those guards back at the lockup. Broke the short man down for his baton and fought his last hundred steps before he got his riot-gear send-off. I'd be picking my teeth out of my teeth right now. I can't say I was that much better off. If I was doped up, I didn't know it. I was thinking straight as a rail. Whatever painkiller they had me on was the first fix I'd had in five days. Right then, a male nurse walked into my room. He put a straw in the plastic cup in front of me.

'Thanks,' I said. 'What hospital—'

He didn't even look at me. He turned heel and was out the door. I wasn't going to get any notice unless I was dying. *All for the better*, I thought. Hell, if I'm going to get all smug in here. Marcus had used a grand hand of pull to lock me up so quiet. If he piled the shit any higher on my sorry ass, flags would start waving, and all his financial tributes would come tumbling down on every louse that helped. I wasn't supposed to be in the hospital. My mouth was supposed to be filled with cock and knives.

'You're like fucking gnats, Frank. Flies at a fucking picnic, the way you're all falling down. I hate hospitals.'

Mary sat on the end of my bed. She held baby Margaret in her lap, one arm around the child's waist.

'There you are. I thought they had you drugged up all asleep. I feel like I have all these fucking maps in my head from walking through hospital lobbies. This wing. That wing. It took us almost an hour to find you. I thought you'd look worse.'

The room was pitch-dark except for two small lights above my bed. My unfinished dinner tray sat on the bed table in front of me.

'Can you lift the bandage?' she said. 'You must've been real scared to do all this.'

'Where's Noni? What are you doing with the baby?'

I went to wipe my eyes. I didn't feel awake. My arm snapped back on the cuffs. This wasn't happening.

'Oh, they cuffed you. I didn't even see that because of the way your arm was there. You can't barely move.'

On the other side of the room, the door was closed. There was no light coming from behind the blinds. Mary dug into her purse. Margaret teetered on her knee while she bent over.

'I can't find it for the life of me,' she said. 'Where are the fucking lights in here?'

In the dark, all I could make out was Mary's curly blonde hair. Margaret was still in the same purple coat and pink winter hat from the prison.

'I'll yell for that fucking guard,' I said. 'Don't think I won't, Mary.'

'Oh, here it is. You want this?'

She held out a blue plastic snort bullet packed with meth.

'Quit with the bullshit—'

'Or what?' she asked. 'You gonna shit your bed?'

Mary leaned over Margaret, and I finally saw her face. She was a scarred shadow of herself. What was left of her famous teased-out blonde hair had thinned to a scalp-showing fried wig. Her wrinkles and hard lines ate the little bit of light in the room, and everything else turned black on her sunken cheeks and around her cherry-bombed-out eyes. Her lipstick was red. Blue smudged retarded across her brow. Her hips and ass—her old highest marks—couldn't fuck the world anymore. She jerked like a victim, like someone left alive and forced to heal on her own.

'How'd you get in here? Where's Noni?' I asked again.

With two fingers, Mary rolled the grinder on the bullet.

'You don't even want to know. You think I just borrowed the fucking kid?'

Her eyes lit up. Her jaw popped between words.

'You're a fucking ass. I killed her, Frank. I cut that bitch up just like you. There, I said it. So fucking dumb.'

I tried to push myself up with the heel of my right hand. She shoved the bullet up her nostril and snorted.

'I was coming—We were coming to see you at the prison, Frank. We get all the way there, and they tell us about this. We drove so fucking fast both ways.'

Margaret started to cry in her lap. Mary wiped her nose with her free hand and dropped the bullet back into her handbag. She got up, held Margaret to her chest, and patted the baby on the back.

'You never showed. Ben says, 'He'll show. He'll show.' Ben shows. You don't show. Nowhere to be found. Then we find you, Frank.'

It was a mess trying to listen to her. She paced back and forth bouncing Margaret at her chest.

'We knew you'd go back to my house because you always loved it so much. You always loved Jon, and he took care of you. He told me everything after you left. He told me about how fucked up you were. He treated you like one of his own. He didn't have anyone.'

'Where is Jon?' I asked.

'He's here . . . close.'

I looked back and forth across the room, ready for Santer to jump out of the shadows. But there was nothing, only Mary breathing heavy, swallowing over and over as the crank hooked.

'Bullshit. He ain't here, and you didn't kill Noni. We both know you ain't got it like that.'

'Chip don't fall far from tree. Isn't that how it goes?' asked Mary. 'That's what the blacks say.'

Mary paced faster and faster. Margaret's head wobbled, snapping up and down like a failing toy.

'Someone needs to pay, Frank. Ben's gone, and someone needs to pay. You owe me. You owe us for what we did. Jon took care of you. He wanted to help you, Frank. He treated you like one of his own.'

'I don't owe you shit.'

'You can't just put all this shit in motion, Frank. Get Jon all riled up, and then just walk away. Ben guaranteed us twenty thousand dollars.'

'If you can't tell, I ain't got shit for you. Go call Ben.'

Mary took Margaret from her shoulder and cradled her close to her chest. She pushed the baby's hat off and stroked through her fine hair. Dried snot and tears crusted Margaret's lip. She wasn't crying anymore, but her eyes wandered around the room, scared.

'I know you still got cash, Frank,' said Mary. 'All that free take from Burning J. You pay us the twenty thousand, and we won't kill your girl. Maybe we'll let this baby alone.'

'You're not seeing it, Mary—the deal's over. I'm locked up. Ben ain't going to Mexico with his boy.'

Mary picked up her purse from the floor and moved to the end of the bed. She was still, staring down at me with her shaking purple-shot eyes.

'No one was ever going to Mexico, Frank.'

Two loud knocks came at the door before a nurse opened it wide. Compared to Mary, she looked like she'd just washed. Her brown hair was pulled back in a ponytail, and her skin was shiny, fed, and pink.

'What's going on in here? We're getting complaints,' she said.

The lights were on in the hallway. Shadows of people walked by the open door.

'Where's that guard?' I asked.

'He's gone for the day. Someone's driving over from county. Is everything all right?'

Mary grabbed her purse and jacket off the chair, scurrying like a giant white rat.

'You got two days, Frank,' she said. 'You don't believe me? Come looking in two days.'

'Lady,' I said to the nurse. 'Grab that baby! That ain't her kid!'

The nurse looked at me and then Mary, scared of what she just walked into.

'That ain't her kid!' I shouted. 'Stop her!'

As Mary went to the door, the nurse took a shaky step towards her.

'Miss, I think I'm going to—'

'Get the fuck outta the way!'

Mary covered Margaret and shoved the nurse back with one arm. She was gone. I wore the cuffs, and no one would listen. The nurse looked at me, scared frozen.

'I'm sorry, but people were calling the station.'

'It's all right,' I said.

'Is she your wife?'

'Is that what she said? Did you let her in?'

'No . . .'

The nurse was lying. One more person scared to tell me the truth.

t felt like there wasn't ever going to be sound again, like Mary gagged the world. After she left, I stayed up and tried to listen to the noise of the hospital, but the thick door of my room shut me in. I wanted to hear electronic phones ringing and plain voices of hospital workers that didn't have a hint of bully or murder. But instead I sat cuffed to the bed repeating two questions to myself like I was chained in a microwave watching my thoughts cook circles on the wall—*What do you believe? Who do you trust?*

Before that day, if you pressed me, I could barely tell you what Mary looked like four years ago. Her curly hair and wide hips were familiar, but her voice and face had cankered from a palsy routine of trash-cooked speed and dirty cocks. She was a scarecrow now. She had skulked in with her stolen child, stood tall in her boots, and blasted crystal right in front of me. And then she menaced down and told me a truth that I didn't want to believe, but the longer I sat with—rubbed me wrong. Right off, I wanted to call Ben, hear him chewing food in my ear, and have a laugh. Tell him that it was quite a hack he pulled having Mary come down, ask him where he found someone that was a ringer for Santer in his prime. But I'd only get that far before the pain in my shredded wrist bit back or the catheter in my dick pinched, letting off piss. I saw baby Margaret's dirty face and dirty clothes, her head bouncing, ready to snap. I remembered I was still waiting to hear from my *good lawyer,* and there was the feeling I'd been fighting—that the last time I'd seen Ben, he was pretty damn comfortable leaving me for dead.

People get greedy. First thing they lose is respect.

That's the truth, old man. Santer never lied to me, I'll give him that. He tore me apart, took me to slaughter, but he always kept his word no matter how high. I wanted to hear his words. In that moment, in that room, I longed to speak to someone who didn't work angles, who was honest even if they were burning for drugs. Mary's word was trash, but she had baby Margaret. Ben promised to help, but my supposed blessed blood brother was gone. What was Mary getting at—*No one was going to Mexico?* Then what was Ben's plan? At the time—any way you cut it—he was getting Sean back. My stomach turned the longer I thought on it. I gagged, felt vomit fighting its way up. As it stood, it didn't matter if it was Mary, Jon, or the whole Shenk family that I needed to burn in a barrel. The only thing that mattered was for me to get out to protect the ones I knew—with no doubts—that I loved.

The guard they sent from county was a regular cop. He was white and looked like a taller version of the short piggy motherfucker that found me bleeding out. His hair was short, balding in the standard fat-head crew cut, and when he walked, he sucked in his gut so his entire body looked like he was holding a buffalo shit. To himself, he was readied and tough. He came in twice through the night. I asked his name both times, but he clammed up. The first time he walked in, he did a once-around the whole room. He pulled the blinds and made me show my arms and cuffs. He had me roll over on my side to check I wasn't squirreling a shank up my ass. The second time, he came in with a small cup of coffee. I asked his name again, but he just pulled the one chair in the room against the wall and sipped his coffee until it was empty. I fell asleep that night with the county guard nodding off in front of me. I slept sound because of the all the hydrocodone. I didn't see Mary's or Jon's face roaring in my dreams. I needed that one night before I ran high again.

I woke up to an older male doctor asking to see my arm. I hadn't met or seen this man. He had a thick head of shaggy hair and a full beard that was covering a peeling sunburn.

John Ethan stood across the room in his uniform. I put my wrist out, and the doctor unwrapped the bandages and examined the needlework.

'How am I looking?'

'How are you feeling?' the doctor asked.

'I can move it, but I just can't grip much.'

I tried to make my hand into a fist. My fingers crunched together but wouldn't come past the start of my palm.

'All right, stop,' said the doctor. 'Relax your hand. Tell me when you feel this.'

He pressed the tip of his pen on each of my fingers. I felt the pressure fine, but I wasn't going to let on.

'Nothing. I don't feel nothing.'

'What about this?'

He put the pen into the center of my palm.

'No. I don't feel it—maybe a little.'

'You don't feel this pen?'

He stabbed down. It smarted something awful, but I just shook my head and let my dick curl up. The doctor let go, grabbed a clipboard next to my bed, and started writing a book of notes. John Ethan stared him down the whole time. He couldn't stand it.

'What's the call then?' said John Ethan. 'When can we take him back?'

The doctor took his glasses from around his neck and put them on. He set the chart down and looked me square in the eye.

'How are you feeling, Frank?' he asked, again.

'I told you. I mean, I can't hardly grip anything.'

'No—altogether. Are you feeling down, emotionally?'

'Oh, this is horseshit!' yelled John Ethan.

'He completely spaghettied his arm, Mr. Ethan.'

'Sergeant.'

'Fine, Sergeant. He's got nerve damage all through his fingers—'

'When can we take him back?'

The doctor took off his glasses and let them drop back around his neck.

'Sergeant, how many suicidal patients have you treated?'

John Ethan got red in the face. It was the same look I'd seen before when I cursed his Jesus. He shifted a few steps in place and took a deep breath. I looked him up and down, searching for that blackjack.

'Don't try to pull rank with me, Doctor,' said John Ethan. 'You won't win. Frank is a *prisoner*, and I would like to return him to *prison* as soon as he is well enough. So, how long?'

The doctor ignored John Ethan and started to wrap my arm back up.

'I'm going to call the nurse down to get you fresh dressings,' he whispered.

'How long?'

The doctor slowly put his glasses on one last time and patted my arm like a good old coach. John Ethan was so pissed, he was chewing on his cheek.

'Two more days . . . At least,' said the doctor. 'Can I speak to you in the hallway?'

They both went out the door, and it wasn't long before they were yelling at the top of their lungs. John Ethan hated not having me in a cell, and the doctor didn't care for his balls getting chopped on his turf. They moved down the hall, their voices turning into a mess the farther they got away. The nurse who had screwed up with Mary came in with a tray of fresh bandages. She still wasn't wearing any makeup, and her ponytail was letting loose across her back. She smiled and rolled her tired eyes at the yelling match outside.

'They're really going at it,' she said.

She sat on the edge of my bed and set a tray of fresh bandages on the rolling table before she started cutting away all the crusted ones from my wrist. The sight of all the crooked stitching made her stop.

'I ran into some furniture,' I said.

She smiled as best she could and went to cleaning off the dried blood.

'So why are you still here?' I asked again.

'Oh, I'm working the turnaround for a friend. She's got kids. She needed a favor.'

'Don't let them walk all over you, now.'

'No, I don't—sorry, I'm not supposed to be talking to you.'

'You weren't supposed to let in my 'wife,' either.'

She stopped and checked the open door behind her.

'You're not going to say anything, are you? I didn't realize—I could lose my job.'

'I'm not saying a word. They'd bust me up worse than this if they knew that woman came around. I could use a favor, though.'

She wrapped the gauze carefully around my wrist.

'You're not going to ask for a scalpel or something? I can't do that.'

'No, no—can you just pop in here a couple of times today and tell me what time it is?'

'Yeah, I can do that, of course.'

'It's just I start to go crazy in here. I don't have a TV. I don't know up from down after an hour.'

She looked down at her watch.

'It's 9:45—AM.'

'Thank you, I appreciate it.'

The nurse taped up her gauze work tight. She started out the room but stopped and went to the window and drew up the middle blind halfway, letting in a shaft of sunlight. She put her finger to her lips in a silent *shh*, and walked out.

Through the window, I saw the gravel-covered roof of a building next door. I couldn't see the sky, but the day looked clear. The sunlight was clean. No cloud shadows moved across the roof. *I ain't Mary*, I told myself. *I got a heart and a few things I love.*

We washed our arms with ammonia. Mary watched us, smiling from the doorway. Santer and I were in the back of her house. We were bent over a big plastic basin next to a clothes washer. Jon scrubbed his forearms with steel wool so hard, his skin was fierce red. His hairs collected at the drain. I poured ammonia from a plastic bottle and rubbed my hands together in a rhythm that made sense to me in my head. We were so high, my eyes were shaking. My temples burst with my heart.

'Didn't I tell you I was good?' he said. 'I know every step like the back of my hand. When Jon Jr. died, I had to gather his black bones before they came. They were hot like dud sticks of dynamite.'

When Jon said that, Mary doubled over laughing. She went behind him, kissed his neck, and said,

'Now it's just us, how it was supposed to be . . .'

I remember walking through the kitchen thinking I was going to die. I couldn't stop sweating, and my whole chest felt empty. I drank a glass of vodka trying to skirt the edge, and then I was sitting in Mary's living room in a big reclining chair. A dim brass lamp sat on the coffee table, and Paul Simon skipped on the stereo. I know it was Paul Simon because I remember wishing I could speak to him about what I'd done. Jon got naked. Mary ran her hands over the PRIMER PADRE tattoo around his neck, scratching, licking at it.

'I want it gone, all gone,' she said.

His dick shook hard in his lap. I was smiling and making sure to laugh when they laughed because I was scared. They sat on the ground smoking a metal pipe of crystal and weed. They handed me the pipe, and Mary got on top of Jon. She fucked him while he hummed to the clipping music. Razor nicks spotted her pussy.

'That's your tight little baby,' she said. 'Like the day I was born.'

He turned her around and winked at me. I walked. I got sick by the front door and slept for two days. Jon woke me up on the naked mattress at the apartment. Mary had set out clothes for me on the bed. I rode in the backseat of a car. I had on an expensive pair of Jon's sunglasses, and my back was wet under my jacket. When we got to the bus station, I remember Jon was happy, so I wasn't worried.

'We did a service, Frank. Them sisters—that family—they ain't gonna fleece another soul. I told you I wasn't out to hurt anyone. Funny how people change.'

I thought I'd see him again, so I didn't say anything important. Mary gave my ticket to the bus driver and made sure I got a good seat. Jon kissed me on the forehead and held me like a girl. He told me to take off my jacket because I'd be more comfortable. I did, and when I turned back around, they were gone.

The nurse dropped off my lunch and told me it was one thirty. She asked me how I felt, and I asked her for more medication. It took her another hour, but she came back with two paper cups of four more hydrocodone. She didn't say much, just set the dixie cups down and left. She looked tired and busy. Nobody noticed the one set of blinds were open until John Ethan was leaving for the day. He didn't ask anything about it and dropped the blinds and checked the locks on the rest of the windows. He told me he and the doctor came to an agreement. In two days—no matter my condition—I'd be bussed back to the prison hospital and monitored for another week.

'Is that all right with you, Frank?' he asked. 'You think you'll be up for heading back?'

'I don't get why you're asking. It ain't like I get my two cents in this shit.'

'Of course you do. I'm telling you so it's not any surprise and you're adjusted to the decision and all that. You understand that, don't you?'

'To be honest, I don't. But that's no care for you.'

'Well, that's where we're at. I want you to get better. I'm going to try and get you a TV.'

'Fine.'

'What do I want to hear, you piece of shit?'

'Thank you.'

He headed out the door, talking over his shoulder as he left.

'That's all I ever want, Frank—that's all. The man from county will be up in an hour. Stay quiet.'

I did. There was nothing else to do besides sit, stare, and piss and shit into my bedpan. If I was going to be staying for two more days, they were going to be on John Ethan's terms. He knew better than to give me any liberties off the cuffs, and I knew better than to ask. In his eyes, if I was well enough to hold my dick and wipe my ass, I was fine to be back at the prison doing the same with those cardboard shit tickets. But that was never going to happen as long as Mary wanted all that ransom—not as long as she had baby Margaret and wanted Maddie dead. I wanted to tell him that so I could return the favor, get him adjusted to the fucking decision and all that. I was moving my cuffed right arm up and down the length of the bed rail when the lady nurse walked in.

'Are you starting a band?' she asked.

'I got one of those itches that I can barely get to.'

She walked over to the right side of my bed and pulled back the sheet.

'Where is it?' she asked.

'Above my left ankle.'

She scratched on my leg and threw the sheet back down.

'Thank you,' I said.

'No need—it's part of the job. I came to say goodbye. It's six o'clock, and I'm done for the day.'

'I appreciate you keeping up your end of the bargain.'

'Wasn't that hard—I got you something. Open your hand.'

She came up close and dropped a kid's digital watch under the rail. It was the kind they gave away at fast food joints. It was green and had a picture of a laughing skeleton on the front, but no wristband.

'Where'd you get this?' I asked.

'The lost and found. There's all sorts of junk in there. It works fine. I set it.'

'How am I supposed to show it off without any bands?'

'I didn't want to get you anything flashy, considering, so I cut them off.'

She watched me fumble with the small watch in my cuffed hand.

'Frank—do you mind if I call you that?' she asked.

'I don't mind, as long as I can get your name.'

'Sarah. It's Sarah.'

She crossed her arms at her chest and shifted in place, nervous.

'Frank, how'd you end up here?'

'In prison or in the hospital?'

'I guess I want to know . . . in prison?'

'To be honest, Sarah, it's none of your business.'

'You're right. I'm sorry—'

'But I think this skeleton watch buys you a single question at least.'

I stuck the watch under my thigh and looked her in the eye.

'I beat up a man real bad who didn't deserve it. So I got mine right here.'

She wanted to hear more—the details of pistol-whipping an East Indian in a motel parking lot—but I wasn't going to let her have all that.

'What about your arm?' she asked.

'Only one, Sarah. You bring me a key to these cuffs, and I'll be happy to tell you my long story, but I promise you, it probably ain't got shit on your favorite TV show.'

'I doubt that . . . You have a good night. Get some rest.'

'Same to you. Don't work so hard.'

She patted me on the arm before she left. She was a nice woman. She saw me for what I was. She was just curious and wanted to hear it out my lips—*I beat up a man who didn't deserve it. I beat up a man real bad who didn't deserve it. So I got mine right here.*

I t was 3:40 AM—close to the robbing hour. I fell in and out of sleep, checking the little watch under my thigh every few minutes, but once the fat-necked guard started snoring, the codone wasn't enough to keep me out. The cop's head was broken over to the side like a rag doll, and his mouth was open just enough to catch the air in his throat and make the pig that much louder.

I pushed the sheet off my legs and slowly rolled my bed table as far away as I could. I kept both eyes on the guard as I put my right leg over the side rail and slid the rest of my body to the edge of the bed. I took a deep breath and pushed all my weight off my right hand. When my bare feet hit the floor, the cold snapped up through my legs, making them sting. For a second, the guard's breath caught in his mouth, and he started hocking up in his sleep. I waited until his snores came back full before I slid down and used my feet to feel around for the wheel locks. The door was still propped open, and the red of an exit sign poured three feet into my room. The only other light came from the murmuring television.

I released the wheel locks on the right and slid my cuffed arm forward and backward to reach the other set. The hospital bed didn't move an inch. I stood and put my shoulder into the frame and pushed the bed till I was right next to the guard. His pistol stuck out the side of his chair, but the keys to the cuffs were tucked deep in his waist. I crouched down and wiped my left hand on my hospital robe. I opened and closed it over and over, wincing each time because it still wasn't good for the weight.

I flipped the button off his holster, grabbed his Glock, and jumped back up as fast as I could. I drew the gun back over his face—ready to jack him with the butt—but the piece of shit still didn't move. I brought the gun close to my body and cocked it with my cuffed hand. I leaned into the bed again and pushed it over to line myself up for a straight shot on the guard's face. My left forearm was already burning from holding the piece up that little bit. I set the nose of the gun on the bed and let my arm relax for a few seconds before I kicked the bottom of the chair. The cop's body wobbled in place. His neck jelly shook, but he just kept breathing heavy, bringing his lips together in his sleep. I took a step back and, with all my weight, drove my heel into his gut. The air went out of him in a long groan before his eyes opened wide. His arms grabbed at his chest, and he started a scream but caught himself when he realized the barrel of his gun on his face.

'Don't! How—please, don't!'

'Gimme the key to the cuffs.'

'I don't have it.'

I took a step forward and pushed the gun into his forehead. My forearm shook with the weight.

'Don't be all smart on me. Gimme me the key.'

He fumbled at his waist trying to fit his fingers under his belly. I could feel the tendons and muscles giving way in my hand. He fished the keys out from his belt and held them up.

'Drop 'em,' I said.

They fell right next to the chair. I pulled them over with my right foot and quickly switched the pistol to my cuffed hand. I crouched down and unlocked the cuff off the rail. I let the other hang from my wrist as I walked backward to the door and closed it slowly.

'Get up.'

The guard pushed himself out of the chair. He was all awake now and wasn't happy about the fix he was in.

'Take off your shoes and your pants.'

'I ain't giving you shit,' he said.

'We can do work like this all night, but you know I don't give a damn. So I'd start moving if I was you.'

His eyes gave up. He kicked off his shoes and unbuckled his holster and belt.

'You can throw that over here,' I said.

He tossed it in front of me, and I kept the gun on him while he dropped his pants.

'Pick it all up, and walk over here to the bathroom.'

He bundled his shoes and clothes in his arms, embarrassed I took him so easy. He walked with his head high, still trying to keep tough.

'Drop all of it against the wall.'

He set the clothes on the ground and tried to take a step towards me as he came back up, but the pistol was still on his chin.

'Just stop,' I said. 'Get in the bathroom.'

He stepped in, and I flipped on the lights and unlocked the cuffs from my right wrist. I threw them across the tiles.

'Cuff yourself on the handle.'

'Where are you going to go?' he said. 'You don't think they'll catch you?'

When he was locked up, I set the gun down and grabbed his pants from the floor. I took out his wallet and pulled the pants up to my waist. They were three sizes too big. I folded them over till they held.

'What hospital is this?' I asked.

'You don't even know where the hell you are? Ha, you're fucked.'

His shoes fit. They were loose but stayed on once I tightened the laces.

'What side of the city are we on? What hospital?' I asked.

'Fuck you. You're not getting any more.'

'The hell I'm not.'

I grabbed a hand towel from next to the sink and beat him over his face with the body of the Glock. Before he could yell, I stuffed the rag into his mouth, gagging him. He screamed and yelled, but it wasn't any louder than the TV in the other room. When he caught his breath, I pulled it out.

'What hospital?'

'. . . Baptist. Phoenix Baptist.'

'Where's your cell phone?'

'On my belt.'

I went back to his holster and pulled his cell phone from its case. I stuck it in my pocket and then went through his wallet and took all sixty dollars of his cash.

'Look, I'm sorry about all the hurt,' I said. 'I need you to tell John Ethan something for me.'

The guard sat on the toilet, holding the swelling side of his face. He looked at me like I was crazy.

'Who?!'

'John Ethan—Sergeant John Ethan. Do you know him?'

'Yeah . . . I know him.'

'You tell him thank you. Thank you for everything, and I mean it.'

I pressed the lock on the bathroom door handle and let the door close. I grabbed the digital watch from the bed, cracked open the door to my room, and peeked down the hall. Lights spilled from the nursing station about thirty yards away. I put my head out and didn't see anyone in either direction. On the ceiling to the right, there was the red exit sign I had seen glowing. I stepped out and followed it, walking as fast as I could. The cop was already pounding at the wall in the bathroom, but when I got a few doors away, he faded away. I didn't look into any other hospital rooms. I kept my eyes on the stairwell door until I touched it. I checked back over my shoulder one more time—nothing.

I was on the fifth floor. I held on to the rail and took the stairs three at a time. When I reached the first floor, I crotched the pistol and held the giant pants up with my right hand. In the lobby, there was a florist and a closed-up gift shop. I looked back and forth, but there wasn't a body or sound except a vacuum running somewhere I couldn't see. I walked past the dark windows of the gift shop. My palms wet with sweat as I walked through the automatic glass doors of the exit. I waited until I was out of the light of the entrance before I ran across the parking lot towards a traffic light that seemed miles away. The cold air made my eyes water at the edges, and I breathed in deep after each step, sucking it all in.

counted the streets, mouthed their names to myself—Vermont, Georgia, Hazelwood, Campbell, Turney. I watched the honest sort of Phoenix get on and off the Nineteenth Avenue bus barely alive but ready for the morning shift of the city. These poor, these Mexicans, these whites and blacks—they all stepped onto the bus the same. The short women muzzled their scarves across their faces. They smiled and laughed, not wanting to ruin their bus rides with cackles and arguments. The men, unshaven and tired, unzipped their coats once all the bodies and window vents put heat back into their faces. They all leaned towards the sun on the left side of the bus. After each stop, morning lit up the inside a hair more until everyone squinted to see the face in front of them, and for ten minutes, everyone was on fire in red. No one looked at me sideways or gave a damn I was still wearing a hospital frock. The Glock was tucked tight at my waist, and I kept my left forearm across my body so no one could see the iodine-soaked stitchwork on my wrist. When the bus crossed under the I-17, I exhaled loud enough that the man sitting next to me glanced over to see if I was bowing up to go nutty on him or if it was just—by the looks of me—my last drunk homeless breath.

I ditched out of the bus when we hit the west side. I knew I'd have an easier time mixing in with the rest of the early-day dry drunks. I made my way east down Indian School Road, looking for somewhere to buy fresh, cheap clothes. It was still early, just getting past six by the skeleton watch. I figured I had another hour—hour and a half at the most—before hell broke and John Ethan put out after me. Word would work itself back up the food chain, and I'd turn around and see Santer, the Jew Goldstein, and the entire Phoenix police force—maybe even that bought-off judge—running me down a back alley into an overgrown chain-linked yard—seen it too many times.

I turned off the guard's phone before I stepped into a Vietnamese donut shop. The place was just getting going. It was empty except for a man who looked at me warily behind the counter. He eyed my hospital robe and brown oversized pants. Anybody could see my shoes were too big for me. I was walking goofy because the shoes slapped the ground ahead of me. I was a strung-out bozo, duck-footing around his tiny donut shop.

'One large coffee,' I said.

The man clocked me up and down and yelled something into the back. He said it so fast I couldn't tell if it was English or not. A moment later, an older bald Vietnamese man came out in a tight Harvard sweatshirt and white apron. He stared me up and down from the kitchen door with his sleeves pulled up to his elbows. They both ignored me and talked back and forth in their language.

'Can I get a coffee?' I asked again. 'A large.'

'Get out,' the Harvard man said in a heavy accent.

Before I could ask again, his counter man got his back.

'Get out!'

I pulled a twenty from my pocket and laid it on the counter. They talked back and forth, arguing in short pissed words. The counter man threw up his arms and pushed Harvard out of the way to get to the back. Harvard smiled and stepped forward. He pulled the twenty towards the register.

'What size?' he asked.

'Large.'

He took a tall Styrofoam cup from a stack and filled it from a steaming urn behind him.

'You want cream?'

I shook my head no. He put a plastic lid on the top of the cup and took a white paper bag and dropped in three donut holes from a tray on the counter.

'Sugar is behind you,' he said, sliding it all over. 'Your money is fine here. I'm sorry for my friend.'

I dropped the silver into the tip jar next to the register.

'Do you know where I can get some clothes?' I said, motioning up and down at my getup. 'I need new clothes.'

'You have money, right?'

I held up the cash from my pocket, and he smiled.

'Nowhere is open. Too early,' he said.

'I know. But do you know a store?'

'You sick, huh? From the hospital.'

'I just need some clothes.'

He nodded up and down, thinking on it, and then he yelled back into the kitchen. There was no answer, so he yelled again—louder and meaner. The other man came out with a scowl on his face. His hands were dusted in flour, and he glared at me, angry I was still there. Harvard talked to him slowly, but the man wasn't having any of it. He yelled back, and Harvard dropped his voice and shamed him quiet-like. The man wiped his hands on his apron and then pulled out his cell phone and started dialing.

'Two blocks that way,' Harvard said, pointing east down the street. 'They have dry cleaning. Only one—you'll see. They help you out.'

'Thanks,' I said. 'Thank you.'

He held out his hand, and it floated between us. I looked at him. He started laughing.

'Shake!' he said.

I put my right hand out and fished my pants up with my left. He grabbed it and shook it hard.

'I'm Tom,' he said.

'Frank. I'm Frank.'

'Frank, your money is fine here. Your money is fine.'

I picked up the coffee and bag of donut holes and started out the door.

'Frank!'

I turned back to Harvard, a big smile on his face.

'Eat the donuts.' He motioned to the bag. 'I make them. They're very sweet and *goood*.'

He drew the last word out long, so it sang up to my ears.

He spoke solid.

His lady's dry cleaner was tucked away into a strip mall just before Seventh Avenue like he'd said. When I opened the door, I knew it was the right place because on the counter was an open box

of donut holes with a handwritten sign, *FREE! SWEET AND GOOD!*
An Asian woman came out from the back with a stack of clothes in
dry cleaning bags folded over her arm. She wasn't hateful like her
husband had been.

'Frank—are you Frank?' she asked.

'That's me.'

'Yes. I'm Roger's wife,' she said.

'Roger?'

'Roger, yes. He's at the donut shop with Tom. You're Frank,
right? My name is Lee Yun.'

Lee had the same singsong accent, but her English was a whole
lot better. She was a put-together little lady in a brown suede vest
and a black shirt to her throat. She didn't blink or stutter when she
looked on me.

'I only met Tom,' I said.

'Do you have money?'

I pulled out the folded cash from my pocket. She smiled, set
down the clothes on the counter, and pulled out a plastic measuring
tape from her pants pocket.

'Arms out,' she said.

'Are those the clothes over there?' I asked, pointing to the pile on
the counter. 'I can go through them.'

'Nooo. We'll find the right size for you—arms out.'

I held the coffee out towards her. She took it, and as soon as she
turned to set it down, I scrambled the Glock from the front of my
pants to my back and prayed it wouldn't drop.

'Arms out.'

Lee wrapped the measuring tape around my chest and brought it together in the front. She peered at the numbers and marked them down on the back of a dry cleaning ticket.

'What happened to your arm?' she asked as she bent down to measure my legs.

'Work—a table saw.'

'Those are very dangerous—'

She stood up and pushed my arms down at my side.

'Relax.'

Lee measured the length of my right arm and marked it down again.

'My father lost two fingers building our house here.'

'With a table saw?'

'No—ah . . . A band saw? The one you hold. He couldn't feed himself for a month. He was still very young. Maybe sixty-two when it happened. We had to feed him like a baby. He couldn't use the chopsticks—all right, done.'

She stepped back behind the counter and started flipping through the pile of clothes, checking the sizes.

'He was very angry when it happened. He wasn't . . . He wasn't, ah . . . He wasn't emotional, you know? He didn't like being fed by us.'

She pulled out two pairs of pants from the stack and set them aside.

'Do you need socks, Frank?'

I lifted up the bottom of my pants and showed her my bare ankles.

'Okay, let me see, okay?'

She turned and walked down a rack of clothes, talking as she searched.

'One night, my father, he stay up all night drinking tea with a bowl of nails. You know, for a hammer? Steel nails. He stay up all night picking the nails with the chopsticks. In the morning, he feed himself fine. He never use the saw again. He drown it in water, let it rust—here. These will work.'

Lee came back to the front with a pair of black socks and a belt. She pulled three shirts from the stack of clothes and set them on top of the pants.

'All these clothes,' she said. 'No one ever comes for them. You want to try them on?'

'How much?' I asked.

'Don't worry. Tom said your money is fine. Come, try them on.'

I followed Lee through the racks into the back. She opened a door to a small bathroom and set the clothes on the sink.

'Go ahead,' she said, waving me in.

I closed the door on Lee's smiling face and emptied my pockets on the top of the toilet. I took the Glock from my pants and set it in the sink while I took off all my clothes. I pulled a pair of blue work pants from their bag and tried them on. The woman knew her trade because they fit swell. I put on a white collared shirt, washed my hands in the sink, splashed water on my face. I dried my face off with the hospital robe and threw all my old clothes into one of the dry cleaning bags.

'How is it, Frank?' Lee asked through the door.

'It's fine, Lee. It's all fine.'

I put the pistol at my back and opened the door. Lee was standing with a black wool coat in her hands.

'Here, try it on,' she said.

'I can't. I don't have money for all that.'

'Come on. Don't worry. It's very cold. It's on me.'

I turned around and let her slip the jacket over my arms.

'Perfect. Good,' she said. 'Big pockets too. Put your hands in. Feel how big.'

She winked at me and walked to the front of the store. She knew I was holding. I threw the old clothes in a trash bin and went up to the front. Lee had the socks and belt out on the counter, ready.

'The jacket looks good, Frank.'

'Thank you, Lee. It's warm. How much?'

She looked me up and down, adding it all up.

'Roger will get mad—do you have ten dollars?'

I handed over the money. She stuck it into her pocket and gave me the socks and the belt.

'Too bad we don't have shoes, huh?' she said, laughing.

She watched me closely as I threaded the belt through my pants. If Lee was scared, she didn't let on. If I disgusted her, I would have never known. I tried to think on what I would have done if an armed, bleeding, hollow-eyed man knocked on my shop. I tried to put together a situation where I wouldn't kick him back from my door and drop a shovel on his face, but there wasn't. Even in a wheelchair, I would've tried to break him again.

'Very good,' she said. 'You can get a job now. Ha!'

She handed me back my coffee and walked me to the door, holding my shoulder.

'Thank you,' I said. 'And tell Tom and Roger thank you, too.'

'Don't worry. Come back when you have a job, and I'll clean the clothes for free.'

She watched from the window as I walked away. Up ahead, the streets looked familiar. I moved the Glock to my jacket pocket and clenched my left fist over and over, readying it for the weight.

I was two blocks from Mary's old tweaker den when my last dose of codone started wearing out. Every few steps, my forearm got warmer till it was a fresh burn under my jacket. The pain knocked at the back of my eyes, reminding me I was awake, on the run, and older. More cars were filling the streets. The city was starting to move. I'd already been off the main road for an hour, had to zigzag my way through neighborhoods just to get to the tall apartment complex I was standing behind. While I counted bullets between two cars, I heard showers running from open windows, and then a TV turned on loud in Spanish on the first floor. The clip was full, but the Glock was in poor shape. The whole machine was oily and chipped. The frame showed a crack just above the trigger. I shoved it back into my coat pocket with no idea if the pistol would even fire.

I got back on the street and kept my eyes on that collapsing apartment on top of the garage where I used to stay. I was trying to look regular—a regular morning man off to work—but I was sweating and felt my face screwing up because of the pain burning my arm. By the time I could see the driveway, I was breathing through my mouth, wanting to hack the thing off. In the daylight, the house looked better. I could see now it was freshly painted, and the few shrubs and bushes were cut and trimmed next to a newly planted tree. That old long Buick that I'd seen was still in the driveway along with a sun-faded Olds, and parked in front of the house on the street was Noni's little Toyota—Colorado tags still expired, wheel wells splattered in mud from speeding to Phoenix through the snow. I breathed in deep, pulled the Glock from my pocket, and cocked it low at my waist. The blinds in every window were drawn closed. As I got closer, I saw a mess of cigarette butts in front of the garage. They scattered from an overflowing coffee can and then trailed off to the cars. They were all Newports stained with bright pink lipstick, and when I got up to the door, I saw a fresh roached blunt on the living room windowsill just behind the burglar bars.

I knocked on the door with the barrel—no sound from inside. I waited another a minute and then kicked hard at the bottom of the door. Voices talked inside the room and then trailed off. Behind me across the street, a teenage neighbor kid came out and went to his car. He pulled his long hair back from his face, stared at me and the pistol, and got into his car—not stirred in the slightest. I kicked at the door again, and this time, I heard straight yelling coming closer.

'What the fuck is this bullshit?'

The door swung open wide. A young-looking black man stood in front of me—the same one I'd seen push Santer off that girl. He didn't have his shirt on, and one of his eyes was busted shut.

'Wrong house, motherfucker!' he yelled.

'Oh, hell no!'

The girl's voice yelled out from the dark room. I put the pistol on the man's chest. His eyes closed, and he held his forehead, shook it back and forth like it wasn't the first time he'd lost it all.

'Motherfucker . . .' he said, holding his hands up and taking a step back.

'Turn on the light,' I said.

In the doorway, I could only see the man standing in front of me. I heard moving around in the living room. When a lamp flipped on, I shut the door.

'Where is she?' I asked. 'Who else is here?'

'Who?' asked the man.

I grabbed him by the back of his neck and drove him with the pistol into a plastic-covered recliner close to the door. As I swept the gun back and forth across the room, memories rushed me. Underneath the choking perfume and stale weed smoke, the house smelled the same. That sour wet—Santer called it cat piss mixed with hot sauce—threaded up my nostrils, snapping at the back of my throat like it used to. A chill shocked through my body. Everything was familiar but different. The ceiling was new, no more molded bannisters peeking out from above. There was wall-to-wall fresh brown carpet. All the bowing splintered hardwood was gone. The walls had been painted, the yellow dripping cigarette stains and ball-point pen graffiti erased. A new fan spun slowly on the ceiling, and a giant box TV wrapped with a big red bow sat across from a brand-new couch still covered in plastic, tags hanging off the end like they were marking the exact spot where Mary and Jon used to fuck on the floor. The black girl was naked, standing in the kitchen doorway. Her hair shot out in different directions, and she still wore caked-on makeup, probably from the night before. She looked like me when I lived here—scared, gripping the wall.

'Noni. Where is she?' I asked. 'Don't bullshit me.'

'Look, I don't know what you're into,' said the man. 'But there ain't no Noni here. Now, you come back around in the afternoon, and we can have Ginger and Honey hook it up on the house.'

'I didn't come here for pussy. She knows that,' I said, tipping the Glock at the girl.

'You know this motherfucker? Is he one of your fucking tricks?!'

The girl ignored her man. The last time I saw her, she hadn't been afraid for one moment. The whole time, she dragged ass like a house cat—even when she was angry, she swung her hips back and forth like life could wait. Now, fear filled her eyes, and her throat swallowed over and over. She looked at me, started to plead.

'*I didn't know.* I promise you, I didn't know.'

'Don't lie to me!' I said, putting the pistol on her. 'What's her fucking car doing here?'

'They left it here a couple days ago,' said the girl. 'The girl was with them, but they didn't even come inside. They just parked it and left.'

'Mary took that girl's baby,' I said. 'Do you know that? Where'd they go?'

'I can't. She ain't right. She'll kill me.'

The man hunched over, put his head back into his hands, and started shaking it back and forth.

'*This is the motherfucker?!* We've been looking to talk to you.'

'Shut up, Keith!' yelled the girl. 'I don't want that lady coming back!'

'Fuck that crazy old bitch! And her old man! I ain't afraid of her!'

Mary had done some kind of work on these two. I lowered the gun, tried to talk straight.

'I don't want to hurt anybody, but I need to know where Mary is.'

'Man, she lives way out, down south in some dump,' said Keith. 'I know that fucking hood.'

'Keith, stop!' the girl said again.

'Fuck a Mary Santer. *I ain't giving her no more shit.* We've been here almost two years, pay our rent in cash, every month, on time. They still come around breaking us down. Bunch of racist-ass junkies, man.'

'I don't want no part of this . . .'

The girl dropped her hands from the doorway and moved fast, picking up her underwear and bra from the living room floor.

'What the fuck is she gonna do, Robbie?' said Keith. 'He's got a gun. I say let him go.'

She grabbed a dress off the couch and pulled it up over her body. It was the tight red hooker dress with her breasts coming out of the top.

'Robbie, is that your name?' I asked.

She didn't look at me and started brushing out her hair in a long mirror above the couch.

'Yes, that's my fucking name,' she said.

'My name's Frank. I'm sorry about all of this, but I need help. Mary's gonna hurt three of mine if I don't find her. She's already got Noni and her baby. She's going after my girl next.'

'You must think I'm crazy—look at him—you see that?'

Keith's right eye was swollen shut. Dark purple bruises—the kind from bats and bars—ran up and down the side of his chest. Same with his bare legs. He'd been stomped. I recognized the work.

'I ain't fucking with that woman . . . *Frank.*'

I clenched the pistol in my hand. Robbie pulled a Kleenex from a box on a side table, wiped the makeup from around her eyes, and balled it up, dropped it on the floor.

'I got money,' I said. 'I'll make it worth your time.'

'That's what you said before. And last I heard, you got locked the fuck up,' said Robbie. 'So for your own sake, you should get the fuck out of our house before I call the cops.'

She grabbed her phone off the coffee table, rubbed at the dial pad. Keith shrugged his shoulders at me, pointed to the door.

'You heard the lady,' he said. 'We don't want no trouble. It ain't worth it.'

I wanted to tell them that it would never end. That as long as Mary and Santer were around, they'd be hassled, rolled, and worse. But they weren't going to listen, they wouldn't believe me, just like Ben.

'They fix up that apartment like this?' I asked, pointing to the garage.

'Nah, they ain't touched it. Been empty since we moved in,' said Keith. 'Water don't work.'

'Go lift that toilet. I'll wait.'

gave it all to them. To me, the rotting eight thousand and change was cursed. There was more from the old cheeva deals, but it was worthless. The few bills that weren't black were glued together with mold or smeared useless with pipe rust. I sat in the living room while they counted the money in the kitchen, talking back and forth low. Robbie still didn't want to go, but to Keith, the money was good faith. I wasn't asking much—help me pick up Maddie and take me to Mary's house. I meant it, too. After ten minutes, Keith came out smiling in a basketball jersey, a creased pair of jeans, and brand-new blue sneakers. He sat down next to me on the couch and asked me if I liked to get high.

I got in the back of Keith's brown '72 Riviera. I wouldn't have known the year if Keith didn't have a small gold plaque screwed into the glove box that read, 'Daddy 1972 Buick Riviera.' After a minute, Robbie came out in the same red leather jacket I'd met her in and a matching red leather skirt. The car scraped the cement as we pulled out the driveway. The suspension was chopped, making it sit low on the road. We got on the highway, drove east. Every bump and crack shimmied through the entire car, shaking the overstuffed brown leather seats like one of those slot massage beds.

Robbie and Keith traded at a White Owl blunt in the front. We drove slower, and the music got louder the higher they got. When we turned into Phoenix Memorial's parking lot, Robbie dug through her purse and pulled out a bottle of Visine. She tilted her head back and dosed both of her eyes. I looked up and down the rows trying to see if there were any police cars—marked or unmarked. Keith parked the Riviera on the second floor overlooking the main entrance of the hospital. I could see a security cruiser parked next to an ambulance in front of the doors, but other than that, there wasn't any more heat. I pulled the skeleton watch from my pocket. It was 8:40 in the morning.

Keith smudged the blunt out in the overflowing ashtray, unbuckled his seatbelt, and turned to me in the back. His good eye was puffy and bloodshot from the dirt weed, and his busted eye was completely shut.

'Say, Frank—what if this girl don't want to go with Robbie?' he asked.

'She will. Don't worry.'

Robbie put on some fresh lipstick in the clouded-out visor mirror. She wiped the extra off her lips and rubbed it into her thigh.

'Robbie,' I said. 'You need to tell her—'

'You told me what to say, but I'm telling you, the last time I saw this girl, she was in no shape to be walking around. You should let her stay and heal up.'

'I can't do that unless I want her looking like Keith or worse.'

'What if old girl is in there?' asked Keith.

Robbie grabbed Keith's hand, both flying high.

'Oh, Keith, I didn't even think of that. You need to let me hold that burner.'

She turned around, held her hand out for my gun.

'I'm not giving you the gun.'

'How you gonna let her go in there with no protection, Frank?' asked Keith. 'That woman will bust her up.'

'I ain't getting busted up *for nobody*,' said Robbie.

'I ain't giving you the gun.'

Robbie turned back around and started fixing her hair in the mirror.

'Then looks like I ain't going in for your girl.'

'Mary's not gonna be in there,' I said.

'You don't know that!' said Robbie. 'That woman is like the exorcist or some shit.'

'Yo, that movie is some scary shit—no joke. You should let her hold that gun, Frank.'

I didn't have the time or the patience. I jumped forward, grabbed Keith's loose seatbelt, and looped it around his neck.

'What the fuck are you doing?' yelled Robbie.

He grabbed at my hands, but I held the choke tight. I dug the pistol into his swollen cheek while he gasped for air.

'You can get paid easy or I can start hurting your man,' I said.

'Let him go!' said Robbie.

'Get out of the car.'

'I will! Let him go!'

I pulled back hard on the belt. Keith's one good eye bulged in the socket, and his neck veins popped out one by one. Robbie opened the door and stepped out of the car.

'Walk!' I shouted.

She pulled her skirt down and zipped up her jacket. She stared me down hard before she started towards the stairs. When she was out of sight, I let the belt slack. Keith grabbed at his neck, coughed, sucking air.

'What the fuck, motherfucker?'

'This is real to me, Keith. No jokes.'

Keith rubbed his neck in the front seat. The skin was red in a thick band across his throat.

'I'm sorry,' I said.

'Fuck your sorry . . . homeless-looking motherfucker.'

He slouched down and pulled the end of the blunt from the ashtray. He lit up and pushed a purple cassette into the radio. He smoked through the giant brown roach, bobbing his head to the music. I pulled up the left sleeve of my jacket and rolled back the cuff of my shirt. Fresh blood seeped through the gauze. When I pulled on Keith's seat belt, I had felt some of the stitches pop. I unwrapped the bandages. Two of the cuts in the small of my arm were opened wide. Dark blood trickled out slow.

'Don't be dripping your shit all over my car,' said Keith.

I rewrapped the bandages as tight as I could and carefully rolled the sleeve back down.

'You know I'm sitting here thinking,' said Keith. 'When I get high, I think about all sorts of deep shit. I listen to the lyrics in a song, and it's like I'm hearing the shit for the first time. Like they're talking directly to me, and I'm the first motherfucker in the world to hear the shit.'

As he talked, I kept my eyes on the hospital's front door. I hated just sitting there and waiting.

'It doesn't even matter what kind of music. It can be R & B, soul, rap, country—I listen to it all when I'm high because I can hear what the motherfuckers had in mind when they wrote the shit. Know what I'm saying?'

'I got an idea,' I said.

'You know what I don't get, Frank?'

I pushed myself back in the seat and looked out the back window to see if there were any police driving into the entrance.

'Why don't you just run? I mean, if it's your ass and the cops ain't after your girl, why don't you just run? Fuck the dumb shit, and don't look back. Shit, you give me money, and I'd go with you. Go to Mexico, get a new name.'

'I can't. I made a promise to Maddie. I told her I'd look after her.'

'How? By getting locked up and having one of your old bitches come after her? That ain't looking after shit.'

'I owe it to her.'

'Like you owe us, huh?'

Keith pinched the roach with both hands, brought it close to his mouth, and took a big deep hit. Ashes sparked up and flew down his throat. He coughed in a fit and quickly rolled his window down and flicked the burning paper out into the parking garage. He grabbed a plastic bottle of Coke from Robbie's empty seat and took down half in one large swallow.

'Damn, my shit is fucked up . . . I'm just saying, Frank . . . Hey, you listening?'

'What's that?' I asked.

'I'm just saying. Maybe all the shit would be better off if you just let it be.'

I wiped the barrel of the Glock on my coat sleeve and kept my eyes on the hospital's entrance.

'There goes your girl with Robbie.'

My chest shook. It had only been five days, and Maddie wasn't the same. Her hair was tied back in a short ponytail. She didn't have any makeup on, and her jean jacket looked two sizes too big for her. Robbie dragged her by the hand across the crosswalk in front of the hospital. They walked fast. Maddie couldn't keep up. Her right arm wrapped around her stomach, and her head wobbled up and down, looking like it would just snap off. A nurse with a wheelchair came running out after them, but Robbie turned and yelled something, scaring her off.

'Start up the car.'

When they got out of the parking lot elevator, I pushed the passenger seat forward and got out. Maddie's face flushed when she saw me. She cried into her hand. Robbie let go, and I ran to her and wrapped my arms around her little body. Her weight collapsed into my arms. I wanted to say so much.

S he was all broken up. Maddie stared out the side window, her head resting on the top of the cracked leather seat. I reached across and put my hand on hers. She held it for a minute and then just let it open underneath mine.

'Maddie, are you hungry?' I asked. 'You want anything?'

'Some water,' she said.

'We're figgin' to stop up here to get some food,' said Keith.

Robbie and Keith stared out the front window. They were acting funny, not talking it up like they were before. I figured they were either scared by the sight of Maddie or their high had let off and they were just stoned quiet. Robbie had put on a pair of giant square gold-rimmed sunglasses, and Keith was leaned back, driving slow with one slacked hand stretching over the top of the steering wheel like he was about to fall asleep.

'Who is she, Frank?' asked Maddie.

I didn't want to lie anymore, but I didn't know how to explain it all.

'Ben made a deal with Santer for help. I didn't want to come. I knew better . . . I was just trying to keep you and Sean safe—'

'You didn't answer my question.'

'Mary is Santer's woman.'

'What happened in Nogales?'

Keith's good eye shot back at me in the rearview. I stared back, unable to look at Maddie in the face.

'Did you kill that family?'

'It's not that simple.'

'But you did, right?'

Two tears ran down Maddie's face not like any I'd seen before. Thick—like syrup—water gathered around each of her eyes before it fell, gentle and heavy, to the edge of her chin.

'I was pregnant, Frank. I miscarried.'

'What are you talking about? That's not what Ben said. He said—'

Maddie squeezed my hand till I looked her in the eye.

'I want to find Noni, and then I want to go home . . . to my parents.'

'Wait, when did—'

'No, that's it,' said Maddie. 'That's all.'

Maddie was pregnant for six weeks when our baby turned on her. The embryo lodged in her fallopian tubes and grew, tearing her open from the inside. Blood filled her abdomen and collected in quarts without her knowing a thing. She passed out when her heart—tuned up and tweaking on that batch of New Year's crystal—called for more blood, but she didn't have any more to give. She fell down on the ground in front of Sean, and by all accounts, just about died. She wanted water now because her body was still trying to heal, and I didn't have one right word to say—there wasn't a damn to make clear. I looked at Robbie and Keith in the front seat. I felt the weight of the stolen gun in my pocket and the sting of the broken suicide stitches in my arm. I honestly wished it was more than that car, those people, and that instant, but it wasn't. Maddie was right. That's it. That was all.

'You want Burger King, baby?' Keith asked Robbie.

'I don't care. Just somewhere I can use . . . the bathroom. I need to use the bathroom.'

Keith took a right into a Burger King and parked the car facing the gas station next door. Robbie got out and rushed inside.

'So all you want is some water?' asked Keith.

Maddie nodded her head, and I reached into my pocket to pull out some cash, but Keith stopped me.

'No, it's all right. I got this.'

He hopped out of the car and headed inside.

'Have you heard from Noni at all?' I asked Maddie.

'She came to the hospital after she saw you. She talked to the doctors and said we were going to leave the next day, but she didn't show. I tried to call her.'

'Did Mary come back after that?'

'She just came that once with this bitch,' said Maddie, kicking the back of Robbie's seat.

'She didn't call again?' I asked.

'No, just that once.'

I didn't tell Maddie that Mary had come to see me with Margaret. I didn't want to scare her any more than she already was.

'Where are we going after this?' she asked.

'We're gonna drop you and Robbie back at their place, and I'm gonna head to Santer's with Keith.'

'You can't leave me with her.'

'Maddie, I can't take you, not like this.'

Maddie pushed herself up and turned to me. It was the first

time she moved since she got in the car. Her right hand strained below the window holding her whole body up.

'Don't leave me with her, Frank. Quit fucking leaving me.'

She let her hand down and fell back against the seat. I didn't know what to do. We had to be gone by night. I didn't have the money or time to start betting against John Ethan's divine calling to hunt me down and, at the same time, find a better place to keep Maddie safe. Outside, Robbie and Keith walked towards the car. Keith carried an open bag of food. When they got in, Robbie handed a bottle of water to Maddie, and Keith took out their food and then handed the bag back to us.

'What's this?' I asked.

'I got y'all some breakfast,' said Keith. 'Just in case you're hungry.'

'Thanks.'

There were two wrapped sandwiches in the bag. I took one out and offered the other to Maddie, but she waved it away.

'After we eat, we're gonna need to head straight over to Santer's,' I said with a mouthful of food.

Robbie stopped chewing and looked at Keith, her eyes wide, throat packed with eggs and bread.

'No, we're not,' she said.

'That wasn't the score, Frank,' said Keith.

'I know, but the sooner we get there, the sooner we're gone. I don't want to get picked up.'

'That girl shouldn't be going over there. She can't walk,' said Robbie.

'I'm fine,' said Maddie.

'She'll stay in the car. She'll be fine,' I said.

'Well, fuck her then. What about me? I ain't going over there.'

'Frank, I don't wanna take Robbie. It ain't safe,' said Keith. 'The two of them are better off at the house.'

'It's not gonna take but a minute,' I said. 'We'll park around the corner. They'll stay in the car.'

'I don't know. It ain't what we talked about,' said Keith.

I took another bite of the sandwich and leaned forward to the front seat.

'You can stay in the car too, Keith. I know Mary has your number.'

'Hey, fuck you. She didn't jack me up. Her man did. And you didn't see the motherfucker—he ain't no slouch.'

Robbie wrapped up her unfinished sandwich and dropped it out the window.

'Well, neither am I,' I said.

As we passed under the 51 freeway and started into west Phoenix, I held my head low and counted police cruisers to see if my escape made a difference. Having Maddie with me didn't make me brave like before. There was just the task in front of me. There's a million country tunes about it—*I did what had to be done . . . So on and so on . . . Don't look back.* I was scared Maddie would tell me she was in so much pain—that her miscarriage and all the surgery afterwards made her hate me more than she already did. She was resolved like only a woman could be. She was strong like I'd always seen her. Now, she understood that everyone wins, everyone loses, and she was just the same. She was smarter. She had finally found me out and had the scars to prove it.

My painkillers had worn off, and I was realizing I was a lot worse off than I first thought. If I moved my left wrist in the slightest, it killed, and my legs were sore from the little bit of walking I had done that morning. I was craving all sorts—even the dirt weed Robbie and Keith had been getting into. Anything to smooth me out and break the mounting edge.

'How much farther?' I asked Keith.

'Not long. She's around the way, off of Sixty-seventh.'

I pulled out the cash and the cell phone from my pocket. I counted out the forty-seven dollars and handed it to Maddie.

'It's all I got. Don't use that phone unless you got to. It's stolen.'

'What a surprise,' said Maddie, sticking the money in the front pocket of her jeans.

'How you feeling?'

She wiped under her eyes and managed half a smile.

'I'm all right—really,' she said.

I rolled up my sleeve and checked the bandages one last time. I tried to roll my left wrist and make a fist, but the slightest move had me seeing stars.

'How are *you* doing?' asked Maddie.

'What do you always say? *We've seen worse.* Just some cat scratches is all.'

She didn't answer. She wanted to say something but stopped herself. As we passed through an intersection, I leaned forward to see what street we were on and felt her hand on my arm.

'What do I do if you don't come back?' she asked.

'Don't worry. I'll be coming back.'

'Stop with the bullshit, Frank. I need to know.'

She'd seen my arm. She was scared. I had told her about John Ethan, but not about cutting myself up.

'Use the money for a bus back to Santa Fe,' I said. 'In our closet, top shelf, there's some boxes of Fiddle Faddle. You'll find everything you need to get back to Colorado.'

'What about Marcus? What if they're there?'

'Marcus doesn't have any problem with you. He's only got eyes for me.'

For a second, Maddie looked like my old girl. Her eyes lit up, and she gave me a big smile.

'What about Sean?'

'Leave that alone, Maddie. Don't go checking on him.'

We passed the 101, and Robbie turned around from the front.

'Just so you know, some shit goes down, you're on your own, white girl.'

'Fuck you,' said Maddie.

Without a blink, Robbie jumped onto her knees in the front seat and started throwing punches on Maddie.

'Who the fuck you think you talking to? I just saved your ass, bitch!'

Maddie covered up. I grabbed Robbie's arms and pushed her back.

'Cut the shit, Robbie!'

'She needs to watch her fucking mouth.'

Robbie turned back around and skulked down. Part of me wished the whole thing would have ended right there. Keith taking the car into a light post, cutting the car in half, hanging our hides off street signs and oncoming traffic.

We took a left off Gilbert onto Baseline Road. On every block, there were low-rent apartment buildings offering one month free in different colored banners. We passed two empty strip malls at one intersection, and it was then I noticed the sides of the roads didn't have nothing but brown dirt and construction trash everywhere. There wasn't a bit of green in any direction. We headed south on Higley and took a left onto East San Angelo into a residential neighborhood. The place was so new, some of the streets didn't even have signs yet. All the curbs were marked with orange paint, separating one empty lot from another. Keith took another right and drove two blocks before he parked.

'The house is supposed to be up there on Northview,' he said, pointing to the street ahead. 'How we doing this?'

There were newly planted palm trees up and down the sidewalk, none of them taller than my waist. The street concrete didn't have a drop of leaked motor oil, and all the houses had flat roofs and the good thick windows to keep the heat in. I was willing to bet they all smelled like fresh paint and torn carpet.

'Frank,' Keith said again. 'How are we doing this?'

'I thought you said she lived in a dump.'

'This ain't all that,' said Keith. 'My mom's got a nicer place.'

'Leave the keys with Robbie, and let's walk up,' I said.

'But I ain't got a gun.'

'I know.'

'Maybe Keith shouldn't go then—without no gun,' said Robbie. 'He can hang back and drive.'

'We don't need a fucking driver. We're not robbing anyone.'

'I ain't even gonna be any good to you, man,' said Keith. 'I can't barely see through this eye.'

'You drove all the way over here,' I said.

Robbie patted him on the knee, kissed him on the cheek.

'Go, baby. Real quick—it's worth it,' she said, winking.

'All you have to do is cover my back, Keith. You don't even have to go inside.'

'Nah, I got you. Pimps don't lose . . .'

He gave the keys to Robbie, leaned over, and kissed her wet on the lips. Maddie pulled me to her, put her arms around my neck, whispered in my ear.

'You always let me off easy.'

When we rounded the corner of Northview, Keith pointed to the second house on the street. It was a smaller model but still had all the signs of being new. The front lawn was dug up with no turf, and there were no address numbers on the curb or mailbox. Keith was walking funny in his oversized Suns jersey, bent over at his waist with his arms out like he was on a tightrope. For all his talk, I could see he hadn't ever gotten dirty for nothing. He was almost ten steps back when I finally stopped and waved him up.

'What the fuck are you doing?' I asked.

'I don't want them to see me.'

'Walking like an ass ain't gonna make you invisible. Stay with me.'

Santer's Harley was parked in the driveway, the gas tank shining in the sun. A rotted-looking red Caprice was parked next to it. An empty baby bottle lay on the front seat. There were a few cars parked half a block down, but other than that, the other homes were unfinished and empty. I motioned for Keith to follow me, and when we were halfway to the door, I stopped.

'Look here,' I said. 'Stay behind me, but not too close. Ain't a damn thing gonna happen, all right?'

Keith shook his head up and down. He was so nervous, he couldn't talk. He kept wringing out his hands like they were wet. I should've sent him back to the car right then. I cocked the pistol and walked to the door. I breathed in deep, grabbed the handle, and pressed the latch down. It was open. I checked behind me to make sure Keith was following. He was leaned forward with his eyes dead on my back. He wet his lips and gave me a quick nod to walk in. I slowly pushed the door open with the pistol out in front of me and took a couple steps into the house. The door opened into an empty living room. I could see clear through to the kitchen out to the unfenced backyard. The floor was bare cement, and the plaster was fresh on the walls. The only signs that anybody had been there were some empty Budweiser bottles and a pallet of paint supplies covered by a plastic drop sheet. A floor lamp was in the center of the room, but even that didn't have a shade or a bulb. When Keith closed the door, I thought I heard a radio on in the back of the house, but it faded away—just a car passing by.

'You sure your man came over here?' I asked Keith.

'Motherfucker . . .'

I heard Keith fumbling with his gun before I turned around. He scrambled, trying to wrangle the piece out of the pocket of his baggy jeans. When I looked at him, I knew. His eyes were frantic, and his whole face was shaking.

'Keith, don't,' I said.

He pulled the pistol out from his pants and raised it on me.

'I'm sorry, Frank. It's you or me—'

A shotgun cocked behind the front door.

'Keith, your back!' I yelled.

The door kicked in. The shotgun opened and sent Keith flying four feet onto the living room floor. The blast sounded like a pipe bomb in the empty house. My ears rang to a buzz, and I didn't bother to look at who I was shooting as I dove to the ground.

'My Dad talked about you right up until the end.'

He couldn't have been older than nineteen. Up close, he was taller, broader across the chest, but still a replica—down to the burning Jim Beam bottle on his left forearm and long red crucifix peeking out from his stained, torn wifebeater. He was Jon before all the meth and murders. His eyes were cranked yellow, but his young face was still full, not starved gaunt by regrets.

'Chip don't fall far from tree, Frank. Ain't that the fucking truth?'

Behind me, Mary walked out from the empty kitchen. With one arm, she carried Margaret on her hip, and had a snub-nosed .38 in her other hand.

'You didn't need to kill him,' I said, pointing to Keith.

'I didn't kill him,' said the kid. 'He got himself shot.'

She stopped ten feet in front of me. Both her and Margaret were still wearing the same dirty clothes from the hospital. Margaret cried at her waist, her little eyes darting around the room.

'Jay, meet your Uncle Frank,' said Mary.

Jay Santer cocked the shotgun at his waist and held it on me as I got back on my feet. I was shaky, the whole house felt like it was on casters. Keith was facedown across the room, blood pooling in the cavity of his back. His face was turned on its side, and his good eye was open on the empty beer bottles.

'How many is it now, Frank? Four? Six?' said Mary. 'I lost count of how many people you killed.'

'Where's Jon?' I asked.

'Dead,' said Mary, jaw grinding away.

'Where's the money?' asked Jay.

Before I could answer, Mary threw her head back and laughed loud. Margaret shook, started to cry in her arm.

'He doesn't have a dime,' said Mary. 'That's not the way Uncle Frank works, is it?'

Sweat broke over Jay's brow, and he shuffled in place, shifting back and forth on his feet.

'It doesn't have to be like this,' I said. 'We can stop right now.'

'That's what Jon said. He said the exact same thing. Then what happened, Jay? Tell your Uncle Frank.'

'I shot him.'

'Why?'

'Because he ruined it.'

'Jon was going to talk, Frank! I finally let him meet Jay, and he still was going to turn us all in, but we saved you. We saved you, and you didn't even know. Just like now—'

'You didn't save shit, Mary.'

Mary stomped at the ground, waving the pistol around Margaret's crying face.

'*Yes, I did!* You think you're so quick! You didn't see this, did you?! You didn't see me pay off your niggers? They wanted to kill you for nothing—for a fucking TV!'

'That ain't saving me.'

'What about Ben? Your precious fucking Ben—you didn't see him coming. He wanted you dead.'

'What do you want from me, Mary? Because I'm sorry to tell you, I ain't got shit. I got nothing for you—'

'Let's go, Mom!' yelled Jay. 'Did you hear him? He doesn't have the money.'

'I want my fucking chance! You got to leave! Why not me?! We were gonna start over, me and Jon, but he couldn't stop fucking. And then he cries and cries, *Why did I kill them? Why did I?* He was ruining it—I loved him, and he was ruining it—'

'Frank . . .'

When I heard Maddie's voice from behind me, my heart fell and fell and fell. Robbie walked her through the front door holding a pistol on Maddie's back. She pushed Maddie forward until she saw Keith's body sprawled out on the bare floor.

'Why? No! He didn't want to come!' Robbie yelled. 'Why? Why'd you kill him? You weren't supposed to kill him! That wasn't the deal!'

Robbie tried to cover her mouth and eyes with her free hand but couldn't turn away. The color fell from her face as she cried. She yanked Maddie's head back hard, forcing the gun into her cheek. Maddie screamed.

'You! You motherfucker!' Robbie yelled at me. 'He said he didn't want to come!'

'Let her go, Robbie!' I said. 'I didn't kill Keith. That man did— Mary's man!'

Without a pause, she pulled the trigger on Jay. He dropped the shotgun, went to his knees holding his branded neck. Blood seeped from between his fingers, eyes still bloodshot yellow, blood soaking the front of his shirt. He struggled for the shotgun on the ground, sucked air out of his open mouth.

'Mom, come on, Mom . . .'

'Always be messin' with us,' cried Robbie. '*Why you people always messin' with us?!*'

Robbie kicked the shotgun from his dead hand and pulled on Maddie's head, trying to get closer to Keith. I lowered my pistol.

'Please, let her go, Robbie. We'll all just leave. We'll get out of here.'

Robbie dropped her gun from Maddie's face and let go of her head as they got to Keith's body. She covered her mouth, shook her head back and forth as if turning Keith into a red and black smear would bring him back to life. Maddie stood frozen. A scared blank look held her face. I put out my hand.

'Come here, baby . . .' I whispered.

I watched Mary's bullets hit Maddie in the chest. I watched Maddie's hands go over her body and her knees buckle underneath her. Her eyes closed, and they stayed closed until her body hit the floor. I turned, raised the Glock, and screamed at Mary as she pulled her trigger on Robbie. I wasn't aiming. I didn't care. I heard Margaret crying as loud as she could. Bursts of fire exploded from the end of the Glock. I pulled the trigger three times and killed Mary with the last two shots. She held on to Margaret as she fell. Blood rushed out of her right side. She didn't make a sound. Yes, I've seen plenty die. Oh, tell it again, Mama. Tell it straight, and say it ain't true.

saw it clear now. For years, Mary had been waiting for anybody to come looking on Jon. It was only a matter of time. Like I said, Jon was the roving pastor of crystal methamphetamine. He never stopped cooking. He couldn't. It was all he had left of his first son. Grand Madre and her family saw that and cheated him solid. The tobacco-skinned daughter wasn't nothing but the Madre's little sister. They let Jon hold that baby boy on that beach in exchange for their own kitchen in Nogales. They took him to the water, fed him the sun, and gave him back the family he'd lost. They watched Jon, sucked him off, and learned how to cook themselves. Jon was so happy, he was willing to look the other way when he found out the women were sisters. For him, the filthy made it real. But when he caught them changing his Burning J to *Fuego Blanco*, he couldn't take the cheek. He gutted them. We gutted them. I took off the oldest boy's head with a handsaw. The cherrywood handle was carved with two laughing doves.

I know Mary loved Jon as much as I loved Maddie because the night he confessed to her about Nogales, she fucked him, forgave him without pause. Poor Jon never healed himself. Again, he'd lost another family over the same haunted drug. He said it before many times—he never wanted to off the world. I don't know when he met Jay, his second son, but clearly it wasn't soon enough. Jon had a kind of conscience that must have finally got the better of him, because after I left, he was set on confessing for that sorry batch of murders. Mary killed Jon because her two worst fears came knocking. She was getting old like me. She was sick of being alone, rough fucking for twenty bags. She saw it all perfect like I had with my dreams for Maddie—her and Jon loving each other forever, going clean, a home free of infection, every door willingly open in a new house. She did what I did. She took stock of her failing body, empty purse, and the sheer amount of drugs moving in and out of her home and decided she wasn't going to risk Jay's and her freedom for anybody. But like me, she couldn't see that a long time ago—like sowing in a drought—her dream was fated to rot.

Mary smoked more and more crank, sucked anyone's cock, and told her story to anyone who'd listen—just changing the names. Mary wanted someone to see and hear—a witness to share the weight of Jon's death and her giant anguish. So she waited, Ben set me up, and I came. And I saw all her hurt and anger. I wouldn't wish it on anyone. I mean it. Believe it or not, the scum report to faith too. They ain't got much else—we don't. We follow the scourge and pray, follow the scourge and pray.

Margaret cried on top of Mary's dead body. The baby was on her back with her head resting on Mary's outstretched right arm. Her legs kicked back and forth in the air, and her arms reached at Mary's dead sunburned face. I picked her up and held her in my arms. Dirt and snot smeared across her face. I carried her to the kitchen sink and wet my hand under the faucet. I wiped her forehead and cheeks. I rocked her, felt her small breath on my cheek, told her not to cry.

My ears still banged from the gunfire, and my whole body was shaky from my knees up. I walked to the back door of the kitchen and looked out on the unfinished backyard. The main road was barely a mile away, and, to the left, I could just make out the rusty brown roof of Keith's Riviera. When I unlatched the door, I heard a muffled slamming—like a mallet hitting the ground. I turned and tried to listen to where it was coming from. It was loud but still tucked under the pinging of my ears.

I went towards the closed door off the kitchen. It opened to a small dark utility room that stank of stale cigarette smoke and burning hair. A makeshift foil pipe and cigarette butts were on the floor against the back wall. Mary had been getting high in there waiting for us to show up. The slamming came clear now from inside the garage. I unlocked the dead bolt and pulled open the door. The only light was coming from a few tiny slats in the garage door. It was pitch-dark besides that. The noise boomed and echoed inside the hollow room, but it stopped quick when I stepped in.

'Noni?' I said.

A muted scream squealed, and the legs of a chair slammed against the floor.

'I can't see a thing. Hold on—'

I went back into the kitchen and bent down to Mary's body. Her blood had soaked her shirt and started two small pools next to her hips. I dug into the pockets of her pants and pulled out a pack of GNC 110s. She had four cigarettes with a small lighter tucked inside the box. As I stood up, Margaret squeezed on my chest knowing her mother was close. I went back into the garage, lit the lighter, and waved it back and forth. I still couldn't see Noni. She was sobbing loud under the gag. I shuffled towards the garage door and walked along the length of it, feeling for the latch. I stuffed the lighter in my pocket and pulled the handle towards me and up. Light poured in from the bottom. Noni was in a chair in the back corner next to a brand-new water heater still wrapped in plastic. Her arms were tied behind her back and each of her legs was duct-taped to a front leg of the chair. Her eyes and mouth were wrapped in long strips of the same tape all the way around her head. She hopped in the chair, hitting the empty water heater behind her. It sent out the booming ping I had heard. I rushed over to Noni, took off my jacket, and put it on the ground for Margaret.

Dummy knots of black tie-line cinched Noni's hands. They had used whatever they could get their hands for the job. I pulled the tape from her eyes first. It stuck against her skin, pinching it raw across her face. She blinked her eyes over and over. Immediately, they welled up with tears.

'It's all right, it's all right,' I said.

When I pulled the tape off her mouth, she took a deep breath and wet her lips before she cried out for her baby.

'Where is she, Frank? Where's Margaret?! Is she here?!— oh, God—'

'She's right here, right here—don't worry.'

I turned the chair so she could see Margaret on the ground.

'Oh my God, Frank! Oh, baby, I'm sorry . . . Mama's sorry.'

I worked through the knots on her hands while she talked. Once the biggest of them came loose, the line unraveled. Noni pulled at the tape on her legs.

'Oh God, Frank! What happened?! I heard shooting and then it got quiet. She said she was going to kill me if I made a sound, but then it got so quiet—'

As soon as she freed her left leg, Noni scrambled to the ground. She held her baby tight and kissed her all over her face.

'I'm so sorry, baby. I'm sorry . . .'

I got her other leg loose. She stood up and paced back and forth inside the empty garage, bouncing Margaret at her chest.

'I need some water. I'm so fucking thirsty—where's Maddie?'

Before I could stop her, Noni walked into the house. I waited for her to scream, but there wasn't a noise. Her footsteps tapped across the kitchen tiles. They died away as she got to the unfinished concrete of the living room. Water filled the pipes in the walls and poured into the kitchen sink. After a few moments, it turned off, and Noni came back into the garage. She bit her lip, looked at me sitting on the floor. She spoke quiet and calm as if nothing had happened.

'I don't want Margaret to be here.'

'Go out the back door and wait for me,' I said. 'I'll be out in a minute.'

I used my good hand to push myself up to my feet. I picked my jacket up and threw it over my shoulder. I stopped and looked on the ground to see if I had dropped anything, but I knew I hadn't. I didn't want to go back inside that house. I picked up all the balls of duct tape and the mess of tie-line off the floor. In the utility room, I squatted down and grabbed Mary's foil pipe. I carried all the trash into the kitchen. The back door was open, and I could see Noni standing in the middle of the backyard holding Margaret. When she saw me, she looked down and started kissing and whispering to her baby.

'Hey,' I said.

'Are we leaving?' she called out.

Noni ran her hand across Margaret's forehead and zipped her little jacket up.

'See that car?' I said, pointing to the roof of Keith's Riviera a couple blocks away. 'Meet me over there.'

I closed the door. Noni stood, looking confused. She glanced back and forth between the house and the car. I waited until she turned around and started making her way through the loose dirt and broken bricks.

I threw the trash into the middle of the living room and laid my jacket on a clean patch of cement. I pulled all the guns from the bodies' hands, trying not to look at their faces. I dropped them all inside my open jacket, folded in the ends, and tied the arms tight. I flipped Robbie's body over and pulled the car keys from her hand. One by one, I went through their pockets for cash and dragged them by their feet to the trash pile in the center of the room. Robbie. Keith. Jay. Mary. Maddie. They all seeped wide stains of blood across the concrete. I doused the pile with two cans of thinner, bent down, and lit the cuff of Maddie's jacket. I picked up the jacket of guns and walked out the back door. There wasn't any ringing in my ears, but I remember my left forearm still stinging from gripping their ankles. I wasn't thinking much as I walked back to the car. I didn't think of much as I dragged those people. I couldn't. If Noni and the baby weren't there, I don't think I would have moved. I'd still be standing in the middle of that brand-new house staring down at Mary's dead face, one arm reaching out to my Madelyne Nicole.

The driver's seat was broken. Noni had to push herself forward to see over the steering wheel and reach the gas pedal. I told her I would drive once we were out of the city, but she didn't understand. She wanted to go back to Keith and Robbie's and pick up her car. She would just run over, she said. Pull the spare key from the wheel well and pick me up.

'. . . I'm pretty sure it's still there. It's a box with a magnet that holds a key. I used to lock my keys in the car all the time, but it's funny—I stopped once I got it.'

She talked and kept talking as we drove north on I-17 out of Phoenix. I told her she'd be fine. I'd get her and Margaret back to Denver. I'd give her all the money she needed to get back. If she heard me, she didn't care.

That's not right. She heard me, but she was scared. The talking made her feel better, and every few moments when she needed a breath, she turned and touched Margaret to make sure her baby was still on my lap.

'. . . They jumped me. What do you call it? Mug. They fucking mugged me, Frank. I went back to the hospital like you said. I was going to take Maddie to her parents the next morning. And they must have followed me the whole time. I parked my car, and I was pulling Margaret out of her seat in the back when that guy—her son—came up to me and asked if I had a cigarette. I was so fucking scared. You saw him. I knew something was wrong—you get that feeling, you know?'

Police sirens came from behind us. I pushed myself up on my elbows to peek out the back window.

'It's okay. It's the highway cops,' said Noni. 'They're pulling someone over . . . Yeah, they were speeding. Assholes . . . Okay, yeah, we're fine. So I didn't say anything. And I should have. I should have fucking screamed as loud as I could. I don't know why I didn't just scream! Fuck!'

Noni slammed her hand on the steering wheel and started to cry.

'Noni, it's all right,' I said. 'There ain't nothing you could have done.'

'Yes, there was—there is, Frank. I could have fucking screamed. That's all I had to do and none of this . . . Oh, fuck. How's my baby?'

She reached back between the seats and squeezed Margaret on her side.

'I'm sorry, baby. I'm sorry. Mama screwed up.'

'You couldn't have done anything.'

'I know, but I should have screamed or ran. He didn't have a gun, but she did. As soon as I looked up, she was right fucking there. And she started saying she was a friend of yours and . . . And I knew she was lying. I just said, 'leave me alone,' or something really fucking stupid because I was so scared. And . . . and . . . yeah . . .'

Noni's lips moved, but she was talking to herself. She went over all the pictures inside her head, breaking her kidnapping down into half seconds and then after that just specks of moments—where her hands were, the temperature dropping in the air. She wasn't sure if she felt sick that night because she hadn't eaten or if the sight of Mary and Jay Santer picking up Margaret barreled her stomach to the floor.

I let Margaret lie on my chest and watched all the tall buildings give way to more and more billboards as we drove out of the city. I pulled the skeleton watch from the pocket of my pants. It was well into the afternoon now—just past two thirty. I closed my eyes, and my body relaxed across the backseat. The rush was gone. All I saw was Maddie falling again and again. I wanted to ask Noni to roll one of the windows down and turn on the radio loud. I wanted to hear something else besides air shocked with gunfire and Maddie's throat swallowing, cracking open for that last bit of air.

'I wish you would have brought her,' said Noni. 'We should have brought her with us.'

Noni wiped the wet from her eyes and let out a chestful of air.

'Do you have a cigarette?' she asked.

I reached into my jacket pocket and handed her Mary's box of GNCs over the front seat. She pulled out a smoke, and I listened to her flick the lighter. She inhaled, and I smelled the smoke like burning cardboard. It filled up the car. She cracked her window, let it rush out. The highway sounded like a knocking river.

'Fuck that woman. I wish I could kill her again,' said Noni.

She took a couple more drags and then flicked the butt out the window.

'Her house was fucking disgusting. There were roaches on the fucking walls. Even in the bathroom. I mean, I'm just thinking about it, and I bet I could have just grabbed Margaret and run out. She didn't tie me up until she blindfolded me and took me to that garage. She just watched me. She'd sit right in front of me and get all fucked up smoking crystal and just sit there and watch me with Margaret. Same thing every night. She'd get all fucked up and start crying about that guy, Santer, and how much she loved him. She just kept telling the same story over and over, almost word for word. And her son, he just ignored it and acted like she wasn't even talking. It was so fucking weird, Frank. He'd be sitting next to her watching TV, and she'd be screaming and throwing shit, and he wouldn't move. She kept saying, *What was I supposed to do? What was I supposed to do?* I wouldn't be surprised if they found some bodies at that woman's house. It was so fucking scary—Are you all right?'

'I'm fine, yeah—'

'Because you're just fucking lying back there. You're just fucking lying back there, and Maddie's dead! She's dead, Frank!'

Noni broke down. Her hands shook, and her face and neck turned beet red.

'What the fuck happened?! How could you let this happen? I'm sorry . . . I just . . . Oh, God.'

I held Margaret, sat up in the backseat, and put my hand on Noni's shoulder.

'I know. I don't know what happened—'

'Lie back down! I don't want to go to jail. They'll take Margaret away. What the fuck are we doing?! *What happened?*'

I didn't answer the question. I wasn't ready. I thought about Keith smoking that White Owl of dirt weed and telling me to run to

Mexico. Leave everyone alone. I wish I could have talked like Noni and made everything better. Maybe she was right. Maybe I should have carried Maddie back to the car, put her in the trunk. Dropped her peaceful-like on her parent's doorstep. But what then? A small fucking note? Some more sorry words? Nothing was enough. *Here, I got your daughter shot up. Here, your baby is dead. Here.* Noni rolled up the window and pushed herself forward again in the seat.

'She loved you so much, Frank, she told me. Because I fucking hated you. But she just kept saying she loved you and that she was waiting for you to be a good man.'

We stopped at the first gas station after Flagstaff. We had to. For the last hour, Margaret had been crying. She needed to be changed and fed, and Noni couldn't hardly stay awake any longer. She had nodded off twice behind the wheel. Both times, she didn't wake up until we were well into the grooved cement of the highway's shoulder. The old Riviera rattled and shook like it was going to explode before Noni got it back on the highway.

'I need some money to get us something to eat,' said Noni, leaning into the driver's window.

She held herself up with both arms on the outside of the door. Her eyelids were purple and swollen, and her lips were a dry crusted white. I pulled out the wadded-up money and handed her two crumpled twenties.

'Get us some gas too,' I said.

Margaret was sleeping next to me on top of Noni's jacket in the backseat. I unfolded all the dead people's money next to her—bill by bill—and counted it out. There was a hundred and twelve dollars and some change to get us back to Santa Fe. I figured if we took it easy and slow, the money just might take the old Riviera home. The sun broke through the car's long back window. It was red-purple and getting ready to set. It warmed the back of my head and lit up all of Robbie and Keith's greasy fingerprints across the dashboard. Dust and weed smoke frosted the windshield.

I watched Noni pay at the register inside. She walked out carrying two plastic bags. I got out of the driver's door and bent my head left and right, letting out the cracks.

'I got some milk and juice and sandwiches for us.'

'You got the keys?' I asked.

She pulled them out and tossed them to me as she got close.

'I'm going to take Margaret to the bathroom and get cleaned up,' she said.

'Which pump?'

'Number four.'

Noni went to the passenger side and pulled the seat forward.

'Hey, baby,' she said, quietly. 'I know. I know. We're going to get you fixed up.'

She picked Margaret up and walked back inside the store. She talked to her as they walked, pointing to the other cars, the people, reminding the baby how cold it was. I started up the Riviera and drove it around to the pumps. There was a newer truck in front of me. It was all jacked-up on fresh tires. The driver, a young-looking white kid, cocked up the folded bill of his baseball hat and stared me down as I got out.

'Nice car,' he said. 'What year?'

I ducked my head down and peeked at the badge on the dash.

''72.'

'It's nice. Needs some paint. My granddad has one of them.'

When I flipped on the pump, lights clipped on all over the station. Gasoline gulped and clicked into the tank. Highway 40 was right in front of me, and the road was steady with cars east and west.

257

Headlamps were on in both directions, so the white and red just melted into glowing rushing lines. The pump stopped at twenty-four dollars. I put the gas cap back on and started it back up.

Noni and Margaret came out looking better. She had washed both their faces and pulled her red hair back into a ponytail. She got into the car and sat down with Margaret in her arms.

'I cleaned her up, but I wish we had some fresh diapers. Once I get some milk in her, she'll feel better.'

We pulled around the truck and turned back onto the service road.

'You going to be all right to drive?' asked Noni.

'I got a little sleep.'

She pulled a diet soda from the bags at her feet. She opened it and looked at the inside of the cap just like Maddie always did. She took a sip and handed it to me. I drank the soda and pressed the gas pedal down as we got back onto the 40 East. Noni fiddled with the heater until hot air poured through all the vents. The Riviera's V8 opened up on the highway and then mellowed to a growl. I turned on the radio and looked for a station without a commercial while Noni held a small plastic bottle of milk up to the center vent on the dash. She held Margaret with her other arm and rocked her gently at her chest.

'Do you want me to tear you off a piece of sandwich? All they had was tuna fish,' she asked.

'I'm all right for now.'

She shook the bottle of milk and held it to her neck, checking the temperature.

'Thanks for coming back for us, Frank.'

Noni stared out the windshield, didn't look at me as she spoke. She opened up the milk, tasted it, and then poured tiny sips into Margaret's mouth. Milk spilled down the side of the baby's face onto Noni's lap.

'Here you go, little girl . . . Come on . . . Just a little bit.'

I stayed in the right lane watching the red needle of the speedometer hover above sixty miles per hour. I could hear Margaret's little mouth open and close as she tried to take down the milk.

'This fucking sucks without a baby bottle, that's for sure,' said Noni.

'We'll stop once we get inside New Mexico.'

'Don't worry, she'll be all right. She's tough, huh? Aren't you?'

Noni kissed Margaret on the forehead and kept feeding her the milk. Then, without a word, she put the cap back onto the bottle and dropped it at her feet. She pulled my right hand from the steering wheel and held it to her heart. She gripped tight and closed her eyes.

'Wherever she is, God, please bless Maddie, and thank you for keeping us all safe. Please don't stop. And if you can hear me, Maddie—'

Her voice broke. She forced out each word through her shaking chest.

'If you can hear me—I love you, and I'm sorry. We're all sending you all the love we got. Be safe.'

NEW MEXICO

don't need to see it. I wrapped this land around my finger a long time ago.

The Riviera was walleyed, and all it gave up was a car-wide swath of cloudy yellow light. While Noni and Margaret slept in the back-seat, I cracked open my window and let the tips of my busted hand feel real native snow. We drove through sharp flurries like fish scales ripping through the air, and I remembered hitting a Jemez deer in Aspen's truck. We were driving up the basin road, tempting a dead man's race with no light but a drowned blizzard moon. In a blink, we hit the animal, and it sailed over the length of the Ford, landed, and ran off into the night of trees. Aspen stopped the truck and pulled out his little revolver to finish the deer. He got out, checked the front end, and then walked a slow ten paces into the pines. After a pop, he came back out, shrugging and yelling,

'Let Colorado have its whiskey mountains! The Texans too! I eat this high desert. Even the Spanish came looking for treasure but only found God, God, and God.'

Highway 40 brought us into Albuquerque's west side just past ten o'clock. Arizona's desert gave up before Gallup, and now, the highway rested on cropped, snowed-in grass. The road was paved on waves here. Asphalt blanketed the rolling ground. The car's chopped suspension creaked up and down over the black humps, and I felt the tires slip more and more as snow collected. It didn't matter. I wasn't going to stop. I was ready to push the Riviera back to Santa Fe, throttle it with my shoulder till the old bumper broke bone. All my doubts had died with Maddie. I had business with Ben.

Noni sat up as I slowed down to a near idle on the slick ramp to the 25. Cars honked behind us, and I let them till we were heading north on the highway again.

'What's their problem?' asked Noni.

'They all want to buy this old car.'

She smiled, reached over the front seat, and grabbed the last smoke out of Mary's box of GNCs.

'Can you crack the window over here?' she asked.

She slid carefully across the backseat trying not to wake Margaret. She lit the smoke and took a long, strong drag, holding it close to the open window. The cherry burned hot on the cheap tobacco, and half the smoke canoed down.

'When'd you quit smoking, Frank?' she asked.

'I didn't. I smoked some of that rat shit while you guys were out.'

Noni held the butt out the window. When it turned to sparks, she let it fly from her fingers. She reached forward and put the window back up as Albuquerque streaked past us. The highway curved a wide left through the city. Compared to Phoenix, all the buildings were short, and the cover of snow made the prefab adobe look like gingerbread. We drove under Paseo del Norte, and I looked out the right window hoping for anything—a shadow, even—of the Sandias.

'We're going to get you some new clothes when we get home, aren't we? A new jacket . . . Some new pants.'

Margaret whined and started to cry. Noni rocked her till she hushed. The air was getting thinner, and after a few miles, the Riviera's engine was starting to run rich. As we reached the end of the city, the gingerbread buildings gave way to black-and-white ground. It looked like the buildings were collapsing under the snow until there wasn't any construction left, just dark and tiny yellow lights of trailer homes freckling east and west off the highway. If I squinted, I could make out the short dirt driveways up to each of the double-wides. *All of them*, I thought, *all of them poor and broke are better off. They got nothing perfect. A swatch of land, four sheets of plaster, a decent roof.* I could make do with an electric heater and cheap wine. We wouldn't have needed much—Maddie and I. A roll of scratch-off tickets and a gas can. A delivery truck and a wife. On my days off, I'd ride a bicycle to save money. Can you believe it? We'd birth our kids on newspaper and try to keep them from crime.

Half a mile up, road flares lit up two parallel lines. Two police cruisers were parked on the shoulder with their lights on a wrecked semi. The little bit of traffic slowed up, and as we rolled closer, we saw three police running back and forth from their cars to the wreck. The truck was headfirst into a low ditch. Its trailer was jack-knifed behind it, torn open after the first axle. Like a steak knife on a pop can, the metal shrieked out in every direction, exposing tall stacks of boxes of I don't know what. Two of the police worked the driver's door with a huge crowbar. They yelled over their shoulders to another man who was talking into a radio on his chest. Their sirens weren't going, so we could hear the two yelling as they counted out each pull on the bar.

'One . . . two . . . three . . . Go, go, go.'

A female Mexican cop stood at the end of the wreck. She slapped her hands together trying to stay warm and stopped each passing car. As she talked to the drivers, she pointed north up the road and shook her head in yes's and no's.

'Get in the front seat with Margaret,' I said.

Noni set the baby down, climbed over, and then reached back and picked her up.

'Put on your seatbelt too.'

The cop slowed us down to a stop and motioned for me to roll down the window.

'Where are you guys heading?' she asked.

'Santa Fe,' I said.

'We're not closing it yet, but the road is getting pretty icy from here on out. There are some really bad patches—especially on the bridges. Just take it slow, all right?'

'Thanks,' I said.

She crouched down and frowned at Noni and Margaret in the front seat.

'You don't have a car seat for that baby?'

'We forgot it back at home,' said Noni.

She shook her head, took a step back, and looked the Riviera over.

'Just take it slow, will you? And get a damn seat for your child, Christ.'

'Thank you,' said Noni. 'Stay warm.'

I rolled the window back up and pushed lightly on the gas.

'Why don't you mind your own fucking business, traffic cop?— what a bitch,' said Noni.

I turned the heater on high and watched the red, blue, and yellow lights fade in the rearview. Out here, the highway was lit only in patches. Under the crooked headlamps, the snow was thousands of marbles scattered on the highway, and when we hit a stretch of orange street lamps, the flakes fell in big clouds and turned to tiny moths sweeping on the pavement, slapping into drops on the hot windshield.

'I hope she doesn't remember this.'

'What's that?' I asked.

'Margaret. I don't want her to remember any of this.'

The baby's eyes were opened wide, staring at Noni.

'She won't,' I said.

'You'd be surprised. I remember all sorts of fucked-up shit. I actually remember more as I get older. First, I'll start remembering the weather. Like I'd say this storm reminds me of this one day growing up—running around in the night. Or a smell will remind me of a day, and then I'll remember specific colors. A week later, I can tell you what I was wearing, what my hair looked like, who was yelling at who. It's all in there in pieces.'

I clicked on the high beams to see better, but all it did was turn the snow into a white-gray wall.

'You know what's funny, though? I always remember the ending first. I know how it felt at the end. Everything else comes in chunks, know what I mean?'

'Like one of them jigsaw puzzles,' I said.

'Yeah, but not one of the hard ones. Those thousand-piece fuckers. They look impossible. I don't know how people do those.'

'They cheat.'

'You can't cheat on a puzzle, Frank.'

'Sure you can. You just jam up the pieces till they fit.'

'But then you don't get the picture on the box.'

'Oh, you get a picture, just not what you're expecting is all.'

Noni rocked Margaret in her arms, humming quietly to the baby.

'Don't worry,' I said. 'If Margaret ever asks, I'll tell her what happened.'

'I don't know if that's better or worse.'

'I'll tell her you saved her life.'

'That's the problem, Frank. I didn't do that.'

'What do you think you're doing right now?'

Noni leaned forward and turned up the radio. She rolled the knob back and forth and found a rock station playing some old Aerosmith.

'His voice was better back then,' she said. 'It sounds hungry.'

I didn't take the car over fifty all the way back to Santa Fe. A few times, I had to drive with one eye peering out my window at the lane marker to make sure I wasn't drifting off the road. Only two cars followed us that I could see. They stayed far back, and when we got close enough to see the first lights of Cerrillos Road, one of them sped up and passed us. The driver honked as he drove by and gave us a thumbs-up and a wave. I kept tapping on the top of the wheel and tried to drive steady.

The weather kept everyone inside. It wasn't till we passed the Texaco and Horseman's Haven at the south end of town that we saw a few cars and trucks creeping along Cerrillos. As we crossed Rodeo and headed into town, my chest gave room, and I could finally breathe deep again. I pulled into a Walgreens and left the car running while Noni went inside to buy diapers and food for Margaret. There was so much I wanted to ask her. I wanted to know what Maddie had told her, what she said about the pregnancy, if she cursed my name. In the seven hours it had taken us to get back to Santa Fe, I had repeated and retold my last hours with Maddie in my head. Every one of her words was drummed into my memory. They snapped like bullwhips.

Noni struggled across the parking lot with four large plastic bags stuffed with diapers. I had given her the last thirty dollars to buy whatever she needed, but I didn't think it afforded all she was carrying. I got out of the car and opened the trunk.

'Lucky us. They had a sale on Pampers. Buy one, get one free. I think I got us enough to get us home. Sorry it took so long. I swear they had a better selection of cat food than baby food. And that woman at the register—fucking zombie. I can't blame her, though—'

Noni froze when she saw the pile of guns in the trunk.

'Close it, Frank.'

'All that's not gonna fit in the backseat,' I said.

'Close the fucking trunk.'

Noni opened the passenger door and picked up Margaret off the seat. She stuffed the bags into the back with one hand, and when I got back in, she slammed her door hard.

'Let's go,' she said.

'I wasn't thinking. I'm sorry.'

'Let's just go. Let's go. Let's go.'

I pulled back onto Cerrillos while Noni dug into one of the Walgreens bags. She pulled out a pack of Camels and packed them on her hand.

'You want one?' she asked.

'Maybe when we get to the house.'

She unwrapped the plastic off the smokes with her teeth and dropped it onto the seat next to her.

'Do you have that lighter?' she asked.

'It's with the other pack.'

'Where's that?'

'It was on the seat. Don't worry. We'll be at the house in a minute.'

'I want to smoke now.'

Noni threw all the trash off the front seat and tore around in the dark looking for the pack of GNCs. Margaret started to cry.

'It's only gonna be a minute,' I said.

'I don't want to fucking wait. You can fucking wait. I can't believe I didn't buy a lighter.'

Noni tossed the unlit smoke out the window. Margaret cried, but Noni didn't do a thing as we took a right on Camino Carlos Rey and passed a neighborhood park. Noni wiped her eyes and took a deep breath.

'I'm sorry, baby. Mama's sorry.'

I took another right onto Alamosa and drove slowly over a set of speed bumps. My neighbors' cars lined both sides of the street. It looked like some of them hadn't moved for days. Thick blankets of dirty snow piled high over everything. When I saw Ben's wrecked Saab in my driveway, I reversed three houses back and parked.

'What are you doing?' asked Noni.

'Did you see that car in the driveway?'

'Frank, I've never been here.'

'It's Ben's car.'

'Doesn't he live with you?'

'He got in a wreck when we left Denver.'

'How? Was Sean in the car?'

'Yeah, he was fine. He was with me—with us—me and Maddie. I'm gonna go around back and check on the house.'

'Don't you have a key?'

I kept forgetting Noni didn't know a thing about what happened after we left her home. Maddie must not have had time to tell her.

'I lost the key,' I said. 'It'll be fine. He probably just got it towed here.'

'Do you want me to go with you?'

Noni was scared. She didn't want to stay in the car and wait. She didn't want to be alone.

'No, you guys stay here.'

'You sure? Because I can keep Margaret quiet.'

I put my hand on her arm that was holding Margaret.

'Noni, it'll be fine—'

'I'm sorry I went nuts on you. Just seeing all that shit in the trunk freaked me out. It's fucking stupid. I know, I know.'

I squeezed tighter on her arm trying to calm her down.

'I should have known better,' I said. 'I wasn't thinking.'

'Okay, okay, we'll be fine . . . Hurry.'

Noni watched me get out and open the trunk. I untied the sleeves of my jacket and dumped the guns onto the floorboard. I grabbed the Glock, shoved it into my waist, and put on my jacket. When I closed the trunk back up, Noni was still staring at me through the back window. She was half-turned around in the front seat with Margaret in her arms.

All the other homes on the street had at least one light on. Most of the people on the block were family folk who kept to themselves. Since I lived there, I'd seen a few hoods cruise up and down—teenage bastards that stole out in their low riders when it was warm. But all in all, I was probably the sorriest one on the block. The house next door to mine still had its Christmas lights on the bushes and around the rain gutters of the roof. It lit up my driveway just enough that I wasn't jumpy. None of the front windows on my house were broken, and the door was latched up tight. I figured Ben's car had been towed in because it was parked in the driveway facing out to the street. Ben never parked there. I couldn't remember one time he didn't leave his car right in the center of the yard. The right side of the Saab's front end was wrecked where he had spun out and hit the ditch. Besides that, the car didn't look all that worse for wear. I walked to the kitchen window and peered inside the house. The sink was still filled with dishes, and my half-handle of Beam sat open on the counter just where I had left it.

I walked around to the side gate. I pushed the trash bins aside and went around to the back. The door off the kitchen was wide open, key still in the lock. I pulled the Glock from my waist and walked slowly inside. Dried dead leaves scattered all over the hardwood, and a lone set of muddy boot prints trailed into the back hallway, didn't turn for the garage. I walked back slow and quiet, followed them straight to mine and Maddie's bedroom, and pushed open the door. I wish I could say I was shocked when I found our closet tossed, the four boxes of Fiddle Faddle ripped apart, and the last of Aspen's match collection and his homemade gauntlets lying on the ground. But I wasn't. I wasn't shocked that nothing else in the house had been touched.

Before Noni and Margaret came inside, I cleaned up our bedroom as best I could. I piled the clothes back in the closet, picked up all the trash from the ground. I let them have our bedroom. I knew I wouldn't be able to sleep with the sheets sweet with Maddie's and my last night. I sat in the living room with an old jam jar half-filled with bourbon. All the other glasses in the house were dirty, and when I turned on the faucet in the kitchen, the water took too long to run clear. I told myself that tomorrow after Noni left, I'd take to cleaning up the entire house and tracking down my truck in whatever rural hack it ended up in.

I waited till Noni went to sleep before I pulled out an old newspaper and opened it across the living room table. I rolled cigarette after cigarette from a stale can of Drum tobacco, and I chain-smoked inside next to a cracked-open window. I was sick of feeling the cold air crack the skin around my mouth and the seams of my face. I only managed two sips of Beam before I passed out. I dreamed in fits—long vivid talks with Maddie in movie theatres and in the middle of streets. We sat on opposite curbs yelling back and forth. My voice went hoarse, and Maddie sounded like a megaphone. Then I walked with Ben and John Ethan through an old mining town. We were old friends there, and when we turned onto such a crowded street, we all laughed. We couldn't move without walking sideways, shoulder to shoulder. Someone said, 'We are sardines.' And I looked up because I wasn't sure I said it, but by then, Ben and John Ethan were laughing, and we were in uniforms, and I can't tell you the significance.

I didn't stir until the afternoon of the next day. I woke up under a blanket and realized Noni must have covered me and taken off my shoes. Warm sunlight shined right on my face from the living room windows. Noni was sitting on a stool at the kitchen island smoking a cigarette and drinking from a mug. I threw the blanket off, sat up on the couch, and rolled my shoulder, trying to wake up my left arm. When I looked down, the forearm of my shirt was stained with pus and blood. It had soaked through and mixed with Ben's bloodstains from two weeks ago. We had left him the same way—passed out, left bleeding arm propped up on the top of the couch.

'How are you feeling?' asked Noni.

'Don't know yet . . . Where'd you get the coffee?'

'It's just hot water. You don't have shit in this house.'

I went to the bathroom and started up the shower. As I took off each piece of my clothing, I counted up all the bruises, scrapes, and crusted scabs all over my body. The stitches on my left arm had mostly held. The tops of two of the deeper cuts had opened up wide in the small of my elbow. They had wept through the night, but now, the blood and infection was dry and came off like powder under my fingernails. The whole right side of my chest from my armpit down was different degrees of purple and red—a keepsake from John Ethan's baptism in the lockup. The color and weight was out of my face and neck. Dirt and blood stained my jawline, and my eyelids were dark pink and swollen. My hands and feet looked like I had been working engines for a couple of days and then taken time to smash every other finger and toe in a car door. I washed in the shower until the hot water ran out, and then wiped the mirror above the sink with a wad of toilet paper. I covered my face with bar soap and rinsed one of Ben's old disposable razors.

The blade tilled into my face, caught in the pits of my cheek, and ripped at the meat of the hairs. I didn't feel when I nicked myself, but when the blood seeped out and mixed with the white film of soap, tears fell slow down my cheeks. Like a mutt's rawboned hackle or a fresh sunk quill, I wanted this wrath out of me. I wanted to put Ben on the block—slowly with meditation and without out a bit of hurry—

I wanted to take that man's head in three drops to the beard of a splitting axe. I'd pike his face in a long day, striking the foot of a fence post once an hour till the wood broke bone. I hurt for Maddie. I hurt for every phony dream that I'd held on to, repeated like a bare parrot in this desert. I wanted more than revenge. I wanted him and all his blood dead.

I took in a chestful of steam from the sink and let it slow me down. I wiped my face with a towel, then wrapped it around my waist and crept into my bedroom, trying to be quiet. Margaret was sleeping on her belly in the bed. I grabbed a T-shirt, sweater, and the cleanest pair of jeans I could find. I pulled on my clothes in the dark hallway and went to the kitchen. Noni was standing at the stove, staring out the window to the front yard.

'I figured we'd go eat when you're ready,' I said.

She didn't answer. She was wearing Maddie's old red puffy jacket and one of my old Sabbath tees.

'Where'd you find all those clothes?' I asked.

'I had to dig, but it was worth it, don't you think?' she said, smiling.

She sat back on the stool and sipped from her mug.

'I cleaned up the living room,' she said. 'Did you have yourself a little party?'

'Tried to, but I can't do it like I used to.'

She picked up a rolling paper, took a pinch of tobacco from the open can, and sprinkled it between her fingers. She rolled the paper up and down with her thumbs before she put her hands to her mouth and sealed the cigarette up.

'Was someone in the house?' she asked.

'Last night? No.'

'You said we were safe, everything was fine—'

'It is.'

She reached down to her feet and set Maddie's vomit-stained purse on the island.

'Then where did this come from?'

She lit up the smoke, waited for my answer. But I had nothing, and she knew it.

'Fuck you, Frank.'

'Noni, whoever it was, they were long gone by the time we got here.'

'That's not the point—'

'It's Ben, Noni. He was—'

'Oh, now it's Ben—it's always something, isn't it?'

Noni went back into the kitchen and slammed the mug on the countertop.

'I want to go home. I need to see if I still have my fucking job.'

'Noni . . .'

'Just shut up! You're a fucking liar—I always said it. *You're a fucking piece-of-shit liar.*'

Her bare feet slapped across the hardwood as she walked back into the bedroom and shut the door. After a few minutes, the cordless house phone turned on with a beep, and I heard her ask for information in Denver, Colorado. I picked up the jar off the living room table and rinsed it out in the kitchen sink. I filled it up with water and drank the whole thing down and then filled it up again. I wanted to go back there and tell Noni off. Remind her who just saved her ass and her precious baby. But she wouldn't have to say much to shut me up, and I knew it—not much at all, actually. She'd only have to ask me why she was in Arizona in the first place and which one of our lovers was dead.

I pulled Maddie's purse in front of me, ran my hand over the Dead Kennedys patch and Misfits skeleton, the last one she'd sewn on before we'd left. I went to open it—grabbed the zipper—but couldn't. I was just too scared. I pushed it away, went to the garage, and flipped on the light. It was exactly the way we'd left it—not a thing moved or touched. From wall to wall, the place was littered with junk and tools. Ben's welding kit was set up in the middle. Two large piles of scrap sheet metal were leaned up against the front garage door. A bicycle was on the ground in pieces next to the welder, and stuffed garbage bags of clothes, magazines, and trash filled the back quarter of the room. I opened the garbage bags near the back, smelled the rotten mulch of Aspen's weed. I dragged the two into the kitchen and ripped them open on the center island next to Maddie's purse. Crumpled and folded bills of every sort poured out onto the countertop. I sat down on the stool and pulled a pen and some paper from a kitchen drawer. I unfolded and smoothed out each bill. It was more than I remembered. There was a time when I first moved into the house that Ben came over every day and forced me to sort and wrap all this cash in little paper sleeves he'd taken from the casino's counting room. I was lazy and hated all the numbers of it, but Ben made me laugh, made it easier. We smoked reefer out of a porcelain lion's head, and he would tell me his ideas and plans. He still had Sean, wasn't sideways on snort, and believed coffee cured cancer and reptiles ruled the world.

I stacked the money in front of me and watched each pile of fives, tens, and twenties get taller and taller. Wouldn't this right here have been enough? I always did my best to keep a stiff lip and talk like a big puncher. I looked down at the dollar-whiskey sacks lamenting over their charity beer. Born losers, I'd say. Fuckery champs. Now, I was the sod thinking on lost cut-ups with my junkie friend, counting the last of my money, frozen scared to open my dead girl's bag. I could have lived off half of it. Look at all that's passed, and I'm still hungry.

gave it all to Noni—close to fourteen thousand dollars—and kept nothing for myself. I wrapped the stacks with two rubber bands and put it in a plastic grocery bag. Noni was sleeping in the bedroom. Margaret was in her arms, and they were both turned on their sides towards the wall. I was just going to set the money on the bed and let her count it alone, but when I bent over to put it down on the mattress, her eyes opened, and she hissed, 'What are you doing?' in this hateful whisper. I dropped the bag on the floor and talked quiet.

'There's a Greyhound leaving for Denver at seven.'

When the clouds smeared into orange and the sun snipped behind all the houses and short desert trees, I backed the Riviera into the driveway and opened the trunk. I packed up Mary's revolver, Jay's shotgun, and Keith and Robbie's matching .25s into a long cardboard box that a long time ago held a dome tent. I carried the box through the house and set it next to the scrap metal and trash in the garage. I went back through all the kitchen drawers and found an old zippered wallet I used to use. It was the kind bikers and mailmen wore, larger than a hand with a thick chain to fasten to your belt loop. I put the little bit of money I had inside the wallet, sat down, and rolled the last of the papers into cigarettes. The bathroom door opened. The fan turned off, and Noni walked into the living room with Margaret in one arm.

'We're ready.'

They both had on their jackets, and Noni had packed paper grocery bags with Margaret's diapers and food.

'I'm sure I got a suitcase or something better for all that,' I said.

'It's all right,' she said. 'These will work.'

'You can go warm up the car. I'll carry these out.'

I handed her the keys, went back to the bedroom, and picked up the dry cleaner's wool coat from the ground. I shook it out, trying to get some of the trunk dust off, before I put it back on. I went back to the kitchen and pulled the Glock from the oven. I had stashed it there out of drunken habit. I wiped it off of before I stuck it back in my jacket pocket and grabbed Maddie's purse and put it under my arm. I locked up the front door and turned off all the lights, and then I picked up Noni's bags and left the way I came in. I didn't lock the back door on purpose this time. If someone came looking on the house ever again, they wouldn't have to bust any windows. They were welcome to walk right in.

'Thank you,' said Noni.

We drove north on St. Francis heading towards the Plaza.

'For the money. Thank you,' she said.

'You should be able to get a decent car. Nothing fancy, but something to get you to work and back—I don't even know where you work. Can you believe that?'

Noni didn't answer. We sped through all the new homes and buildings on the south side of town. When we crossed St. Michael's Drive, all the adobe stopped looking like painted concrete and appeared more like the old imperfect mud it was. We passed Cerrillos, took a right onto Paseo de Peralta, and slowly made our way down the two-lane road. The homes kissed the street here. Their front yards went right up to the curb. Traffic was walled-in on the tight street, like a chain-link and driftwood corridor that dumped into the middle of downtown. We took a left on South Guadalupe, and I parked the car at a meter in front of that famous local spot, the Cowgirl Hall of Fame.

'Where's the bus station?' asked Noni.

'A couple blocks up. We have to walk—parking gets hairy up and down here.'

Noni bent forward with Margaret in her arms and looked at the night sky through the front windshield.

'Doesn't look like there's gonna be any snow tonight,' I said. 'You guys will probably have easy going all the way to Denver.'

Noni opened up the door and got out. She pushed her seat forward with her free hand and reached for the grocery bags in the back. I grabbed her hand, stopping her.

'I'll get these.'

'Let go of my arm,' she said.

'Noni, I don't want you going off like this.'

'Let go of my fucking arm.'

I let her loose, and she picked up the two bags and set them on the sidewalk. I ran around to the other side to help, but as soon as I got close, she stopped me.

'Don't, Frank.'

'You're just gonna walk them two blocks with all that? I would have dropped you off, if I'd known that.'

Noni stood frozen looking at me.

'What, Noni? Will you talk to me?' I begged.

'You don't get it, Frank.'

'What?—I'm sorry. What do you want?'

Noni bent over and threaded her left arm through the bag handles.

'I don't want anything from you,' she said.

'I'm sorry about lying to you, but I didn't want to worry you. Don't you think we've had enough worry? I mean, shit . . .'

Margaret looked at me from Noni's arms. The spark was back in her eyes along with the color in her face.

'I know I have enough worry,' said Noni. 'Maddie had enough too. But you—I don't know, Frank. I don't know when you're going to be done. It's a shame.'

Her face flushed and a few tears fell down her cheeks, but she wiped them away quick, refusing to break down on another street.

'Let me help you,' I said.

'Goodbye, Frank. God bless.'

That's the last time I ever saw Noni and baby Margaret. The last I heard of them too. For as much as she had in her arms, she didn't struggle. She talked to her daughter at her chest and looked back and forth for traffic as she crossed the street. She turned back once, waved and smiled. One of those sad smiles like she just couldn't bear to watch my life.

took the long way there. I drove south down Cerrillos through the whole of Santa Fe. I passed Maddie and my favorite Allsup's, where no matter the hour, the cashiers always fried our burritos fresh. I smiled driving by the State School for the Deaf, remembering the night when Ben convinced me the mutes needed us to make a rope out of cash and string it like holly on the fence. I saw the old Lamplighter liquor store and Baja Tacos. There'd be afternoons I'd walk back and forth between the two, eating Styrofoam cups of green chile stew on one end and chasing them with shot flasks of Cuervo at the other. Traffic slowed down to twenty as I got to Cheeks, the only titty club in town. When I first got to Santa Fe— before I knew a soul—I met a long-haired Los Alamos scientist there. We bought each other lap dances from the same girl till the place closed. Back and forth, song by song, after four hours, I told him my name. The lights came on in the middle of Fleetwood Mac. Stevie Nicks faded away while the stripper stood up between us, tied the sashes of her white satin bra, and shook both our hands like we'd played a good game. I left with the scientist. He told me he had something I'd like in his car. I walked behind him, fist clenched, thinking he was gonna yank his cock from his sweat-pants. Instead, he kicked his back bumper, made his trunk pop open like the Fonz, and showed me a nuclear bomb. It looked like a roasted eleven-year-old wrapped in towels, beeping green lights for eyes, still smoking-hot to the touch.

I veered off onto Airport Road, followed it to the end of town, and hopped on the 599 North. I didn't touch the radio. I enjoyed the echo of Keith's car off the empty snowfields. For an hour I drove on the highways, got on the 285 again, and pressed on the gas till the old big block filled my body, numbed my legs, and shook Maddie's purse on the seat. The roads were near empty. The Buick's crooked headlights made the pavement look like a well-worn trail. As I passed through Española, I turned the heater to my feet and lit up one of the two cigarettes I'd rolled at the house. All the history I'd ever learned was from strangers at rest stops and gas stations like the ones I passed. Two separate times, people told me the Anasazi carved this land themselves. They told me the Mustang was a wild Spanish horse who fell in love with the land, and when he first looked across Rio Grande, he reared up and came down with such force—all the canyons became deeper and quiet rivers turned to rapids. I told them both I didn't understand. One gave up, walked away cursing me under his breath. The other grabbed my face—his hands like claws—turned me around, and yelled into my ear at the top of his lungs,

'All this hatched from the ground, Bodaway Bruce. Like the very first raptor, naked, hungry against the sky.'

I pulled off the 68. The gate to Aspen's land was open, chained back, and locked to the fence. I turned onto the road slow, but the Riviera still bottomed out—metal screamed over the drainage grates. I turned the headlights on high and watched in the rearview as the gravel and dust turned into a red brake-lit cloud. The Buick shivered on the dirt road, threatening to fall apart. The engine light came on, and the cherry of the cigarette fell onto my lap like the whole wide world wanted me to stop and turn around. I licked my palm and pressed the burning coal into my jacket, spit the rest of the smoke onto the dash. As I rounded the first hill, I saw Aspen's backhoe lighting up the land with floodlights, black smoke coming out its stacks. I pulled close, turned the Buick off. Ben waved at me from the backhoe's driver's seat, coaxing me to get out. I pulled the Glock from my jacket and opened the door. My boot sank into the ground. In front of the backhoe, water shot high into the sky from the destroyed wellhead.

'Did you get the purse?' Ben yelled over the engine.

He had on some of my clothes, a thick denim work jacket and a green flannel shirt. Between the shadows and all the howling smoke, he looked like a diseased monster—pale skin, black for eyes. His arms moved back and forth, forcing the machine's rusted teeth into the ground. I motioned for him to shut it down. He shook his head no.

'Took me all night to get it started!'

I pulled the pistol and let a round off into the backhoe's tire. Air hissed, and watery mud spat up and showered over Ben. He reached forward, turned off the engine, and held up his hands.

'I wanted you to have the purse,' he said. 'I didn't open it. I didn't touch a thing.'

'She's dead, Ben.'

'I know. It's all over the news.'

He crumpled forward, put his head to the steering wheel. His long hair tossed over the levers of the backhoe. Mud dropped over everything. It hit my arms and shoulders, beaded up on the wool like black plastic paint.

'Come down,' I said.

'You can do it from down there.'

'Come down.'

Slowly, he climbed out of the machine. He held on to the handles and lowered himself down. He walked towardss me, thousand-dollar shoes flooding with water, arms open, wanting to embrace. I raised the gun.

'I would have given it to you, Ben,' I said. 'If you'd just asked, I would have signed over the deed.'

He nodded his head, listening. He was high like always, sniffing, sucking all his bitter snot back up.

'I know—I knew when you took Sean from my car.'

The pistol shook. The barrel vibrated in front of me. I lifted my other hand, steadied the Glock.

'I wanted to get started,' said Ben. 'Show him I could work. Marcus says a huge fountain is going to be where we're standing. People are gonna walk into the casino through a wall of gold and glass doors.'

Tears dropped one after another from my friend's face. He didn't shudder or sob, just talked fast, held his cruddy hands together and bounced his body, trying to stay warm.

'He told me I could have him back, Frank. I get him this land, and Sean and I could leave. No more Ali, no more fucking house— just me and Sean.'

The gun slacked to his stomach. I wanted to take him in my arms, hold him close, pat him on the back another time.

'He says I'm not fit to be a dad. I just wanted to show him that I was strong—cold like him. Just once, I wanted to get it right.'

The sound of another car came from behind us. Its tires bouncing, ringing the drainage grates. Behind us, bright headlights lit up the remains of Aspen's blown-up double-wides. The trailers were torn apart, arching from their centers like a pair of broken arms. My body shook, fighting for a full breath of air. Ben stepped closer, steadied the gun with his chest.

'Do it. So Sean doesn't see.'

As the front of Goldstein's Benz rounded the back of the hill, I felt Ben's hand close over mine.

'You got straight, Frank. Straighter than I ever thought.'

We pulled the trigger.

The shot snapped loud, stopping the Benz thirty yards away. Ben dropped. His head splashed at my feet, drowning in black and dark. A car door opened. I turned, held my hand up shielding my eyes from the Benz's lights.

'Is it done?' a voice called out.

'Yes.'

'Her remains will arrive in Colorado tomorrow.'

The car door closed. The Benz slowly reversed out. I kicked the body from my shoes, got back in the Riviera, and grabbed Maddie's purse from the seat. I pulled on the zipper—had to run it back and forth because the teeth were still glued-up with vomit. One by one, I reached in and pulled everything out. There was still a can of beer in there, her rainbow plastic bracelets, her leather wallet—her father's with a hunting hound painted on the front—nickels, dimes, pennies, and a few quarters, a blank Utah postcard with drawings of the Salt Lake capital and sego lilies—the state flower—on the front, Chap-Stick, pink glitter lip gloss, two old children's tattoos in plastic, two tampons, and a pregnancy test stick—the two blue lines clear even in the dark car. In the inside pocket, I found the roll of cash I'd given her at the motel the night I'd left. And at the bottom by itself, I felt our ring. I closed my fist around it, didn't look, put it straight into my pocket with the gun.

© KORY ALDEN

Born in Canada to Jamaican immigrant parents and raised in Texas, Wally Rudolph smoked marijuana for the first time at the age of fourteen. The joint, rolled from the Book of Revelations of a pocket-sized bible, was the start of a fifteen year affair with illicit drugs that had him drop out of college and took him back and forth across the American Midwest. Along the way he studied fiction and poetry with Jack Butler, Pulitzer finalist for *Living in Little Rock with Miss Little Rock*, and Walt Whitman Award Winner and former NEA fellow, Greg Glazner, in New Mexico at the now defunct College of Santa Fe. In 2007, he was recognized by The Ford Theatre Foundation in Los Angeles as part of its New and Emerging Voices Reading Series for his unpublished collection of short stories, *The World's Princess*. He also was a finalist and honorable mention for *Glimmer Train's* August 2009 Short Story Award for New Writers and their March 2010 Open Fiction contest. His fiction can be found in the literary journals, *Milk Money, Lines + Stars, Palooka, Slush Pile, The Brooklyner,* and the anthology, *Literary: Pasadena.* He is a graduate of The Second City Conservatory in Chicago and now resides with his family in Los Angeles. As an actor, he has appeared in numerous films and TV shows including *Street Kings, Bang Bang,* and *Sons of Anarchy.*